Walter Scott, Mary Harriott Norris

Sir Walter Scott's Marmion

Volume 1

Walter Scott, Mary Harriott Norris

Sir Walter Scott's Marmion
Volume 1

ISBN/EAN: 9783337389888

Printed in Europe, USA, Canada, Australia, Japan

Cover: Foto ©Andreas Hilbeck / pixelio.de

More available books at **www.hansebooks.com**

The Students' Series of English Classics.

SIR WALTER SCOTT'S

MARMION

EDITED BY

MARY HARRIOTT NORRIS,

INSTRUCTOR IN ENGLISH
EDITOR OF GEORGE ELIOT'S "SILAS MARNER,"
AUTHOR OF "PHEBE," "DOROTHY DELAFIELD," "DANIEL OF THE
EIGHTEENTH CENTURY"

LEACH, SHEWELL
BOSTON AND

C. J. PETERS & SON,
TYPOGRAPHERS AND ELECTROTYPERS.

PRESS OF BERWICK & SMITH.

PREFACE. .

THE prolific genius of Walter Scott has seldom had a parallel. Under the stress of grief and need, Johnson composed Rasselas in a week. Lope de Vega wrote whole dramas in a day, and exhibited something of the marvellous uniform capacity for composition in both quality and quantity that characterized the great Scotch romance writer. But Walter Scott was also a singular example of versatility, — a gift, indeed, which is seldom attended by either profundity or great achievement. Scotland's revealer, however, while not highly original or philosophical in conception, was notably and meritoriously successful as poet and romancist; if not profound, he was highly dramatic in his instincts and writings. He left to his contemporaries and posterity poems and tales which will always place him among the foremost masters in English literature of the nineteenth century. He covered the whole field of Scotch folk-lore in which Macpherson and Bishop Percy were worthy pioneers.

In preparing "Marmion" for the "Students' Series of English Classics," the editor, conscious of the mass of information open to the general reader concerning Scott's life from its beginning to its close, has deemed it best to confine herself — by means of compilation chiefly, from the author himself and his sympathetic biographer, Lockhart — to a picture of the poet's literary development and bias till the time of the publication of "Marmion." This sketch is supplemented by a synopsis of the leading subsequent events in Scott's life. The notes also include, as far as possible consistently with this edition, the poet's own notes. The editor has endeavored to make her annotation of the poem so complete that the student will find works of reference unnecessary; and it is therefore her earnest hope that the present edition will be found eminently suitable, not only for college preparatory examinations, but also for study in high schools and seminaries. She has also thought it advisable to present, continuously, first the poem proper of Marmion, and secondly the six epistles.

MARY HARRIOTT NORRIS.

NEW YORK, AUGUST, 1891.

SIR WALTER SCOTT.

BIOGRAPHICAL SKETCH.

(1771-1832.)

WALTER SCOTT, one of a family of twelve children, was born in Edinburgh, Aug. 15, 1771. He died at Abbotsford, Sept. 21, 1832.

"Every Scottishman has a pedigree. It is a national prerogative as unalienable as his pride and his poverty. My birth was neither distinguished nor sordid. According to the prejudices of my country, it was esteemed gentle, as I was connected, though remotely, with ancient families both by my father's and my mother's side." — *Autobiography.*

[During Walter Scott's second year, owing to the loss of power in his right leg, he was sent to the country, to his grandfather's farm of Sandy-Knowe.]

"It is here at Sandy-Knowe, in the residence of my paternal grandfather, that I have the first consciousness of existence. . . . The local information, which I conceive had some share in forming my future tastes and pursuits, I derived from the old songs and tales which then formed the amusement of a retired country family. . . . The ballad of Hardyknute I was early master of."

" I was in my fourth year when my father was advised that the Bath waters might be of some advantage to my lameness. . . . After being a year at Bath, I returned first to Edinburgh, and afterwards for a season to Sandy-Knowe; and thus the time whiled away till about my eighth year, when it was thought sea-bathing might be of service to my lameness. . . . For this purpose I remained some weeks at Prestonpans. . . . From Prestonpans I was transported back to my father's house in George's Square [Edinburgh], which continued to be my most established place of residence until my marriage, in 1797. I felt the change from being a single indulged brat to becoming a member of a large family very severely. . . . I had sense enough, however, to bend my temper to my new circumstances; but such was the agony I internally experienced that I have guarded against nothing more in the education of my own family than against their acquiring habits of self-willed caprice and domination."

" My lameness and solitary habits had made me a tolerable reader, and my hours of leisure were usually spent in reading aloud to my mother Pope's translation of Homer, which, excepting a few traditionary ballads and the songs in Allan Ramsay's 'Evergreen,' was the first poetry which I perused."

" In 1778 I was sent to the second class of the grammar school, or high school of Edinburgh. . . . Among my companions my good-nature and a flow of ready imagination rendered me very popular. . . . After having been three years under Mr. Fraser [at the high school], our class was, in the usual routine of the school, turned over to Dr. Adam, the rector. It was from this respectable man that I first learned the value of the knowledge I had hitherto considered only as a burdensome task. It was the fashion to remain two years at his class, where we read Cæsar, and Livy, and Sallust, in prose; Virgil, Horace, and Terence, in verse. I had by this time mastered, in some degree, the difficulties of the language, and began to be sensible of its beauties. This was really gathering grapes from thistles; nor shall I soon forget the swelling of my little pride when the rector pronounced that, though many of my schoolfellows understood the Latin better, Gualterus Scott was behind few in following and enjoying the author's meaning. Thus encouraged, I distinguished myself by some attempts at poetical versions from Horace and Virgil. . . .

"As I had always a wonderful facility in retaining in my memory whatever verses pleased me, the quantity of Spenser's stanzas which I could repeat was really marvellous. But this memory of mine was a very fickle ally, and has, through my whole life, acted merely upon its own capricious motion. . . . It seldom failed to preserve most tenaciously a favorite passage of poetry, playhouse ditty, or, above all, a Border-raid ballad; but names, dates, and the other technicalities of history, escaped me in a most melancholy degree.

"Among the valuable acquisitions I made about this time was an acquaintance with Tasso's 'Jerusalem Delivered.' . . . But above all, I then first became acquainted with Bishop Percy's 'Reliques of Ancient Poetry.' . . . I remember well the spot where I read these volumes for the first time. It was beneath a huge platanus-tree, in the ruins of what had been intended for an old-fashioned arbour. The summer-day sped onward so fast that, notwithstanding the sharp appetite of thirteen, I forgot the hour of dinner, was sought for with anxiety, and was still found entranced in my intellectual banquet. . . . About this period also I became acquainted with the works of Richardson and those of Mackenzie, — with Fielding, Smollett, and some others of our best novelists. To this period also I can trace distinctly the awaking of that delightful feeling for the beauties of natural objects which has never since deserted me." — *Autobiography.*

[After leaving the High School, Walter Scott went to college at Edinburgh. His acquirements in Greek and mathematics were slight.]

YOUTH.

"In other studies I was rather more fortunate. I made some progress in ethics. . . . I was farther instructed in mental philosophy at the close of 'Mr. Dugald Stewart.' . . . To sum up my academical studies, I attended the class of history, and, as far as I remember, no others, except those of the civil and municipal law. . . . I imagine my father's reason for sending me to so few classes in the college was a desire that I should apply myself particularly to my legal studies. He had not determined whether I should fill the situation of an advocate or a writer; but judiciously considering the technical knowledge of the latter to be useful at least, if not essential, to a barrister, he resolved I should serve the ordinary apprenticeship of five years to his own profession. I accordingly entered into indentures with my father about 1785–86, and entered upon the dry and barren wilderness of forms and conveyances."

"I cannot reproach myself with being entirely an idle apprentice. . . . The drudgery, indeed, of the office I disliked, and the confinement I altogether detested ; but I loved my father, and I felt the rational pride and pleasure of rendering myself useful to him. I was ambitious also. . . . Other circumstances reconciled me in some measure to the confinement. The allowance for copy-money furnished a little fund for the *menus plaisirs* of the circulating library and the theatre. . . . My desk usually contained a store of most miscellaneous volumes, especially works of fiction of every kind, which were my supreme delight. I might except novels, except those of the better and higher class."

"A part of my earnings was dedicated to an Italian class which I attended twice a week, and rapidly acquired some proficiency. I had previously renewed and extended my knowledge of the French language, from the same principle of romantic research. Tressan's romances, the *Bibliothèque Bleue* and *Bibliothèque de Romans*, were already familiar to me, and I now acquired similar intimacy with the works of Dante, Boiardo, Pulci, and other eminent Italian authors. I fastened also like a tiger upon every collection of old

songs or romances which chance threw in my way, or
which my scrutiny was able to discover on the dusty
shelves of James Sibbald's circulating library, in the
Parliament Square. . . .

"Excursions on foot or horseback formed by far my
most favorite amusement. . . . My principal object in
these excursions was the pleasure of seeing romantic
scenery, or what afforded me at least equal pleasure, the
places which had been distinguished by remarkable historical events. Yet to me, the wandering over the field
of Bannockburn was the source of more exquisite pleasure than gazing upon the celebrated landscape, from the
battlements of Stirling Castle. I do not by any means
infer that I was dead to the feeling of picturesque
scenery; on the contrary, few delighted more in its
general effect. But I was unable, with the eye of a
painter, to dissect the various parts of the scene, to
comprehend how the one bore upon the other, to esti-
mate the effect which various features of the view had
in producing its leading and general effect. . . . But
show me an old castle, or a field of battle, and I was at
home at once, filled it with its combatants in their proper
costume, and overwhelmed my hearers by the enthusiasm
of my description. . . . I mention this to show the distinction between a sense of the picturesque in action and
in scenery. If I have since been able in poetry to trace
with some success the principles of the latter, it has
always been with reference to its general and leading
features, or under some alliance with moral feeling; and
even this proficiency has cost me study.

"About 1788 I began to feel and take my ground in society. A ready wit, a good deal of enthusiasm, and a perception that soon ripened into tact and observation of character, rendered me an acceptable companion to many young men whose acquisitions in philosophy and science were infinitely superior to anything I could boast. . . . In this society I was naturally led to correct my former useless course of reading; for — feeling myself greatly inferior to my companions in metaphysical philosophy and other branches of regular study — I laboured, not without some success, to acquire at least such a portion of knowledge as might enable me to maintain my rank in conversation. In this I succeeded pretty well; but unfortunately then, as often since through my life, I incurred the deserved ridicule of my friends from the superficial nature of my acquisitions, which being, in the mercantile phrase, *got up* for society, very often proved flimsy in the texture; and thus the gifts of an uncommonly retentive memory and acute powers of perception were sometimes detrimental to their possessor, by encouraging him to a presumptuous reliance upon them. Amidst these studies, and in this society, the time of my apprenticeship elapsed; and in 1790, or thereabouts, it became necessary that I should seriously consider to which department of the law I was to attach myself.

"My father behaved with the most parental kindness. He offered, if I preferred his own profession, immediately to take me into partnership with him.

"The bar, though I was conscious of my deficiencies

as a public speaker, was the line of ambition and liberty; it was that also for which most of my contemporary friends were destined. And, lastly, although I
would willingly have relieved my father of the labours of
his business, yet I saw plainly we could not have agreed
in some particulars if we had attempted to conduct it
together, and that I should disappoint his expectations
if I did not turn to the bar. So to that object my
studies were directed with great ardour and perseverance
during the years 1789, 1790, 1791, 1792." — *Autobiography.*

EARLY MANHOOD.

In 1792 Scott had expressed a desire to penetrate
the wild regions of Liddesdale, in order to visit the
ruins of "the famous Castle of hermitage, and to pick
up some of the ancient riding ballads."

The descendants of the ancient clans of Scott and
Kerr lived in the same portion of Scotland, and it was
Walter Scott's old friend, Charles Kerr, who introduced
the young antiquarian to a near relative of the Kerrs,
Mr. Robert Shortreed, who had many connections in
Liddesdale.

"During seven successive years Scott made a raid, as
he called it, into Liddesdale, with Mr. Shortreed as his
guide, exploring every rivulet to its source, and every
ruined *peel* from foundation to battlement. At this
time no wheeled carriage had ever been seen in the
district — the first, indeed, that ever appeared there was
a gig, driven by Scott himself, for a part of his way,
when on the last of these seven excursions. There was

no inn or public-house of any kind in the whole valley; the travellers passed from the shepherd's hut to the minister's manse, and again from the cheerful hospitality of the manse to the rough and jolly welcome of the homestead, gathering, wherever they went, songs and tunes, and occasionally more tangible relics of antiquity — even such 'a rowth of auld nicknackets' as Burns ascribes to Captain Grose. To these rambles Scott owed much of the materials of his 'Minstrelsy of the Scottish Border;' and not less of that intimate acquaintance with the living manners of these unsophisticated regions, which constitutes the chief charm of one of the most charming of his prose works. But how soon he had any definite object before him in his researches seems very doubtful. 'He was *makin' himsell* a' the time,' said Mr. Shortreed; 'but he didna ken maybe what he was about till years had passed. At first, he thought o' little, I dare say, but the queerness and the fun.'"

In 1795, while visiting Edinburgh, Mrs. Barbauld "entertained a party at Mr. Dugald Stewart's, by reading Mr. William Taylor's then unpublished version of Bürger's 'Lenore.'" Although Scott was not present, he became so interested in a friend's version of the poem, that he obtained a copy of the original in German, and one evening, between supper and bedtime, made his own translation. He carried this translation to his friend the next morning, who, in a letter on the matter, wrote thus: "Upon my word, Walter Scott is going to turn out a poet — something of a cross, I think, between Burns and Gray." If several effusions composed ten years before be excepted, this was the first attempt at poetry of Scotland's future minstrel.

In October, 1796, Scott "was 'prevailed on,' as he playfully expresses it, by the request of friends, to indulge his own vanity, by publishing the translation of 'Lenore,' with that of the 'Wild Huntsman,' also from Bürger, in a thin quarto. . . . The reception of the two ballads had, in the mean time, been favorable, in his own circle at least. The many inaccuracies and awkwardnesses of rhyme and diction to which he alludes in republishing them towards the close of his life did not prevent real lovers of poetry from seeing that no one but a poet could have transposed the daring imagery of the German in a style so free, bold, masculine, and full of life.

"His friend, Charles Kerr of Abbotrule, had been residing a good deal about this time in Cumberland : indeed, he was so enraptured with the scenery of the lakes as to take a house in Keswick. . . . His letters to Scott (March, April, 1797) abound in expressions of wonder that he should continue to devote so much of his vacations to the Highlands of Scotland, with every crag and precipice of which, says he, 'I should imagine you would be familiar by this time.' . . . After the rising of the Court of Session in July, Scott accordingly set out on a tour to the English lakes."

In later years, "The Bridal of Triermain" commemorated this journey. His visit to Cumberland and adjacent districts was, however, of special importance because it was there that he met Charlotte Margaret Carpenter, who shortly afterward became his wife.

Walter Scott and his wife mingled intimately in their early married life in both military and literary circles in Edinburgh. "Perhaps no where could have been found a society on so small a scale, including more of vigorous intellect, varied information, elegant tastes, and real virtue, affection, and confidence. How often have I heard its members, in the midst of the wealth and honours which most of them in due season attained, sigh over the recollection of those humbler days. . . . In the summer of this year [1798] Scott had hired a pretty cottage at Lasswade, on the Esk. . . . It was here, that when his warm heart was beating with young and happy love, and his whole mind and spirit were nerved by new motives for exertion — it was here, that in the ripened glow of manhood he seems to have first felt something of his real strength, and poured himself out in those splendid original ballads which were at once to fix his name."

In February, 1799, Scott's translation of Goethe's *Goetz von Berlichingen* appeared; and this is important only because, quoting Lockhart still further — " But who does not recognize in Goethe's drama the true original of the death-scene of Marmion and the storm in Ivanhoe."

One morning, in the autumn of 1799, James Ballantyne called on Walter Scott to induce him to write on some legal question of the day for the newspaper Ballantyne then printed. On this occasion Ballantyne warmly

praised Scott's poetry. At parting, the young lawyer and
poet combined "threw out a casual observation, that he
wondered his old friend did not try to get some little
booksellers' work, 'to keep his types in play during the
rest of the week.' Ballantyne answered that such an
idea had not before occurred to him. . . . Scott, 'with
his good-humoured smile,' said, 'You had better try what
you can do.' Ballantyne assented," and the result of this
little experiment changed wholly the course of his worldly
fortune as well as of his friend's.

Thus began the great printing-house of Ballantyne
Brothers, thus was laid the foundation of Scott's fortune,
and thus, through his secret partnership with this house,
was the scene prepared for the last pathetic, tragic chapters of his life, when, with declining health, and an
overwhelming debt, through the failure of three large
publishing houses, severally propping one another, he
struggled against illness, palsied mental powers and
debt, to retrieve his name from dishonor, and to retain
the princely manor and estate of Abbotsford for his
eldest son.

During 1800 and 1801 his literary occupation was
the completion of Border Ballads, and during 1801–02
the first and second volumes of these appeared. An
edition of eight hundred copies was exhausted in the
course of a year. The third volume was published in
1803. At this period in Scott's career he still "retained
in features and form an impress of that elasticity and
youthful vivacity which, he used to complain, wore off
after he was forty. . . . He had now, indeed, somewhat

of a boyish gayety of look, and in person was tall, slim, and extremely active."

To the "Minstrelsy of the Scottish Border," the name under which the Border Ballads was published, Scott requested Ballantyne to append in substance the following notice : "In the press and will speedily be published, 'The Lay of the Last Minstrel,' by Walter Scott, Esq., editor of the 'Minstrelsy of the Scottish Border.' Also 'Sir Tristrem,' a Metrical Romance, by Thomas of Ercildoune, called The Rhymer, edited from an ancient manuscript, with an introduction and notes by Walter Scott, Esq."

The ancients ballads in the Minstrelsy, never before printed, were forty-three. Scott's editions of the others "were superior in all respects to those that had preceded them. He had, I firmly believe, interpolated hardly a line or even an epithet of his own; but his diligent zeal had put him in possession of a variety of copies in different stages of preservation; and to the task of selecting a standard text among such a diversity of materials he brought a knowledge of old manners and phraseology, and a manly simplicity of taste, such as had never before been united in the person of a poetical antiquary. From among a hundred corruptions he seized, with instinctive tact, the primitive diction and imagery."

In the spring of 1805 Scott took a lease of the house and grounds of Ashestiel, which belonged to his cousin, as a summer home for his family. With Ashestiel he rented a small farm. This property overlooked the

Tweed; and, though seven miles either from "kirk or market," the poet delighted in supplying both mundane and celestial needs, — the first by killing his own mutton and poultry, the second by adopting, to quote his own words, "the goodly practice of reading prayers every Sunday, to the great edification of my household." Lockhart further says concerning the new home: "Ashestiel will be visited by many, for his sake, as long as Waverley and Marmion are remembered. A more beautiful situation for the residence of a poet could not be conceived. Here Scott busied himself about the farm, the care of his absent relative's woods, and with hunting. . . . He had long, solitary evenings for the uninterrupted exercise of his pen; perhaps, on the whole, better opportunities of study than he had ever enjoyed before, or was to meet with elsewhere in later days.

"In the first week of January, 1805, 'The Lay' [of the Last Minstrel] was published; and its success at once decided that literature should form the main business of Scott's life. . . . The favour which it at once attained had not been equalled in the case of any one poem of considerable length during at least two generations; it certainly had not been approached in the case of any narrative poem since the days of Dryden. Before it was sent to the press it had received warm commendation from the ablest and most influential critic of the time; but when Mr. Jeffrey's reviewal appeared, a month after publication, laudatory as its language was, it scarcely came up to the opinion which had already taken root in the public mind." Previous to the publi-

cation of the edition of 1830, nearly 44,000 copies of the
'Lay of the Last Minstrel' were sold in Great Britain.
In the history of British poetry nothing had ever
equalled the demand for the 'Lay of the Last Minstrel.' "

During the year 1805 Scott also wrote several articles for the *Edinburgh Review*, as well as the opening
chapters of *Waverley*. The novel, however, was laid
aside long before it was finished, and the illustrious
author had almost forgotten it, when, accidentally un-
earthing it, he concluded to complete it. In so doing, he
opened another pathway to fame. It was at this date
also that Scott conceived the first outlines of the "Lady
of the Lake." Some of his inspiration for this delightful
narrative poem was doubtless due to his youthful and
enthusiastic study of Spenser and Ossian. In passing,
it is perhaps just to Scott to say, that in later years,
while recognizing James Macpherson's talent, he was
"compelled to admit that incomparably the greater
part of the English Ossian must be ascribed to Macpherson himself."

In November of 1806, when Scott was thirty-five
years old and still under the stimulus of success which
had attended the "Lay of the Last Minstrel," he began
"Marmion." Constable the publisher "offered a thousand guineas for the poem shortly after it was begun,
without having seen one line of it. . . . The news that
a thousand guineas had been paid for an unseen and
unfinished manuscript appeared in those days portentous."

"I had formed," Scott says, "the prudent resolution

to bestow a little more labour than I had yet done on my productions, and to be in no hurry to announce myself as a candidate for literary fame. Accordingly, particular passages of a poem which was finally called 'Marmion' were laboured with a good deal of care by one by whom much care was seldom bestowed. Whether the work was worth the labour or not, I am no competent judge; but I may be permitted to say, that the period of its composition was a very happy one in my life; so much so, that I remember with pleasure at this moment (1830) some of the spots in which particular passages were composed. It is probably owing to this that the introductions to the several cantos assumed the form of familiar epistles to my intimate friends, in which I alluded, perhaps more than was necessary or graceful, to my domestic occupations and amusements,—a loquacity which may be excused by those who remember that I was still young, light-hearted, and happy, and that 'out of the abundance of the heart the mouth speaketh.' "

"Marmion" was not published till February, 1808; but between the inception and completion of the poem, Scott had written many fugitive articles, and had been engrossed with special business incident to his profession. An author's work does not always blossom on the lofty plateau of inspiration, and in January, 1808, we find the poet humourously writing to Lady Louisa Stuart: "Marmion is, at this instant, gasping upon Flodden Field, and there I have been obliged to leave him for these few days in the death pangs. I hope I shall find time enough this morning to knock him on the head with two or three thumping stanzas."

Among contemporary criticisms of this new poem, those of Southey and Jeffrey are interesting. Southey says: "The story is made of better materials than 'The Lay,' yet they are not so well fitted together. As a whole, it has not pleased me so much — in parts, it has pleased me more. There is nothing so finely conceived in your former poem as the death of Marmion: there is nothing finer in its conception anywhere. The introductory epistles I did not wish away, because, as poems, they gave me great pleasure; but I wished them at the end of the volume, or at the beginning — anywhere except where they were."

Jeffrey says, in a criticism of "Marmion," in the *Edinburgh Review* for April, 1808: "The characteristics of both [the 'Lay of the Last Minstrel' and 'Marmion'] are evidently the same; a broken narrative — a redundancy of minute description — bursts of unequal and energetic poetry — and a general tone of spirit and animation, unchecked by timidity or affectation, and unchastened by any great delicacy of taste or elegance of fancy."

Lockhart considers Jeffrey's criticism, of which only an extract is here given, and one which appears to the editor a just summary, as exceedingly severe and unwarranted. The poet himself felt that his analytic friend had dropped a caustic pen in blacker ink than "Marmion" required. Lockhart considers "Marmion" "as, on the whole, the greatest of Scott's poems."

Professor Minto of the University of Aberdeen said: "Scott's resuscitation of the four-beat measure of the old 'gestours' afforded a signal proof of the justness of their instinct in choosing this vehicle for their recitations. The four-beat lines of 'Marmion' took possession of the public like a kind of madness; they not only clung to the memory, but they would not keep off the tongue: people could not help spouting them in solitary places and muttering them as they walked about the streets."

For variety of metre, the judicious intermixture of light and gay passages, and a realistic reproduction of the over-wrought chivalric spirit of the ancient clans of Scotland, "Marmion" must always be admired. The poem betrays, with all the added labor its author gave it, the carelessness characteristic of his writings. The poet, however, never aimed at Dutch fidelity in details as regards fact, composition, or a literary style. He was, in these respects, notwithstanding the length and elaboration of his tales, whether in prose or verse, an impressionist. He needed a large canvas, a free brush, and a distant perspective.

Like all men of true genius, he had an immense capacity for work; and composition, whether of a romance or a poem, was a recreation. He was fortunate in being the predecessor of Byron, and this he appreciated. He was sufficiently free from the unhappy egotism which marks so many authors to realize when he had exhausted the vein from which was wrought "The Lay" and "Marmion" and the "Lady of the Lake."

It was then that Scott turned novelist. The genius of a man who could write poems like these, and novels like "The Heart of Mid-Lothian" and "Guy Mannering," must touch the imagination as epic in its proportions, and ally its possessor in versatility with Shakspeare and Goethe.

M. H. N.

IMPORTANT FACTS IN THE LIFE OF WALTER SCOTT,

AFTER THE PUBLICATION OF MARMION.

———————•———————

1806–1808. The poet edited the Works of John Dryden.

1808–1812. He edited the Works of Jonathan Swift.

1808. He with others projected the *Quarterly Review* in opposition to the *Edinburgh Review*.

1810. Lady of the Lake published, and the composition of Waverley, the poet's first novel, resumed.

1811. Poem of Don Roderick published, and the nucleus of the estate, which the poet named Abbotsford, bought.

1813. Rokeby published; also the Bridal of Triermain. The Poet Laureateship declined.

1814. Waverley published.

1815. Poem, the Lord of the Isles, and second romance, Guy Mannering, published. A visit to the Continent, where, on the field of Waterloo and in Paris, Scott collected much material for Life of Napoleon.

1816. The Antiquary, Tales of my Landlord, the Black Dwarf, and Old Mortality published.

1817. Harold the Dauntless [poem] published. The poet's first serious illness. Rob Roy published.

1818. Heart of Mid-Lothian published. Offer of a baronetcy accepted.

1819. Ivanhoe published.

1820. The Monastery published. A visit at Abbotsford from Prince Gustavus Vasa of Sweden. Scott made a baronet. His portrait painted at the request of the King by Sir Thomas Lawrence, for the great gallery at Windsor Castle. Offered honorary degrees by Oxford and Cambridge. Many distinguished literary and scientific guests received at Abbotsford. The Abbot published. Scott elected president of Royal Society of Edinburgh.

1821. Kenilworth published. At this date Scott estimated that his yearly net income from new literary work was about $75,000. He continued to improve and enlarge his beautiful chateau and estate at Abbotsford. The Pirate published.

1822. Fortunes of Nigel published. Edinburgh visited by George IV. Scott almost daily the King's guest at dinner at Dalkeith Palace.

1823. Peveril of the Peak published. First novel of Continental Life, Quentin Durward, and St. Ronan's Well published.

1824. Red Gauntlet published. Maida, "the noblest and most celebrated of all his dogs," died.

1825. Marriage of the poet's older son, Lieutenant Scott. Abbotsford, with the reservation of Sir Walter Scott's life-rent, settled by marriage contract on Lieutenant Scott and wife. Expenses to Scott connected with the marriage of his son about $25,000. Poet's library at this time contained at least fifteen thousand volumes. Great entrance hall of Abbotsford now finished, and ornamented below the cornice with the shields of the ancient clans, such as those of Douglas, Kerr, Hume, etc. Visited Ireland and received with great honor. Diary begun.

1826. Failure of the three great publishing houses of Hunt
& Robinson, Constable, and Ballantyne. Scott a silent
partner in the last two. His losses, $585,000. United lia-
bilities of the three houses about $3,365,000. Death of
Lady Scott. Woodstock published and sold for about
$40,000, which sum was applied to Scott's debts. Wood-
stock written in less than three months. Town house
offered for sale. Scott's visit to London and Paris for materials for Life of Napoleon. Received with distinguished
honor and respectful sympathy everywhere. Returned to
Scotland cheered and rested for his life-and-death battle
with his debt.

1827. Life of Napoleon published. First and second editions
brought for Scott's creditors $90,000. Chronicles of the
Canongate, First Series, — also, First Series of Tales of
a Grandfather published. Scott sold some of his copyrights
for $23,750, which he applied to his debt. By January,
1828, debt reduced nearly $200,000. Fair Maid of Perth
published. Second Series of Tales of a Grandfather published.

1829. Anne of Geierstein published. Third Series of Tales
of a Grandfather published.

1830. Fourth Series of Tales of a Grandfather published;
also, Letters on Demonology and Witchcraft. Rank of
privy councillor offered to him by George IV. and declined.
Second dividend of three shillings declared by the Ballantyne estate; first dividend was six shillings. Creditors send
Scott a vote of thanks and pass a resolution — "That Sir
Walter Scott be requested to accept of his furniture, plate,
linens, paintings, library, and curiosities of every description, as the best means the creditors have of expressing
their very high sense of his most honourable conduct, and in

grateful acknowledgment for the unparalleled and most successful exertions he has made, and continues to make, for them."

1831. His health continuing to fail, Scott left home in September for the Continent. Winter of 1831–32 passed in Naples. He started for home on April 16, reached Abbotsford on July 11, and died from overwork on September 21, 1832.

MARMION.

To the Right Honorable HENRY LORD MONTAGU, etc., this romance is inscribed by the author.

ADVERTISEMENT TO THE FIRST EDITION.

It is hardly to be expected, that an Author whom the Public have honored with some degree of applause, should not be again a trespasser on their kindness. Yet the Author of MARMION must be supposed to feel some anxiety concerning its success, since he is sensible that he hazards, by this second intrusion, any reputation which his first Poem may have procured him. The present story turns upon the private adventures of a fictitious character; but is called a Tale of Flodden Field, because the hero's fate is connected with that memorable defeat, and the causes which led to it. The design of the Author was, if possible, to apprise his readers, at the outset, of the date of his Story, and to prepare them for the manners of the Age in which it is aid. Any Historical Narrative, far more an attempt at Epic composition, exceeded his plan of a Romantic Tale; yet he may be permitted to hope, from the popularity of THE LAY OF THE LAST MINSTREL, that an attempt to paint the manners of the feudal times, upon a broader scale, and in the course of a more interesting story, will not be unacceptable to the Public.

The Poem opens about the commencement of August, and concludes with the defeat of Flodden, 9th September, 1513.

ASHESTIEL, 1808.

> Alas! that Scottish maid should sing
> The combat where her lover fell!
> That Scottish bard should wake the string,
> The triumph of our foes to tell!
> .   — LEYDEN.

24

CANTO FIRST. .

The Castle.

I.

DAY set on Norham's castled steep,
And Tweed's fair river, broad and deep,
  And Cheviot's mountains lone:
The battled towers, the donjon keep,
The loophole grates, where captives weep,
The flanking walls that round it sweep,
  In yellow lustre shone.
The warriors on the turrets high,
Moving athwart the evening sky,
  Seem'd forms of giant height:
Their armour, as it caught the rays,
Flash'd back again the western blaze,
  In lines of dazzling light.

II.

Saint George's banner, broad and gay,
Now faded, as the fading ray
  Less bright, and less, was flung;
The evening gale had scarce the power
To wave it on the Donjon Tower,
  So heavily it hung.
The scouts had parted on their search,
  The Castle gates were barr'd;

Above the gloomy portal arch,
Timing his footsteps to a march,
  The Warder kept his guard;
Low humming, as he paced along,
Some ancient Border gathering song.

III.

A distant trampling sound he hears:
He looks abroad, and soon appears,
O'er Horncliff-hill a plump of spears,[1]
  Beneath a pennon gay;
A horseman, darting from the crowd,
Like lightning from a summer cloud,
Spurs on his mettled courser proud,
  Before the dark array.
Beneath the sable palisade,
That closed the Castle barricade,
  His bugle horn he blew;
The warder hasted from the wall,
And warn'd the Captain in the hall,
  For well the blast he knew;
And joyfully that knight did call,
To sewer, squire, and seneschal.

IV.

·'Now broach ye a pipe of Malvoisie,[2]
  Bring pasties of the doe,
And quickly make the entrance free,
And bid my heralds ready be,
And every minstrel sound his glee,
  And all our trumpets blow;

And, from the platform, spare ye not
To fire a noble salvo-shot:
   Lord MARMION waits below !"
Then to the Castle's lower ward
   Sped forty yeomen tall,
The iron-studded gates unbarr'd
Raised the portcullis' ponderous guard,
The lofty palisade unsparr'd
   And let the drawbridge fall.

V.

Along the bridge Lord Marmion rode,
Proudly his red-roan charger trode,
His helm hung at the saddlebow ;
Well by his visage you might know
He was a stalworth knight, and keen,
And had in many a battle been ;
The scar on his brown cheek reveal'd
A token true of Bosworth field ;
His eyebrow dark, and eye of fire,
Show'd spirit proud, and prompt to ire ;
Yet lines of thought upon his cheek
Did deep design and counsel speak.
His forehead, by his casque worn bare,
His thick moustache, and curly hair,
Coal-black, and grizzled here and there,
   But more through toil than age ;
His square-turn'd joints, and strength of limb,
Show'd him no carpet knight so trim,
But in close fight a champion grim,
   In camps a leader sage.

VI.

Well was he arm'd from head to heel,
In mail and plate of Milan steel;
But his strong helm, of mighty cost,
Was all with burnish'd gold emboss'd ·
Amid the plumage of the crest,
A falcon hover'd on her nest,
With wings outspread, and forward breast;
E'en such a falcon, on his shield,
Soar'd sable in an azure field:
The golden legend bore aright, —
𝕮𝖍𝖔 𝖈𝖍𝖊𝖈𝖐𝖘 𝖆𝖙 𝖒𝖊, 𝖙𝖔 𝖉𝖊𝖆𝖙𝖍 𝖎𝖘 𝖉𝖎𝖌𝖍𝖙.
Blue was the charger's broider'd rein;
Blue ribbons deck'd his arching mane;
The knightly housing's ample fold
Was velvet blue, and trapp'd with gold.

VII.

Behind him rode two gallant squires,
Of noble name, and knightly sires;
They burn'd the gilded spurs to claim;
For well could each a war-horse tame,
Could draw the bow, the sword could sway,
And lightly bear the ring away;
Nor less with courteous precepts stored,
Could dance in hall, and carve at board,
And frame love-ditties passing rare,
And sing them to a lady fair.

VIII.

Four men-at-arms came at their backs,
With halbert, bill, and battle-axe;

They bore Lord Marmion's lance so strong,
And led his sumpter-mules along,
And ambling palfrey, when at need
Him listed ease his battle-steed.
The last and trustiest of the four,
On high his forky pennon bore;
Like swallow's tail, in shape and hue,
Flutter'd the streamer glossy blue,
Where, blazon'd sable, as before,
The towering falcon seem'd to soar.
Last, twenty yeomen, two and two,
In hosen black, and jerkins blue,
With falcons broider'd on each breast,
Attended on their lord's behest.
Each, chosen for an archer good,
Knew hunting-craft by lake or wood;
Each one a six-foot bow could bend,
And far a cloth-yard shaft could send;
Each held a boar-spear tough and strong,
And at their belts their quivers rung.
Their dusty palfreys, and array,
Show'd they had march'd a weary way.

IX.

'Tis meet that I should tell you now,
How fairly arm'd, and order'd how,
    The soldiers of the guard,
With musket, pike, and morion,
To welcome noble Marmion,
    Stood in the Castle-yard;
Minstrels and trumpeters were there,
The gunner held his linstock yare,
    For welcome-shot prepared:

Enter'd the train, and such a clang,
As then through all his turrets rang,
  Old Norham never heard.

X.

The guards their morrice-pikes advanced,
  The trumpets flourish'd brave,
The cannon from the ramparts glanced,
  And thundering welcome gave.
A blithe salute, in martial sort,
  The minstrels well might sound,
For, as Lord Marmion cross'd the court,
  He scatter'd angels round.
" Welcome to Norham, Marmion !
  Stout heart, and open hand !
Well dost thou brook thy gallant roan,
  Thou flower of English land ! "

XI.

Two pursuivants, whom tabarts deck,
With silver scutcheon round their neck,
  Stood on the steps of stone,
By which you reach the donjon gate,
And there, with herald pomp and state,
  They hail'd Lord Marmion :
They hail'd him Lord of Fontenaye,
Of Lutterward, and Scrivelbaye,
  Of Tamworth tower and town ;
And he, their courtesy to requite,
Gave them a chain of twelve marks' weight,
  All as he lighted down.

" Now, largesse, largesse, Lord Marmion,
  Knight of the crest of gold!
A blazon'd shield, in battle won,
  Ne'er guarded heart so bold."

XII.

They marshall'd him to the Castle-hall,
  Where the guests stood all aside,
And loudly flourish'd the trumpet-call,
  And the heralds loudly cried,
— " Room, lordings, room for Lord Marmion,
  With the cres and helm of gold !
Full well we know the trophies won
  In the lists of Cottiswold:
There, vainly Ralph de Wilton strove
  'Gainst Marmion's force to stand;
To him he lost his lady-love,
  And to the King his land.
Ourselves beheld the listed field,
  A sight both sad and fair;
We saw Lord Marmion pierce his shield,
  And saw his saddle bare;
We saw the victor win the crest
  He wears with worthy pride;
And on the gibbet-tree, reversed,
  His foeman's scutcheon tied.
Place, nobles, for the Falcon-Knight !
  Room, room, ye gentles gay,
For him who conquer'd in the right,
  Marmion of Fontenaye ! "

XIII.

Then stepp'd to meet that noble Lord,
  Sir Hugh the Heron bold,
Baron of Twisell, and of Ford,
  And Captain of the Hold.
He led Lord Marmion to the deas,
  Raised o'er the pavement high,
And placed him in the upper place —
  They feasted full and high ;
The whiles a Northern harper rude
Chanted a rhyme of deadly feud,
  "*How the fierce Thirwalls, and Ridlays all,*
    Stout Willimondswick,
    And Hardriding Dick,
  And Hughie of Hawdon, and Will o' the Wall,
Have set on Sir Albany Featherstonhaugh,
And taken his life at the Deadman's-shaw."
  Scantly Lord Marmion's ear could brook
    The harper's barbarous lay ;
  Yet much he prais'd the pains he took,
    And well those pains did pay :
For lady's suit, and minstrel's strain,
By knight should ne'er be heard in vain.

XIV.

"Now, good Lord Marmion," Heron says,
  "Of your fair courtesy,
I pray you bide some little space
  In this poor tower with me.
Here may you keep your arms from rust,
  May breathe your war-horse well ;
Seldom hath pass'd a week but giust
  Or feat of arms befell :

The Scots can rein a mettled steed;
  And love to couch a spear; —
Saint George! a stirring life they lead,
  That have such neighbours near.
Then stay with us a little space,
  Our northern wars to learn;
I pray you, for your lady's grace!"
  Lord Marmion's brow grew stern.

XV.

The Captain mark'd his alter'd look,
  And gave a squire the sign;
A mighty wassail-bowl he took,
  And crown'd it high in wine.
" Now pledge me here, Lord Marmion:
  But first I pray thee fair,
Where thou hast left that page of thine,
That used to serve thy cup of wine,
  Whose beauty was so rare?
When last in Raby towers we met,
  The boy I closely eyed,
And often mark'd his cheeks were wet,
  With tears he fain would hide:
His was no rugged horse-boy's hand,
To burnish shield or sharpen brand,
  Or saddle battle-steed;
But meeter seem'd for lady fair,
To fan her cheek, or curl her hair,
Or through embroidery, rich and rare,
  The slender silk to lead;
His skin was fair, his ringlets gold,
  His bosom — when he sigh'd,
The russet doublet's rugged fold
  Could scarce repel its pride!

Say, hast thou given that lovely youth
  To serve in lady's bower!
Or was the gentle page, in sooth,
  A gentle paramour?"

XVI.

Lord Marmion ill could brook such jest;
  He roll'd his kindling eye,
With pain his rising wrath suppress'd,
  Yet made a calm reply:
"That boy thou thought'st so goodly fair,
He might not brook the northern air;
More of his fate if thou wouldst learn,
I left him sick in Lindisfarn:
Enough of him.—But, Heron, say,
Why does thy lovely lady gay
Disdain to grace the hall to-day?
Or has that dame, so fair and sage,
Gone on some pious pilgrimage?"
He spoke in covert scorn, for fame
Whisper'd light tales of Heron's dame.

XVII.

Unmark'd, at least unreck'd, the taunt,
  Careless the Knight replied,
"No bird, whose feathers gayly flaunt,
  Delights in cage to bide:
Norham is grim and grated close,
Hemm'd in by battlement and fosse,
  And many a darksome tower;
And better loves my lady bright
To sit in liberty and light,
  In fair Queen Margaret's bower.

We hold our greyhound in our hand,
   Our falcon on our glove;
But where shall we find leash or band,
   For dame that loves to rove?
Let the wild falcon soar her swing,
She'll stoop when she has tired her wing." —

XVIII.

" Nay, if with Royal James's bride,
The lovely Lady Heron bide,
Behold me here a messenger,
Your tender greetings prompt to bear;
For, to the Scottish court address'd,
I journey at our King's behest,
And pray you, of your grace, provide
For me, and mine, a trusty guide.
I have not ridden in Scotland since
James back'd the cause of that mock prince
Warbeck, that Flemish counterfeit,
Who on the gibbet paid the cheat.
Then did I march with Surrey's power,
What time we razed old Ayton tower."

XIX.

" For such-like need, my lord, I trow,
Norham can find you guides enow;
For here be some have prick'd as far,
On Scottish ground, as to Dunbar;
Have drunk the monks of St. Bothan's ale,
And driven the beeves of Lauderdale;
Harried the wives of Greenlaw's goods,
And given them light to set their hoods."

XX.

" Now, in good sooth," Lord Marmion cried,
" Were I in warlike wise to ride,
A better guard I would not lack,
Than your stout forayers at my back.
But, as in form of peace I go,
A friendly messenger, to know,
Why through all Scotland, near and far,
Their king is mustering troops for war,
The sight of plundering border spears
Might justify suspicious fears,
And deadly feud, or thirst of spoil,
Break out in some unseemly broil :
A herald were my fitting guide ;
Or friar, sworn in peace to bide ;
Or pardoner, or travelling priest,
Or strolling pilgrim, at the least."

XXI.

The Captain mused a little space,
And pass'd his hand across his face.
— " Fain would I find the guide you want,
But ill may spare a pursuivant,
The only men that safe can ride
Mine errands on the Scottish side :
And though a bishop built this fort,
Few holy brethren here resort ;
Even our good chaplain, as I ween,
Since our last siege we have not seen :
The mass he might not sing or say,
Upon one stinted meal a-day ;
So, safe he sat in Durham aisle,
And pray'd for our success the while.

Our Norham vicar, woe betide,
Is all too well in case to ride;
The priest of Shoreswood — he could rein
The wildest war-horse in your train;
But then, no spearman in the hall
Will sooner swear, or stab, or brawl.
Friar John of Tillmouth were the man:
A blithesome brother at the can,
A welcome guest in hall and bower,
He knows each castle, town, and tower,
In which the wine and ale is good,
'Twixt Newcastle and Holy-Rood.
But that good man, as ill befalls,
Hath seldom left our castle walls,
Since, on the Vigil of St. Bede,
In evil hour he cross'd the Tweed,
To teach Dame Alison her creed.
Old Bughtrig found him with his wife;
And John, an enemy to strife,
Sans frock and hood, fled for his life.
The jealous churl hath deeply swore,
That, if again he venture o'er,
He shall shrive penitent no more.
Little he loves such risks, I know;
Yet in your guard perchance will go."

XXII.

Young Selby, at the fair hall-board,
Carved to his uncle and that lord,
And reverently took up the word.
" Kind Uncle, woe were we each one,
If harm should hap to Brother John.

He is a man of mirthful speech,
Can many a game and gambol teach;
Full well at tables can he play,
And sweep at bowls the stake away.
None can a lustier carol bawl,
The needfullest among us all,
When time hangs heavy in the hall,
And snow comes thick at Christmas tide,
And we can neither hunt, nor ride
A foray on the Scottish side.
The vowed revenge of Bughtrig rude,
May end in worse than loss of hood.
Let Friar John, in safety, still
In chimney-corner snore his fill,
Roast hissing crabs, or flagons swill:
Last night, to Norham there came one,
Will better guide Lord Marmion." —
" Nephew," quoth Heron, " by my fay,
Well hast thou spoke; say forth thy say."

XXIII.

" Here is a holy Palmer come,
From Salem first, and last from Rome;
One that hath kiss'd the blessed tomb,
And visited each holy shrine
In Araby and Palestine;
On hills of Armenie hath been,
Where Noah's ark may yet be seen;
By that Red Sea, too, hath he trod,
Which parted at the prophet's rod;
In Sinai's wilderness he saw
The mount where Israel heard the law,
'Mid thunder-dint, and flashing levin,
And shadows, mists, and darkness, given.

He shows Saint James's cockle-shell,
Of fair Montserrat, too, can tell;
   And of that Grot where Olives nod,
Where, darling of each heart and eye,
From all the youth of Sicily,
   Saint Rosalie retired to God.

XXIV.

" To stout Saint George of Norwich merry,
Saint Thomas, too, of Canterbury,
Cuthbert of Durham and Saint Bede,
For his sins' pardon hath he pray'd.
He knows the passes of the North,
And seeks far shrines beyond the Forth;
Little he eats, and long will wake,
And drinks but of the stream or lake.
This were a guide o'er moor and dale;
But, when our John hath quaffed his ale,
As little as the wind that blows,
And warms itself against his nose,
Kens he, or cares, which way he goes." —

XXV.

" Gramercy!" quoth Lord Marmion,
" Full loath were I, that Friar John,
That venerable man, for me,
Were placed in fear or jeopardy.
If this same Palmer will me lead
   From hence to Holy-Rood,
Like his good saint, I'll pay his meed,
Instead of cockle-shell, or bead,
With angels fair and good.

I love such holy ramblers; still
They know to charm a weary hill,
   With song, romance, or lay:
Some jovial tale, or glee, or jest,
Some lying legend, at the least,
   They bring to cheer the way." —

XXVI.

" Ah! noble sir," young Selby said,
And finger on his lip he laid,
" This man knows much, perchance e'en more
Than he could learn by holy lore.
Still to himself he's muttering,
And shrinks as at some unseen thing.
Last night we listen'd at his cell;
Strange sounds we heard, and, sooth to tell,
He murmur'd on till morn, howe'er
No living mortal could be near.
Sometimes I thought I heard it plain,
As other voices spoke again.
I cannot tell — I like it not —
Friar John hath told us it is wrote,
No conscience clear, and void of wrong,
Can rest awake, and pray so long.
Himself still sleeps before his beads
Have mark'd ten aves, and two creeds."

XXVII.

— " Let pass," quoth Marmion; " by my fay,
This man shall guide me on my way,
Although the great arch-fiend and he
Had sworn themselves of company.

So please you, gentle youth, to call
This Palmer to the Castle-hall."
The summon'd Palmer came in place;
His sable cowl o'erhung his face;
In his black mantle was he clad,
With Peter's keys, in cloth of red,
  On his broad shoulders wrought;
The scallop shell his cap did deck:
The crucifix around his neck
  Was from Loretto brought;
His sandals were with travel tore,
Staff, budget, bottle, scrip, he wore;
The faded palm-branch in his hand
Show'd pilgrim from the Holy Land.

XXVIII.

When as the Palmer came in hall,
No lord, nor knight, was there more tall,
Nor had a statelier step withal,
  Or look'd more high and keen;
For no saluting did he wait,
But strode across the hall of state,
And fronted Marmion where he sate,
  As he his peer had been.
But his gaunt frame was worn with toil;
His cheek was sunk, alas the while!
And when he struggled at a smile,
  His eye look'd haggard wild:
Poor wretch! the mother that him bare,
If she had been in presence there,
In his wan face, and sun-burn'd hair,
  She had not known her child.

Danger, long travel, want, or woe,
Soon change the form that best we know —
For deadly fear can time outgo,
   And blanch at once the hair;
Hard toil can roughen form and face,
And want can quench the eye's bright grace,
Nor does old age a wrinkle trace
   More deeply than despair.
Happy whom none of these befall,
But this poor Palmer knew them all.

XXIX.

Lord Marmion then his boon did ask;
The Palmer took on him the task,
So he would march with morning tide,
To Scottish court to be his guide.
"But I have solemn vows to pay,
And may not linger by the way,
   To fair Saint Andrews bound,
Within the ocean-cave to pray,
Where good Saint Rule his holy lay,
From midnight to the dawn of day,
   Sung to the billows' sound;
Thence to Saint Fillan's blessed well,
Whose spring can frenzied dreams dispel,
   And the crazed brain restore:
Saint Mary grant, that cave or spring
Could back to peace my bosom bring,
   Or bid it throb no more!"

XXX.

And now the midnight draught of sleep,
Where wine and spices richly steep,

In massive bowl of silver deep,
  The page presents on knee.
Lord Marmion drank a fair good rest,
The Captain pledged his noble guest,
The cup went through among the res⁺
  Who drained it merrily;
Alone the Palmer pass'd it by,
Though Selby press'd him courteously.
This was a sign the feast was o'er;
It hush'd the merry wassel roar,
  The minstrels ceased to sound.
Soon in the castle nought was heard,
But the slow footstep of the guard,
  Pacing his sober round.

XXXI.

With early dawn Lord Marmion rose:
And first the chapel doors unclose;
Then, after morning rites were done,
(A hasty mass from Friar John,)
And knight and squire had broke their fast,
On rich substantial repast,
Lord Marmion's bugles blew to horse:
Then came the stirrup-cup in course:
Between the Baron and his host,
No point of courtesy was lost;
High thanks were by Lord Marmion paid,
Solemn excuse the Captain made,
Till, filing from the gate, had pass'd
That noble train, their Lord the last.
Then loudly rung the trumpet call,
Thunder'd the cannon from the wall
  And shook the Scottish shore;

Around the castle eddied slow,
Volumes of smoke as white as snow,
   And hid its turrets hoar;
Till they roll'd forth upon the air,
And met the river breezes there,
Which gave again the prospect fair.

CANTO SECOND.

The Convent.

I.

THE breeze which swept away the smoke,
  Round Norham Castle roll'd,
When all the loud artillery spoke,
With lightning-flash and thunder-stroke,
As Marmion left the Hold.
It curl'd not Tweed alone, that breeze,
For, far upon Northumbrian seas,
  It freshly blew, and strong,
Where, from high Whitby's cloister'd pile,
Bound to Saint Cuthbert's Holy Isle,
  It bore a bark along.
Upon the gale she stoop'd her side,
And bounded o'er the swelling tide,
  As she were dancing home;
The merry seamen laugh'd, to see
Their gallant ship so lustily
  Furrow the green sea-foam.
Much joy'd they in their honour'd freight;
For, on the deck, in chair of state,
The Abbess of Saint Hilda placed,
With five fair nuns, the galley graced.

II.

'Twas sweet to see these holy maids,
Like birds escaped to green-wood shades,
   Their first flight from the cage,
How timid, and how curious too,
For all to them was strange and new,
And all the common sights they view,
   Their wonderment engage.
One eyed the shrouds and swelling sail,
   With many a benedicite;
One at the rippling surge grew pale,
   And would for terror pray;
Then shriek'd, because the sea-dog, nigh,
His round black head, and sparkling eye,
   Rear'd o'er the foaming spray;
And one would still adjust her veil,
Disorder'd by the summer gale,
Perchance lest some more worldly eye
Her dedicated charms might spy;
Perchance, because such action graced
Her fair-turn'd arm and slender waist.
Light was each simple bosom there,
Save two, who ill might pleasure share, —
The Abbess and the Novice Clare.

III.

The Abbess was of noble blood,
But early took the veil and hood,
Ere upon life she cast a look,
Or knew the world that she forsook.
Fair too she was, and kind had been
As she was fair, but ne'er had seen

For her a timid lover sigh,
Nor knew the influence of her eye.
Love, to her ear, was but a name,
Combined with vanity and shame;
Her hopes, her fears, her joys, were all
Bounded within the cloister wall:
The deadliest sin her mind could reach,
Was of monastic rule the breach;
And her ambition's highest aim
To emulate Saint Hilda's fame.
For this she gave her ample dower,
To raise the convent's eastern tower;
For this, with carving rare and quaint,
She deck'd the chapel of the saint,
And gave the relic-shrine of cost,
With ivory and gems emboss'd.
The poor her Convent's bounty blessed,
The pilgrim in its halls found rest.

IV.

Black was her garb, her rigid rule
Reform'd on Benedictine school;
Her cheek was pale, her form was spare;
Vigils, and penitence austere,
Had early quench'd the light of youth,
But gentle was the dame, in sooth;
Though, vain of her religious sway,
She loved to see her maids obey.
Yet nothing stern was she in cell,
And the nuns loved their Abbess well.
Sad was this voyage to the dame;
Summon'd to Lindisfarne, she came,

There, with St. Cuthbert's Abbot old,
And Tynemouth's Prioress, to hold
A chapter of Saint Benedict,
For inquisition stern and strict,
On two apostates from the faith,
And, if need were, to doom to death.

V.

Nought say I here of Sister Clare,
Save this, that she was young and fair;
As yet, a novice unprofess'd,
Lovely and gentle, but distress'd.
She was betroth'd to one now dead,
Or worse, who had dishonour'd fled.
Her kinsmen bade her give her hand
To one, who loved her for her land:
Herself, almost heart-broken now,
Was bent to take the vestal vow,
And shroud within Saint Hilda's gloom,
Her blasted hopes and wither'd bloom.

VI.

She sate upon the galley's prow,
And seem'd to mark the waves below;
Nay, seem'd, so fix'd her look and eye,
To count them as they glided by.
She saw them not — 'twas seeming all —
Far other scene her thoughts recall, —
A sun-scorch'd desert, waste and bare,
Nor waves, nor breezes, murmur'd there;
There saw she, where some careless hand
O'er a dead corpse had heap'd the sand,

To hide it till the jackals come,
To tear it from the scanty tomb. —
See what a woful look was given,
As she raised up her eyes to heaven!

VII.

Lovely, and gentle, and distress'd —
These charms might tame the fiercest breast;
Harpers have sung, and poets told,
That he, in fury uncontrolled,
The shaggy monarch of the wood,
Before a virgin fair and good,
Hath pacified his savage mood.
But passions in the human frame,
Oft put the lion's rage to shame:
And jealousy, by dark intrigue,
With sordid avarice in league,
Had practised with their bowl and knife,
Against the mourner's harmless life.
This crime was charged 'gainst those who lay
Prison'd in Cuthbert's islet gray.

VIII.

And now the vessel skirts the strand
Of mountainous Northumberland;
Towns, towers, and halls, successive rise,
And catch the nuns' delighted eyes.
Monk-Wearmouth soon behind them lay;
And Tynemouth's priory and bay;
They mark'd, amid her trees, the hall
Of lofty Seaton-Delaval;
They saw the Blythe and Wansbeck floods
Rush to the sea through sounding woods;

They pass'd the tower of Widderington,
Mother of many a valiant son;
At Coquet-isle their beads they tell
To the good saint who own'd the cell;
Then did the Alne attention claim,
And Warkworth, proud of Percy's name;
And next, they cross'd themselves, to hear
The whitening breakers sound so near,
Where, boiling through the rocks, they roar,
On Dunstanborough's cavern'd shore;
Thy tower, proud Bamborough, mark'd they there,
King Ida's castle, huge and square,
From its tall rock look grimly down,
And on the swelling ocean frown;
Then from the coast they bore away,
And reach'd the Holy Island's bay.

IX.

The tide did now its flood-mark gain,
And girdled in the Saint's domain:
For, with the flow and ebb, its style
Varies from continent to isle;
Dry-shod, o'er sands, twice every day,
The pilgrims to the shrine find way;
Twice every day, the waves efface
Of staves and sandall'd feet the trace.
As to the port the galley flew,
Higher and higher rose to view
The Castle, with its battled walls,
The ancient Monastery's halls,
A solemn, huge, and dark-red pile,
Placed on the margin of the isle.

X.

In Saxon strength that abbey frown'd,
With massive arches broad and round,
  That rose alternate, row and row,
  On ponderous columns, short and low,
    Built ere the art was known,
  By pointed aisle and shafted stalk,
  The arcades of an alley'd walk
    To emulate in stone.
On the deep walls, the heathen Dane
Had pour'd his impious rage in vain :
And needful was such strength to these,
Exposed to the tempestuous seas,
Scourged by the winds' eternal sway,
Open to rovers fierce as they,
Which could twelve hundred years withstand
Winds, waves, and northern pirates' hand.
Not but that portions of the pile,
Rebuilded in a later style,
Show'd where the spoiler's hand had been ;
Not but the wasting sea-breeze keen
Had worn the pillar's carving quaint,
And moulder'd in his niche the saint,
And rounded, with consuming power,
The pointed angles of each tower ;
Yet still entire the Abbey stood,
Like veteran, worn, but unsubdued.

XI.

Soon as they near'd his turrets strong,
The maidens raised Saint Hilda's song,
  And with the sea-wave and the wind,
  Their voices, sweetly shrill, combined,
    And made harmonious close ;

Then, answering from the sandy shore,
Half drown'd amid the breakers' roar,
   According chorus rose:
Down to the haven of the Isle,
The monks and nuns in order file,
   From Cuthbert's cloisters grim;
Banner, and cross, and relics there,
To meet Saint Hilda's maids, they bare;
And, as they caught the sounds on air,
   They echoed back the hymn.
The islanders, in joyous mood,
Rush'd emulously through the flood,
   To hale the bark to land;
Conspicuous by her veil and hood,
Signing the cross, the Abbess stood,
   And bless'd them with her hand.

XII.

Suppose we now the welcome said,
Suppose the Convent banquet made:
   All through the holy dome,
Through cloister, aisle, and gallery,
Wherever vestal maid might pry,
Nor risk to meet unhallow'd eye,
   The stranger sisters roam:
Till fell the evening damp with dew,
And the sharp sea-breeze coldly blew,
For there, even summer night is chill.
Then, having stray'd and gazed their fill,
   They closed around the fire;
And all, in turn, essay'd to paint
The rival merits of their saint,
   A theme that ne'er can tire

A holy maid; for, be it known,
That their saint's honor is their own.

XIII.

Then Whitby's nuns exulting told,
How to their house three Barons bold
   Must menial service do;
While horns blow out a note of shame,
And monks cry " Fye upon your name!
In wrath, for loss of sylvan game,
   Saint Hilda's priest ye slew." —
" This, on Ascension-day, each year,
While labouring on our harbour-pier,
Must Herbert, Bruce, and Percy hear." —
They told, how in their convent cell
A Saxon Princess once did dwell,
   The lovely Edelfled;
And how, of thousand snakes, each one
Was changed into a coil of stone,
   When holy Hilda pray'd;
Themselves, within their holy bound,
Their stony folds had often found.
They told, how sea-fowls' pinions fail
As over Whitby's towers they sail,
And, sinking down, with flutterings faint,
They do their homage to the saint.

XIV.

Nor did Saint Cuthbert's daughters fail,
To vie with these in holy tale;
His body's resting-place, of old,
How oft their patron changed, they told;

How, when the rude Dane burn'd their pile,
The monks fled forth from Holy Isle;
O'er northern mountain, marsh, and moor,
From sea to sea, from shore to shore,
Seven years Saint Cuthbert's corpse they bore.
They rested them in fair Melrose;
   But though, alive, he loved it well,
Not there his relics might repose;
   For, wondrous tale to tell!
In his stone coffin forth he rides,
A ponderous bark for river tides,
Yet light as gossamer it glides,
   Downward to Tilmouth cell.
Nor long was his abiding there,
For southward did the saint repair;
Chester-le-Street and Rippon saw
His holy corpse, ere Wardilaw
   Hail'd him with joy and fear;
And, after many wanderings past,
He chose his lordly seat at last,
Where his cathedral, huge and vast,
   Looks down upon the Wear:
There, deep in Durham's Gothic shade,
His relics are in secret laid;
   But none may know the place,
Save of his holiest servants three,
Deep sworn to solemn secrecy,
   Who share that wondrous grace.

XV.

Who may his miracles declare!
Even Scotland's dauntless king, and heir
   (Although with them they led

Galwegians, wild as ocean's gale,
And Lodon's knights, all sheathed in mail,
And the bold men of Teviotdale,)
　　Before his standard fled.
'Twas he, to vindicate his reign,
Edged Alfred's falchion on the Dane,
And turn'd the Conqueror back again,
When, with his Norman bowyer band,
He came to waste Northumberland.

XVI.

But fain Saint Hilda's nuns would learn
If, on a rock by Lindisfarne,
Saint Cuthbert sits, and toils to frame
The sea-born beads that bear his name:
Such tales had Whitby's fishers told,
And said they might his shape behold,
　　And hear his anvil sound;
A deaden'd clang, — a huge dim form,
Seen but, and heard, when gathering storm
　　And night were closing round.
But this, as tale of idle fame,
The nuns of Lindisfarne disclaim.

XVII.

While round the fire such legends go,
Far different was the scene of woe,
Where, in a secret aisle beneath,
Council was held of life and death.
　　It was more dark and lone, that vault,
　　　　Than the worst dungeon cell:
　　Old Colwulf built it, for his fault,
　　　　In penitence to dwell,

When he, for cowl and beads, laid down
The Saxon battle-axe and crown.
This den, which, chilling every sense
   Of feeling, hearing, sight,
Was call'd the Vault of Penitence,
   Excluding air and light,
Was, by the prelate Sexhelm, made
A place of burial for such dead,
As, having died in mortal sin,
Might not be laid the church within
'Twas now a place of punishment;
Whence if so loud a shriek were sent,
   As reach'd the upper air,
The hearers bless'd themselves, and said,
The spirits of the sinful dead
   Bemoan'd their torments there.

XVIII.

But though, in the monastic pile,
Did of this penitential aisle
   Some vague tradition go.
Few only, save the Abbot, knew
Where the place lay; and still more few
Were those, who had from him the clew
   To that dread vault to go,
Victim and executioner
Were blindfold when transported there.
In low dark rounds the arches hung,
From the rude rock the side-walls sprung;
The grave-stones, rudely sculptured o'er,
Half sunk in earth, by time half wore,
Were all the pavement of the floor;

The mildew-drops fell one by one,
With tinkling plash, upon the stone.
A cresset,[1] in an iron chain,
Which served to light this drear domain,
With damp and darkness seem'd to strive,
As if it scarce might keep alive;
And yet it dimly served to show
The awful conclave met below.

XIX.

There, met to doom in secrecy,
Were placed the heads of convents three:
All servants of Saint Benedict,
The statutes of whose order strict
   On iron table lay;
In long black dress, on seats of stone,
Behind were these three judges shown
   By the pale cresset's ray:
The Abbess of Saint Hilda's there
Sat for a space with visage bare,
Until, to hide her bosom's swell,
And tear-drops that for pity fell,
   She closely drew her veil:
Yon shrouded figure, as I guess,
By her proud mien and flowing dress,
Is Tynemouth's haughty Prioress,
   And she with awe looks pale:
And he, that Ancient Man, whose sight
Has long been quench'd by age's night,
Upon whose wrinkled brow alone,
Nor ruth, nor mercy's trace, is shown,
   Whose look is hard and stern, —

Saint Cuthbert's Abbot is his style ;
For sanctity call'd, through the isle,
   The Saint of Lindisfarne.

XX.

Before them stood a guilty pair ;
But, though an equal fate they share,
Yet one alone deserves our care.
Her sex a page's dress belied ;
The cloak and doublet, loosely tied,
Obscured her charms, but could not hide.
   Her cap down o'er her face she drew ;
     And, on her doublet breast,
   She tried to hide the badge of blue,
     Lord Marmion's falcon crest.
But, at the Prioress' command,
A monk undid the silver band,
   That tied her tresses fair,
And raised the bonnet from her head,
And down her slender form they spread,
   In ringlets rich and rare.
Constance de Beverley they know,
Sister profess'd of Fontevraud,
Whom the church number'd with the dead,
For broken vows, and convent fled.

XXI.

When thus her face was given to view,
(Although so pallid was her hue,
It did a ghastly contrast bear
To those bright ringlets glistering fair,)
Her look composed, and steady eye,
Bespoke a matchless constancy ;

And there she stood so calm and pale,
That, but her breathing did not fail,
And motion slight of eye and head,
And of her bosom, warranted
That neither sense nor pulse she lacks,
You might have thought a form of wax,
Wrought to the very life, was there;
So still she was, so pale, so fair.

XXII.

Her comrade was a sordid soul,
  Such as does murder for a meed;
Who, but of fear, knows no control,
Because his conscience, sear'd and foul,
  Feels not the import of his deed;
One, whose brute-feeling ne'er aspires
Beyond his own more brute desires.
Such tools the Tempter ever needs,
To do the savagest of deeds;
For them no vision'd terrors daunt,
Their nights no fancied spectres haunt,
One fear with them, of all most base,
The fear of death, — alone finds place.
This wretch was clad in frock and cowl,
And shamed not loud to moan and howl,
His body on the floor to dash,
And crouch, like hound beneath the lash;
While his mute partner, standing near,
Waited her doom without a tear.

XXIII.

Yet well the luckless wretch might shriek,
Well might her paleness terror speak!

For there were seen in that dark wall,
Two niches, narrow, deep, and tall ; —
Who enters at such grisly door,
Shall ne'er, I ween, find exit more.
In each a slender meal was laid,
Of roots, of water, and of bread :
By each, in Benedictine dress,
Two haggard monks stood motionless ;
Who, holding high a blazing torch,
Show'd the grim entrance of the porch :
Reflecting back the smoky beam,
The dark-red walls and arches gleam.
Hewn stones and cement were display'd,
And building tools in order laid.

XXIV.

These executioners were chose,
As men who were with mankind foes,
And with despite and envy fired,
Into the cloister had retired ;
  Or who, in desperate doubt of grace,
  Strove, by deep penance, to efface
    Of some foul crime the stain ;
  For, as the vassals of her will,
  Such men the Church selected still,
  As either joy'd in doing ill,
    Or thought more grace to gain,
If, in her cause, they wrestled down
Feelings their nature strove to own.
By strange device were they brought there,
They knew not how, nor knew not where.

XXV.

And now that blind old Abbot rose,
  To speak the Chapter's doom,
On those the wall was to enclose,
  Alive, within the tomb,
But stopp'd, because that woful Maid,
Gathering her powers, to speak essay'd.
Twice she essay'd, and twice in vain ;
Her accents might no utterance gain ;
Nought but imperfect murmurs slip
From her convulsed and quivering lip ;
  'Twixt each attempt all was so still,
  You seem'd to hear a distant rill —
    'Twas ocean's swells and falls ;
  For though this vault of sin and fear
  Was to the sounding surge so near,
  A tempest there you scarce could hear,
    So massive were the walls.

XXVI.

At length, an effort sent apart
The blood that curdled to her heart,
  And light came to her eye,
And color dawn'd upon her cheek,
A hectic and a flutter'd streak,
Like that left on the Cheviot peak,
  By Autumn's stormy sky ;
And when her silence broke at length,
Still as she spoke she gather'd strength,
  And arm'd herself to bear.
It was a fearful sight to see
Such high resolve and constancy,
  In form so soft and fair,

XXVII.

" I speak not to implore your grace ;
Well know I, for one minute's space
   Successless might I sue :
Nor do I speak your prayers to gain ;
For if a death of lingering pain,
To cleanse my sins, be penance vain,
   Vain are your masses too. —
I listen'd to a traitor's tale,
I left the convent and the veil ;
For three long years I bow'd my pride,
A horse-boy in his train to ride ;
And well my folly's meed he gave,
Who forfeited, to be his slave,
All here, and all beyond the grave. —
He saw young Clara's face more fair,
He knew her of broad lands the heir,
Forgot his vows, his faith forswore,
And Constance was belov'd no more.—
   'Tis an old tale, and often told ;
     But did my fate and wish agree,
   Ne'er had been read, in story old,
   Of maiden true betray'd for gold,
   That loved, or was avenged, like me !

XXVIII.

" The King approved his favorite's aim ;
In vain a rival barr'd his claim,
   Whose fate with Clare's was plight,
For he attaints that rival's fame
With treason's charge — and on they came,
   In mortal lists to fight.

Their oaths are said,
Their prayers are pray'd,
Their lances in the rest are laid,
They meet in mortal shock;
And, hark! the throng, with thundering cry,
Shout 'Marmion, Marmion! to the sky,
De Wilton to the block!'
Say ye, who preach Heaven shall decide
When in the lists two champions ride,
Say, was Heaven's justice here?
When, loyal in his love and faith,
Wilton found overthrow or death,
Beneath a traitor's spear?
How false the charge, how true he fell,
This guilty packet best can tell."—
Then drew a packet from her breast,
Paused, gather'd voice, and spoke the rest.

XXIX.

" Still was false Marmion's bridal staid;
To Whitby's convent fled the maid,
The hated match to shun.
'Ho! shifts she thus?' King Henry cried.
' Sir Marmion, she shall be thy bride,
If she were sworn a nun.'
One way remained — the King's command
Sent Marmion to the Scottish land:
I linger'd here, and rescue plann'd
For Clara and for me:
This caitiff Monk, for gold, did swear,
He would to Whitby's shrine repair,
And, by his drugs, my rival fair
A saint in heaven should be.

But ill the dastard kept his oath,
Whose cowardice has undone us both.

XXX.

" And now my tongue the secret tells,
Not that remorse my bosom swells,
But to assure my soul that none
Shall ever wed with Marmion.
Had fortune my last hope betray'd,
This packet, to the King convey'd,
Had given him to the headsman's stroke,
Although my heart that instant broke. —
Now, men of death, work forth your will,
For I can suffer, and be still;
And come he slow, or come he fast,
It is but Death who comes at last

XXXI.

" Yet dread me, from my living tomb,
Ye vassal slaves of bloody Rome!
If Marmion's late remorse should wake,
Full soon such vengeance will he take,
That you shall wish the fiery Dane
Had rather been your guest again.
Behind, a darker hour ascends!
The altars quake, the crosier bends,
The ire of a despotic King
Rides forth upon destruction's wing;
Then shall these vaults, so strong and deep,
Burst open to the sea-winds' sweep;
Some traveller then shall find my bones
Whitening amid disjointed stones,
And, ignorant of priests' cruelty,
Marvel such relics here should be."

XXXII.

Fix'd was her look, and stern her air:
Back from her shoulders stream'd her hair;
The locks, that wont her brow to shade,
Stared up erectly from her head;
Her figure seem'd to rise more high;
Her voice, despair's wild energy
Had given a tone of prophecy.
Appall'd the astonish'd conclave sate;
With stupid eyes, the men of fate
Gazed on the light inspired form,
And listen'd for the avenging storm;
The judges felt the victim's dread;
No hand was moved, no word was said,
Till thus the Abbot's doom was given,
Raising his sightless balls to heaven: —
" Sister, let thy sorrows cease;
Sinful brother, part in peace !"
    From that dire dungeon, place of doom,
      Of execution too, and tomb,
        Paced forth the judges three;
Sorrow it were, and shame, to tell
The butcher-work that there befell,
When they had glided from the cell
        Of sin and misery.

XXXIII.

An hundred winding steps convey
That conclave to the upper day;
But, ere they breathed the fresher air,
They heard the shriekings of despair,
    And many a stifled groan:

With speed their upward way they take,
(Such speed as age and fear can make,)
And cross'd themselves for terror's sake,
    As hurrying, tottering on :
Even in the vesper's heavenly tone,
They seem'd to hear a dying groan,
And bade the passing knell to toll
For welfare of a parting soul.
Slow o'er the midnight wave it swung,
Northumbrian rocks in answer rung ;
To Warkworth cell the echoes roll'd,
His beads the wakeful hermit told,
The Bamborough peasant raised his head,
But slept ere half a prayer he said :
So far was heard the mighty knell,
The stag sprung up on Cheviot Fell,
Spread his broad nostril to the wind,
Listed before, aside, behind,
Then couch'd him down beside the hind,
And quaked among the mountain fern,
To hear that sound so dull and stern.

CANTO THIRD.

The Hostel, or Inn.

1.

THE livelong day Lord Marmion rode:
The mountain path the Palmer show'd,
By glen and streamlet winded still,
Where stunted birches hid the rill.
They might not choose the lowland road,
For the Merse forayers were abroad,
Who, fired with hate and thirst of prey,
Had scarcely fail'd to bar their way.
Oft on the trampling band, from crown
Of some tall cliff, the deer look'd down;
On wing of jet, from his repose
In the deep heath, the black-cock rose;
Sprung from the gorse the timid roe,
Nor waited for the bending bow;
And when the stony path began,
By which the naked peak they wan,
Up flew the snowy ptarmigan.
The noon had long been pass'd before
They gain'd the height of Lammermoor;
Thence winding down the northern way
Before them, at the close of day,
Old Gifford's towers and hamlet lay.

II.

No summons calls them to the tower,
To spend the hospitable hour.
To Scotland's camp the Lord was gone;
His cautious dame, in bower alone,
Dreaded her castle to unclose,
So late, to unknown friends or foes,
On through the hamlet as they paced,
Before a porch, whose front was graced
With bush and flagon trimly placed,
   Lord Marmion drew his rein:
The village inn seem'd large, though rude;
Its cheerful fire and hearty food
   Might well relieve his train.
Down from their seats the horsemen sprung,
With jingling spurs the court-yard rung;
They bind their horses to the stall,
For forage, food, and firing call,
And various clamour fills the hall:
Weighing the labour with the cost,
Toils everywhere the bustling host.

III.

Soon, by the chimney's merry blaze,
Through the rude hostel might you gaze;
Might see, where, in dark nook aloof,
The rafters of the sooty roof
   Bore wealth of winter cheer;
Of sea-fowl dried, and solands store,
And gammons of the tusky boar,
   And savoury haunch of deer.
The chimney arch projected wide;
Above, around it, and beside,
   Were tools for housewives' hand,

Nor wanted, in that martial day,
The implements of Scottish fray,
　　The buckler, lance, and brand.
Beneath its shade, the place of state,
On oaken settle Marmion sate,
And view'd around the blazing hearth.
His followers mix in noisy mirth;
Whom with brown ale, in jolly tide,
From ancient vessels ranged aside,
Full actively their host supplied.

IV.

Theirs was the glee of martial breast,
And laughter theirs at little jest;
And oft Lord Marmion deign'd to aid,
And mingle in the mirth they made;
For though, with men of high degree,
The proudest of the proud was he,
Yet, trained in camps, he knew the art
To win the soldier's hardy heart.
They love a captain to obey,
Boisterous as March, yet fresh as May;
With open hand, and brow as free,
Lover of wine and minstrelsy;
Ever the first to scale a tower,
As venturous in a lady's bower: —
Such buxom chief shall lead his host
From India's fires to Zembla's frost.

V.

Resting upon his pilgrim staff,
　　Right opposite the Palmer stood;
His thin dark visage seen but half,
　　Half hidden by his hood.

Still fix'd on Marmion was his look,
Which he, who ill such gaze could brook,
   Strove by a frown to quell;
But not for that, though more than once
Full met their stern encountering glance,
   The Palmer's visage fell.

VI.

By fits less frequent from the crowd
Was heard the burst of laughter loud;
For still, as squire and archer stared
On that dark face and matted beard,
   Their glee and game declined.
All gazed at length in silence drear,
Unbroke, save when in comrade's ear
Some yeoman, wondering in his fear,
   Thus whisper'd forth his mind: —
" Saint Mary ! saw'st thou e'er such sight?
How pale his cheek, his eye how bright,
Whene'er the firebrand's fickle light
   Glances beneath his cowl !
Full on our Lord he sets his eye;
For his best palfrey would not I
   Endure that sullen scowl."

VII.

But Marmion, as to chase the awe
Which thus had quell'd their hearts, who saw
The ever-varying fire-light show
That figure stern and face of woe,
   Now call'd upon a squire: —
" Fitz-Eustace, know'st thou not some lay,
To speed the lingering night away?
   We slumber by the fire." —

VIII.

" So please you," thus the youth rejoined,
" Our choicest minstrel's left behind.
Ill may we hope to please your ear,
Accustom'd Constant's strains to hear.
The harp full deftly can he strike,
And wake the lover's lute alike ;
To dear Saint Valentine, no thrush
Sings livelier from a spring-tide bush,
No nightingale her love-lorn tune
More sweetly warbles to the moon.
Woe to the cause, whate'er it be,
Detains from us his melody,
Lavish'd on rocks, and billows stern,
Or duller monks of Lindisfarne.
Now must I venture, as I may,
To sing his favourite roundelay."

IX.

A mellow voice Fitz-Eustace had,
The air he chose was wild and sad ;
Such have I heard, in Scottish land
Rise from the busy harvest band,
When falls before the mountaineer,
On Lowland plains, the ripen'd ear.
Now one shrill voice the notes prolong,
Now a wild chorus swells the song :
Oft have I listen'd, and stood still,
As it came soften'd up the hill,
And deem'd it the lament of men
Who languish'd for their native glen ;
And thought how sad would be such sound
On Susquehanna's swampy ground,

Kentucky's wood-encumber'd brake,
Or wild Ontario's boundless lake,
Where heart-sick exiles, in the strain,
Recall'd fair Scotland's hills again!

X.

Song.

Where shall the lover rest
   Whom the fates sever
From his true maiden's breast,
   Parted forever!
Where, through groves deep and high,
   Sounds the far billow,
Where early violets die,
   Under the willow.

CHORUS.

Eleu loro, &c.   Soft shall be his pillow.

There, through the summer day,
   Cool streams are laving;
There, while the tempests sway,
   Scarce are boughs waving;
There, thy rest shalt thou take,
   Parted forever,
Never again to wake,
   Never, O never!

CHORUS.

Eleu loro, &c.   Never, O never'

XI.

Where shall the traitor rest,
  He, the deceiver,
Who could win maiden's breast,
  Ruin, and leave her?
In the lost battle,
  Borne down by the flying,
Where mingles war's rattle
  With groans of the dying.

CHORUS.

Eleu loro, &c. There shall he be lying.

Her wing shall the eagle flap
  O'er the false-hearted;
His warm blood the wolf shall lap,
  Ere life be parted.
Shame and dishonour sit
  By his grave ever;
Blessings shall hallow it, —
  Never, O never!

CHORUS.

Eleu loro, &c. Never, O never!

XII.

It ceased, the melancholy sound;
And silence sunk on all around.
The air was sad; but sadder still
  It fell on Marmion's ear,
And plain'd as if disgrace and ill,
  And shameful death, were near.

He drew his mantle past his face,
  Between it and the band,
And rested with his head a space,
  Reclining on his hand.
His thoughts I scan not; but I ween,
That, could their import have been seen,
The meanest groom in all the hall,
That e'er tied courser to a stall,
Would scarce have wish'd to be their prey,
For Lutterward and Fontenaye.

XIII.

High minds, of native pride and force,
Most deeply feel thy pangs, Remorse!
Fear, for their scourge, mean villains have,
Thou art the torturer of the brave!
Yet fatal strength they boast to steel
Their minds to bear the wounds they feel,
Even while they writhe beneath the smart
Of civil conflict in the heart.
For soon Lord Marmion raised his head,
And, smiling, to Fitz-Eustace said, —
"Is it not strange, that, as ye sung,
Seem'd in mine ear a death-peal rung,
Such as in nunneries they toll
For some departing sister's soul?
  Say, what may this portend?"
Then first the Palmer silence broke,
(The livelong day he had not spoke,)
  "The death of a dear friend."

XIV.

Marmion, whose steady heart and eye
Ne'er changed in worst extremity;

Marmion, whose soul could scantly brook,
Even from his King, a haughty look ;
Whose accent of command controll'd,
In camps, the boldest of the bold —
Thought, look, and utterance failed him now,
Fall'n was his glance, and flush'd his brow ;
   For either in the tone,
Or something in the Palmer's look,
So full upon his conscience strook,
   That answer he found none.
Thus oft it haps, that when within
They shrink at sense of secret sin,
   A feather daunts the brave ;
A fool's wild speech confounds the wise,
And proudest princes veil their eyes
   Before their meanest slave.

XV.

Well might he falter ! — By his aid
Was Constance Beverley betray'd.
Not that he augur'd of the doom,
Which on the living closed the tomb :
But, tired to hear the desperate maid
Threaten by turns, beseech, upbraid ;
And wroth, because in wild despair,
She practised on the life of Clare ;
Its fugitive the Church he gave,
Though not a victim, but a slave ;
And deem'd restraint in convent strange
Would hide her wrongs, and her revenge.
Himself, proud Henry's favourite peer,
Held Romish thunders idle fear,

Secure his pardon he might hold,
For some slight mulct of penance-gold.
Thus judging, he gave secret way,
When the stern priests surprised their prey.
His train but deem'd the favourite page
Was left behind, to spare his age;
Or other if they deem'd, none dared
To mutter what he thought and heard:
Woe to the vassal, who durst pry
Into Lord Marmion's privacy!

XVI.

His conscience slept — he deem'd her well,
And safe secured in distant cell;
But, waken'd by her favourite lay,
And that strange Palmer's boding say,
That fell so ominous and drear,
Full on the object of his fear,
To aid remorse's venom'd throes,
Dark tales of convent-vengeance rose;
And Constance, late betray'd and scorn'd,
All lovely on his soul return'd;
Lovely as when, at treacherous call,
She left her convent's peaceful wall,
Crimson'd with shame, with terror mute,
Dreading alike escape, pursuit,
Till love, victorious o'er alarms,
Hid fears and blushes in his arms.

XVII.

" Alas ! " he thought, " how changed that mien !
How changed these timid looks have been,

Since years of guilt, and of disguise,
Have steel'd her brow, and arm'd her eyes!
No more of virgin terror speaks
The blood that mantles in her cheeks;
Fierce and unfeminine, are there,
Frenzy for joy, for grief despair;
And I the cause — for whom were given
Her peace on earth, her hopes in heaven! —
Would," thought he, as the picture grows,
" I on its stalk had left the rose!
Oh, why should man's success remove
The very charms that wake his love!
Her convent's peaceful solitude
Is now a prison harsh and rude.
And, pent within the narrow cell,
How will her spirit chafe and swell!
How brook the stern monastic laws!
The penance how — and I the cause!
Vigil and scourge — perchance even worse!" —
And twice he rose to cry, " To horse!" —
And twice his Sovereign's mandate came,
Like damp upon a kindling flame;
And twice he thought, " Gave I not charge
She should be safe, though not at large?
They durst not, for their island, shred
One golden ringlet from her head."

XVIII.

While thus in Marmion's bosom strove
Repentance and reviving love,
Like whirlwinds, whose contending sway
I've seen Loch Vennachar obey,

Their Host the Palmer's speech had heard,
And, talkative, took up the word:
   " Ay, reverend Pilgrim, you, who stray
From Scotland's simple land away,
   To visit realms afar,
Full often learn the art to know
   Of future weal, or future woe,
   By word, or sign, or star;
Yet might a knight his fortune hear,
If, knight-like, he despises fear,
Not far from hence; — if fathers old
Aright our hamlet legend told." —
These broken words the menials move,
(For marvels still the vulgar love,)
And, Marmion giving license cold,
His tale the host thus gladly told: —

XIX.

The Host's Tale.

" A clerk could tell what years have flown
Since Alexander filled our throne,
(Third monarch of that warlike name,)
And eke the time when here he came
To seek Sir Hugo, then our lord:
A braver never drew a sword;
A wiser never, at the hour
Of midnight spoke the word of power:
The same, whom ancient records call
The founder of the Goblin-Hall.
I would, Sir Knight, your longer stay
Gave you that cavern to survey.
Of lofty roof, and ample size,
Beneath the castle deep it lies:

To hew the living rock profound,
The floor to pave, the arch to round,
There never toil'd a mortal arm,
It all was wrought by word and charm;
And I have heard my grandsire say,
That the wild clamour and affray
Of those dread artisans of hell,
Who labour'd under Hugo's spell,
Sounded as loud as ocean's war,
Among the caverns of Dunbar.

XX.

" The King Lord Gifford's castle sought,
Deep labouring with uncertain thought;
Even then he muster'd all his host,
To meet upon the western coast:
For Norse and Danish galleys plied
Their oars within the Frith of Clyde.
There floated Haco's banner trim,
Above Norweyan warriors grim,
Savage of heart, and large of limb;
Threatening both continent and isle,
Bute, Arran, Cunninghame, and Kyle.
Lord Gifford, deep beneath the ground,
Heard Alexander's bugle sound,
And tarried not his garb to change,
But, in his wizard habit strange,
Came forth, — a quaint and fearful sight;
His mantle lined with fox-skins white;
His high and wrinkled forehead bore
A pointed cap, such as of yore
Clerks say that Pharaoh's Magi wore:

His shoes were mark'd with cross and spell,
Upon his breast a pentacle;
His zone, of virgin parchment thin,
Or, as some tell, of dead man's skin,
Bore many a planetary sign,
Combust, and retrograde, and trine;
And in his hand he held prepared,
A naked sword without a guard.

XXI.

" Dire dealings with the fiendish race
Had mark'd strange lines upon his face;
Vigil and fast had worn him grim,
His eyesight dazzled seem'd and dim,
As one unused to upper day;
Even his own menials with dismay
Beheld, Sir Knight, the grisly Sire,
In his unwonted wild attire;
Unwonted, for traditions run,
He seldom thus beheld the sun. —
' I know,' he said — his voice was hoarse,
And broken seem'd its hollow force, —
' I know the cause, although untold,
Why the King seeks his vassal's hold:
Vainly from me my liege would know
His kingdom's future weal or woe;
But yet, if strong his arm and heart,
His courage may do more than art.

XXII.

" ' Of middle air the demons proud,
Who ride upon the racking cloud,

Can read, in fix'd or wandering star,
The issue of events afar;
But still their sullen aid withhold,
Save when by mightier force controll'd.
Such late I summon'd to my hall;
And though so potent was the call,
That scarce the deepest nook of hell
I deem'd a refuge from the spell,
Yet, obstinate in silence still,
The haughty demon mocks my skill.
But thou — who little know'st thy might,
As born upon that blessed night
When yawning graves, and dying groan,
Proclaim'd hell's empire overthrown, —
With untaught valour shalt compel
Response denied to magic spell.'
' Gramercy,' quoth our Monarch free,
' Place him but front to front with me,
And, by this good and honour'd brand,
The gift of Cœur-de-Lion's hand,
Soothly I swear that, tide what tide,
The demon shall a buffet bide.' —
His bearing bold the wizard view'd,
And thus, well pleased, his speech renew'd: —
' There spoke the blood of Malcolm! mark:
Forth pacing hence, at midnight dark,
The rampart seek, whose circling crown
Crests the ascent of yonder down:
A southern entrance shalt thou find;
There halt, and there thy bugle wind.
And trust thine elfin foe to see,
In guise of thy worst enemy:

Couch then thy lance, and spur thy steed —
Upon him, and St. George to speed!
If he go down, thou soon shalt know
Whate'er these airy sprites can show; —
If thy heart fail thee in the strife,
I am no warrant for thy life.'

XXIII.

" Soon as the midnight bell did ring,
Alone and arm'd, forth rode the King
To that old camp's deserted round:
Sir Knight, you well might mark the mound,
Left hand the town, — the Pictish race,
The trench, long since, in blood did trace;
The moor around is brown and bare,
The space within is green and fair.
The spot our village children know,
For there the earliest wild-flowers grow;
But woe betide the wandering wight,
That treads its circle in the night!
The breadth across, a bowshot clear,
Gives ample space for full career:
Opposed to the four points of heaven,
By four deep gaps are entrance given.
The southernmost our Monarch past,
Halted, and blew a gallant blast;
And on the north, within the ring,
Appear'd the form of England's King,
Who then, a thousand leagues afar,
In Palestine waged holy war:
Yet arms like England's did he wield,
Alike the leopards in the shield,

Alike his Syrian courser's frame,
The rider's length of limb the same :
Long afterwards did Scotland know,
Fell Edward was her deadliest foe.

XXIV.

" The vision made our Monarch start,
But soon he mann'd his noble heart,
And in the first career they ran,
The Elfin Knight fell, horse and man ;
Yet did a splinter of his lance
Through Alexander's visor glance,
And razed the skin — a puny wound.
The King, light leaping to the ground,
With naked blade his phantom foe
Compell'd the future war to show.
Of Largs he saw the glorious plain,
Where still gigantic bones remain,
    Memorial of the Danish war ;
Himself he saw, amid the field,
On high his brandish'd war-axe wield,
    And strike proud Haco from his car,
While all around the shadowy Kings
Denmark's grim ravens cower'd their wings.
'Tis said, that, in that awful night,
Remoter visions met his sight,
Foreshowing future conquests far,
When our sons' sons wage northern war ;
A royal city, tower and spire,
Redden'd the midnight sky with fire,
And shouting crews her navy bore,
Triumphant to the victor shore.
Such signs may learned clerks explain,
They pass the wit of simple swain.

XXV.

"The joyful King turn'd home again,
Headed his host, and quell'd the Dane;
But yearly, when return'd the night
Of his strange combat with the sprite,
  His wound must bleed and smart;
Lord Gifford then would gibing say,
'Bold as ye were, my liege, ye pay
  The penance of your start.',
Long since, beneath Dunfermline's nave,
King Alexander fills his grave,
  Our Lady give him rest!
Yet still the knightly spear and shield
The Elfin Warrior doth wield,
  Upon the brown hill's breast;
And many a knight hath proved his chance,
In the charm'd ring to break a lance,
  But all have foully sped;
Save two, as legends tell, and they
Were Wallace wight and Gilbert Hay. —
Gentles, my tale is said."

XXVI.

The quaighs were deep, the liquor strong,
And on the tale the yeoman-throng
Had made a comment sage and long,
  But Marmion gave a sign:
And, with their lord, the squires retire;
The rest, around the hostel fire,
  Their drowsy limbs recline:
For pillow, underneath each head,
The quiver and the targe were laid.

Deep slumbering on the hostel floor,
Oppress'd with toil and ale, they snore:
The dying flame, in fitful change,
Threw on the group its shadows strange.

XXVII.

Apart, and nestling in the hay
Of a waste loft, Fitz-Eustace lay;
Scarce, by the pale moonlight, were seen
The foldings of his mantle green:
Lightly he dreamt, as youth will dream,
Of sport by thicket, or by stream,
Of hawk or hound, of ring or glove,
Or, lighter yet, of lady's love.
A cautious tread his slumber broke,
And, close beside him, when he woke,
In moonbeam half, and half in gloom,
Stood a tall form, with nodding plume;
But, ere his dagger Eustace drew,
His master Marmion's voice he knew.

XXVIII.

— " Fitz-Eustace! rise, I cannot rest;
Yon churl's wild legend haunts my breast,
And graver thoughts have chafed my mood:
The air must cool my feverish blood;
And fain would I ride forth to see
The scene of Elfin chivalry.
Arise, and saddle me my steed;
And, gentle Eustace, take good heed
Thou dost not rouse these drowsy slaves;
I would not, that the prating knaves

Had cause for saying, o'er their ale,
That I could credit such a tale." —
Then softly down the steps they slid,
Eustace the stable door undid,
And, darkling, Marmion's steed array'd,
While, whispering, thus the Baron said : —

XXIX.

" Did'st never, good my youth, hear tell,
   That on the hour when I was born,
Saint George, who graced my sire's chapelle,
Down from his steed of marble fell,
   A weary wight forlorn?
The flattering chaplains all agree,
The champion left his steed to me.
I would, the omen's truth to show,
That I could meet this Elfin Foe!
Blithe would I battle, for the right
To ask one question at the sprite : —
Vain thought! for elves, if elves there be,
An empty race, by fount or sea,
To dashing waters dance and sing,
Or round the green oak wheel their ring."
Thus speaking, he his steed bestrode,
And from the hostel slowly rode.

XXX.

Fitz-Eustace followed him abroad,
And mark'd him pace the village road,
   And listen'd to his horse's tramp,
     Till, by the lessening sound,
   He judged that of the Pictish camp
     Lord Marmion sought the round.

Wonder it seem'd, in the squire's eyes,
That one, so wary held, and wise, —
Of whom 'twas said he scarce received
For gospel, what the church believed, —
  Should, stirr'd by idle tale,
Ride forth in silence of the night,
As hoping half to meet a sprite,
Array'd in plate and mail.
For little did Fitz-Eustace know,
That passions, in contending flow,
  Unfix the strongest mind ;
Wearied from doubt to doubt to flee,
We welcome fond credulity,
Guide confident, though blind.

XXXI.

Little for this Fitz-Eustace cared,
But, patient, waited till he heard,
At distance, prick'd to utmost speed,
The foot-tramp of a flying steed,
  Come town-ward rushing on ;
First, dead, as if on turf it trode,
Then, clattering, on the village road, —
In other pace than forth he yode,
  Returned Lord Marmion.
Down hastily he sprung from selle,
And, in his haste, well-nigh he fell ;
To the squire's hand the rein he threw,
And spoke no word as he withdrew :
But yet the moonlight did betray,
The falcon-crest was soil'd with clay ;
And plainly might Fitz-Eustace see,
By stains upon the charger's knee.

And his left side, that on the moor
He had not kept his footing sure.
Long musing on these wondrous signs,
At length to rest the squire reclines,
Broken and short; for still, between,
Would dreams of terror intervene:
Eustace did ne'er so blithely mark
The first notes of the morning lark.

CANTO FOURTH.

The Camp.

I.

EUSTACE, I said, did blithely mark
The first notes of the merry lark.
The lark sang shrill, the cock he crew,
And loudly Marmion's bugles blew,
And with their light and lively call,
Brought groom and yeoman to the stall.
  Whistling they came, and free of heart,
    But soon their mood was changed;
  Complaint was heard on every part,
    Of something disarranged.
Some clamoured loud for armour lost;
Some brawl'd and wrangled with the host;
" By Becket's bones," cried one, " I fear,
That some false Scot has stolen my spear!" —
Young Blount, Lord Marmion's second squire,
Found his steed wet with sweat and mire;
Although the rated horse-boy sware,
Last night he dress'd him sleek and fair.
While chafed the impatient squire like thunder,
Old Hubert shouts, in fear and wonder, —
" Help, gentle Blount! help, comrades all!
Bevis lies dying in his stall:
To Marmion who the plight dare tell,
Of the good steed he loved so well?"

Gaping for fear and ruth, they saw
The charger panting on his straw;
Till one, who would seem wisest cried —
" What else but evil could betide,
With that cursed Palmer for our guide?
Better we had through mire and bush
Been lantern-led by Friar Rush."

II.

Fitz-Eustace, who the cause but guess'd,
    Nor wholly understood,
His comrades' clamourous plaints suppress'd;
    He knew Lord Marmion's mood.
Him, ere he issued forth, he sought,
And found deep plunged in gloomy thought,
    And did his tale display
Simply as if he knew of nought
    To cause such disarray.
Lord Marmion gave attention cold,
Nor marvell'd at the wonders told, —
Pass'd them as accidents of course,
And bade his clarions sound to horse.

III.

Young Henry Blount, meanwhile, the cost
Had reckoned with their Scottish host;
And, as the charge he cast and paid,
" Ill thou deserv'st thy hire," he said:
" Dost see, thou knave, my horse's plight?
Fairies have ridden him all the night,
    And left him in a foam!
I trust that soon a conjuring band,
With English cross and blazing brand,

Shall drive the devils from this land,
  To their infernal home:
For in this haunted den, I trow,
All night they trample to and fro."
The laughing host looked on the hire, —
" Gramercy, gentle southern squire,
And if thou comest among the rest,
With Scottish broadsword to be blest,
Sharp be the brand, and sure the blow,
And short the pang to undergo."
Here stay'd their talk, — for Marmion
Gave now the signal to set on.
The Palmer showing forth the way,
They journey'd all the morning day.

IV.

The green-sward way was smooth and good,
Through Humbie's and through Saltoun's wood;
A forest glade, which varying still,
Here gave a view of dale and hill,
There narrower closed, till overhead,
A vaulted screen the branches made.
" A pleasant path," Fitz-Eustace said;
" Such as where errant-knights might see
Adventures of high chivalry;
Might meet some damsel flying fast,
With hair unbound and looks aghast;
And smooth and level course were here,
In her defence to break a spear.
Here, too, are twilight nooks and dells;
And oft, in such, the story tells,
The damsel kind, from danger freed,
Did grateful pay her champion's meed."

He spoke to cheer Lord Marmion's mind:
Perchance to show his lore design'd;
   For Eustace much had pored
Upon a huge romantic tome,
In the hall window of his home,
Imprinted at the antique dome
   Of Caxton, or De Worde.
Therefore he spoke, — but spoke in vain,
For Marmion answer'd nought again.

V.

Now sudden, distant trumpets shrill,
In notes prolong'd by wood and hill,
   Were heard to echo far;
Each ready archer grasp'd his bow,
But by the flourish soon they know,
   They breathed no point of war.
Yet cautious, as in foeman's land,
Lord Marmion's order speeds the band,
   Some opener ground to gain;
And scarce a furlough had they rode,
When thinner trees, receding, show'd
   A little woodland plain,
Just in that advantageous glade,
The halting troop a line had made,
As forth from the opposing shade
   Issued a gallant train.

VI.

First came the trumpets at whose clang
So late the forest echoes rang;
On prancing steeds they forward press'd,
With scarlet mantle, azure vest;

Each at his trump a banner wore,
Which Scotland's royal scutcheon bore :
Heralds and pursuivants, by name
Bute, Islay, Marchmount, Rothsay, came,
In painted tabards, proudly showing
Gules, Argent, Or, and Azure glowing,
 Attendant on a King-at-arms,
Whose hand the armorial truncheon held
That feudal strife had often quell'd,
 When wildest its alarms.

VII.

He was a man of middle age ;
In aspect manly, grave, and sage,
 As on King's errand come ;
But in the glances of his eye,
A penetrating, keen, and sly
 Expression found its home ;
The flash of that satiric rage,
Which, bursting on the early stage,
Branded the vices of the age,
 And broke the keys of Rome.
On milk-white palfrey forth he paced ;
His cap of maintenance was graced
 With the proud heron-plume.
From his steed's shoulder, loin, and breast,
 Silk housings swept the ground,
With Scotland's arms, device, and crest,
 Embroider'd round and round.
The double treasure might you see,
 First by Achaius borne,
The thistle and the fleur-de-lis,
 And gallant unicorn.

So bright the King's armorial coat,
That scarce the dazzled eye could note,
In living colours, blazon'd brave,
The Lion, which his title gave;
A train which well beseem'd his state,
But all unarm'd around him wait.
 Still is thy name in high account,
  And still thy verse has charms,
 Sir David Lindesay of the Mount,
  Lord Lion King-at-arms !

VIII.

Down from his horse did Marmion spring,
Soon as he saw the Lion-King;
For well the stately Baron knew
To him such courtesy was due,
Whom royal James himself had crown'd,
And on his temples placed the round
 Of Scotland's ancient diadem :
And wet his brow with hallow'd wine,
And on his finger given to shine
 The emblematic gem.
Their mutual greetings duly made,
The Lion thus his message said : —
"Though Scotland's King hath deeply swore
Ne'er to knit faith with Henrp more,
And strictly hath forbid resort
From England to his royal court;
Yet, for he knows Lord Marmion's name,
And honours much his warlike fame,
My liege hath deem'd it shame, and lack
Of courtesy, to turn him back;

And, by his order, I, your guide,
Must lodging fit and fair provide,
Till finds King James meet time to see
The flower of English chivalry."

IX.

Though inly chafed at this delay,
Lord Marmion bears it as he may.
The Palmer, his mysterious guide,
Beholding thus his place supplied,
   Sought to take leave in vain;
Strict was the Lion-King's command,
That none, who rode in Marmion's band,
   Should sever from the train:
"England has here enow of spies
In Lady Heron's witching eyes;"
To Marchmount thus, apart, he said,
But fair pretext to Marmion made.
The right hand path they now decline,
And trace against the stream the Tyne.

X.

At length up that wild dale they wind,
   Where Crichtoun Castle crowns the bank;
For there the Lion's care assigned
   A lodging meet for Marmion's rank.
That Castle rises on the steep
   Of the green vale of Tyne:
And far beneath, where slow they creep,
From pool to eddy, dark and deep,
Where alders moist, and willows weep,
   You hear her streams repine.

The towers in different ages rose;
Their various architecture shows
   The builders' various hands;
A mighty mass, that could oppose,
When deadliest hatred fired its foes,
   The vengeful Douglas bands.

XI.

Crichtoun! though now thy miry court
   But pens the lazy steer and sheep,
   Thy turrets rude, and totter'd Keep,
Have been the minstrel's loved resort.
Oft have I traced, within thy fort,
   Of mouldering shields the mystic sense,
   Scutcheons of honour, or pretence,
Quarter'd in old armorial sort,
   Remains of rude magnificence.
Nor wholly yet had time defaced
   Thy lordly gallery fair;
Nor yet the stony cord unbraced,
Whose twisted knots, with roses laced,
   Adorn thy ruin'd stair.
Still rises unimpair'd below,
The courtyard's graceful portico;
Above its cornice, row and row
   Of fair hewn facets richly show
     Their pointed diamond form,
   Though there but houseless cattle go,
     To shield them from the storm.
And, shuddering, still may we explore,
     Where oft whilom were captives pent,
   The darkness of the Massy More;
     Or, from thy grass-grown battlement,

May trace, in undulating line,
The sluggish mazes of the Tyne.

XII.

Another aspect Crichtoun show'd,
As through its portal Marmion rode;
But yet 'twas melancholy state
Received him at the outer gate;
For none were in the Castle then,
But women, boys, or aged men.
With eyes scarce dried, the sorrowing dame,
To welcome noble Marmion, came;
Her son, a stripling twelve years old,
Proffer'd the Baron's rein to hold;
For each man that could draw a sword
Had march'd that morning with their lord,
Earl Adam Hepburn, he who died
On Flodden, by his sovereign's side.
Long may his Lady look in vain!
She ne'er shall see his gallant train
Come sweeping back through Crichtoun-Dean,
'Twas a brave race, before the name
Of hated Bothwell stain'd their fame.

XIII.

And here two days did Marmion rest,
    With every rite that honour claims,
Attended as the King's own guest: —
    Such the command of Royal James,
Who marshall'd then his land's array,
Upon the Borough-moor that lay.

Perchance he would not foeman's eye
Upon his gathering host should pry,
Till full prepared was every band
To march against the English land.
Here while they dwelt, did Lindesay's wit
Oft cheer the Baron's moodier fit;
And, in his turn, he knew to prize
Lord Marmion's powerful mind, and wise. —
Train'd in the lore of Rome and Greece,
And policies of war and peace.

XIV.

It chanced, as fell the second night,
  That on the battlements they walk'd,
And, by the slowly fading light,
  Of various topics talked;
And, unaware, the Herald-bard
Said, Marmion might his toil have spared,
  In travelling so far;
For that a messenger from heaven
In vain to James had counsel given
  Against the English war;
And, closer question'd, thus he told
A tale, which chronicles of old
In Scottish story have enroll'd: —

XV.

Sir David Lindesay's Tale.

" Of all the palaces so fair,
  Built for the royal dwelling,
In Scotland, far beyond compare
  Linlithgow is excelling;

And in its park in jovial June,
How sweet the merry linnet's tune,
  How blithe the blackbird's lay !
The wild buck bells from ferny brake,
The coot dives merry on the lake,
The saddest heart might pleasure take
    To see all nature gay.
But June is to our sovereign dear
The heaviest month in all the year :
Too well his cause of grief you know,
June saw his father's overthrow.
Woe to the traitors who could bring
The princely boy against his King !
Still in his conscience burns the sting.
In offices as strict as Lent,
King James's June is ever spent.

XVI.

" When last this ruthful month was come,
And in Linlithgow's holy dome
  The King, as wont, was praying ;
While, for his royal father's soul,
The chanters sung, the bells did toll,
  The Bishop mass was saying —
For now the year brought round again
The day the luckless king was slain —
In Katharine's aisle the Monarch knelt,
With sackcloth-shirt, and iron belt,
  And eyes with sorrow streaming ;
Around him in their stalls of state,
The Thistle's Knight-Companions sate,
  Their banners o'er them beaming.

I too was there, and, sooth to tell,
Bedeafen'd with the jangling knell,
Was watching where the sunbeams fell,
   Through the stain'd casement gleaming;
But, while I mark'd what next befell,
   It seem'd as I were dreaming.
Stepp'd from the crowd a ghostly wight,
In azure gown, with cincture white;
His forehead bald, his head was bare,
Down hung at length his yellow hair. —
Now, mock me not, when, good my Lord,
I pledge to you my knightly word,
That, when I saw his placid grace,
His simple majesty of face,
His solemn bearing, and his pace
   So stately gliding on, —
Seem'd to me ne'er did limner paint
So just an image of the Saint,
Who propp'd the Virgin in her faint, —
   The loved Apostle John!

XVII.

" He stepp'd before the Monarch's chair,
And stood with rustic plainness there,
   And little reverence made;
Nor head, nor body, bow'd nor bent,
But on the desk his arm he leant,
   And words like these he said,
In a low voice, but never tone
So thrill'd through vein, and nerve and bone : —
' My mother sent me from afar,
Sir King, to warn thee not to war, —
   Woe waits on thine array;

If war thou wilt, of woman fair,
Her witching wiles and wanton snare,
James Stuart, doubly warn'd, beware:
   God keep thee as he may!'
     The wondering Monarch seem'd to seek
      For answer, and found none;
     And when he raised his head to speak,
      The monitor was gone.
The Marshal and myself had cast
To stop him as he outward pass'd;
But, lighter than the whirlwind's blast,
   He vanish'd from our eyes,
Like sunbeam on the billow cast,
   That glances but, and dies."

XVIII.

While Lindesay told his marvel strange,
   The twilight was so pale,
He mark'd not Marmion's colour change,
   While listening to the tale;
But, after a suspended pause,
The Baron spoke: — " Of nature's laws
   So strong I held the force,
   That never superhuman cause
     Could e'er control their course.
And, three days since, had judged your aim
Was but to make your guest your game.
But I have seen, since past the Tweed,
What much has changed my sceptic creed,
And made me credit aught." — He staid,
And seem'd to wish his words unsaid:
But, by that strong emotion press'd
Which prompts us to unload our breast,
   Even when discovery's pain,

To Lindesay did at length unfold
The tale his village host had told,
    At Gifford, to his train.
Nought of the Palmer says he there,
And nought of Constance, or of Clare;
The thoughts, which broke his sleep, he seems
To mention but as feverish dreams.

XIX.

" In vain," said he, " to rest I spread
My burning limbs, and couch'd my head:
    Fantastic thoughts return'd;
 And, by their wild dominion led,
    My heart within me burn'd.
So sore was the delirious goad,
I took my steed, and forth I rode,
And, as the moon shone bright and cold,
Soon reach'd the camp upon the wold.
The southern entrance I pass'd through,
And halted, and my bugle blew.
Methought an answer met my ear, —
Yet was the blast so low and drear,
So hollow, and so faintly blown,
It might be echo of my own.

XX.

" Thus judging, for a little space
I listen'd, ere I left the place;
    But scarce could trust my eyes,
Nor yet can think they served me true,
When sudden in the ring I view,
In form distinct of shape and hue,
    A mounted champion rise. —

I've fought, Lord-Lion, many a day,
In single fight, and mix'd affray,
And ever, I myself may say,
   Have borne me as a knight;
But when this unexpected foe
Seem'd starting from the gulf below, —
I care not though the truth I show, —
   I trembled with affright;
And as I placed in rest my spear
My hand so shook for very fear,
   I scarce could couch it right.

XXI.

" Why need my tongue the issue tell ?
We ran our course, — my charger fell; —
What could he 'gainst the shock of hell? —
   I roll'd upon the plain.
High o'er my head, with threatening hand,
The spectre shook his naked brand, —
   Yet did the worst remain:
My dazzled eyes I upward cast, —
Not opening hell itself could blast
   Their sight, like what I saw !
Full on his face the moonbeams strook, —
A face could never be mistook !
I knew the stern vindictive look,
   And held my breath for awe.
I saw the face of one who, fled
To foreign climes, has long been dead, —
   I well believe the last;
For ne'er, from visor raised, did stare
A human warrior, with a glare
   So grimly and so ghast.

Thrice o'er my head he shook the blade;
But when to good St. George I pray'd,
(The first time e'er I ask'd his aid,)
  He plunged it in the sheath;
And, on his courser mounting light,
He seem'd to vanish from my sight:
The moonbeam droop'd, and deepest night
  Sunk down upon the heath. —
  'Twere long to tell what cause I have
    To know his face, that met me there,
  Call'd by his hatred from the grave,
    To cumber upper air:
Dead or alive, good cause had he
To be my mortal enemy."

XXII.

Marvell'd Sir David of the Mount;
Then, learn'd in story, 'gan recount
  Such chance had happ'd of old,
When once, near Norham, there did fight
A spectre fell of fiendish might,
In likeness of a Scottish knight,
  With Brian Bulmer bold,
And train'd him nigh to disallow
The aid of his baptismal vow.
" And such a phantom, too, 'tis said,
With Highland broadsword, targe, and plaid,
  And fingers red with gore,
Is seen in Rothiemurcus glade,
Or where the sable pine-trees shade
Dark Tomantoul, and Auchnaslaid,
  Dromouchty, or Glenmore.

And yet, whate'er such legends say,
Of warlike demon, ghost, or fay,
  On mountain, moor, or plain,
Spotless in faith, in bosom bold,
True son of chivalry should hold
  These midnight terrors vain ;
For seldom have such spirits power
To harm, save in the evil hour,
When guilt we meditate within,
Or harbor unrepented sin." —
Lord Marmion turn'd him half aside,
And twice to clear his voice he tried,
  Then press'd Sir David's hand, —
But nought, at length, in answer said ;
And here their farther converse staid,
  Each ordering that his band
Should bowne them with the rising day,
To Scotland's camp to take their way. —
  Such was the King's command.

XXIII.

Early they took Dun-Edin's road,
And I could trace each step they trode.
Hill, brook, nor dell, nor rock, nor stone,
Lies on the path to me unknown.
Much might it boast of storied lore ;
But, passing such digression o'er,
Suffice it that the route was laid
Across the furzy hills of Braid.
They pass'd the glen and scanty rill,
And climb'd the opposing bank, until
They gain'd the top of Blackford Hill

XXIV.

Blackford! on whose uncultured breast,
　Among the broom, and thorn, and whin,
A truant-boy, I sought the nest,
Or listed, as I lay at rest,
　While rose, on breezes thin,
The murmur of the city crowd,
And, from his steeple jangling loud,
　Saint Giles's mingling din.
Now, from the summit to the plain,
Waves all the hill with yellow grain;
　And o'er the landscape as I look,
Nought do I see unchanged remain,
　Save the rude cliffs and chiming brook,
To me they make a heavy moan,
Of early friendships past and gone.

XXV.

But different far the change has been,
　Since Marmion, from the crown
Of Blackford, saw that martial scene
　Upon the bent so brown:
Thousand pavilions, white as snow,
Spread all the Borough-moor below,
　Upland, and dale, and down: —
A thousand did I say?　I ween,
Thousands on thousands there were seen,
That chequer'd all the heath between
　The streamlet and the town;
In crossing ranks extending far,
Forming a camp irregular;
Oft giving way, where still there stood
Some relics of the old oak wood,

That darkly huge did intervene,
And tamed the glaring white with green :
In these extended lines there lay
A martial kingdom's vast array.

XXVI.

For from Hebudes, dark with rain,
To eastern Lodon's fertile plain,
And from the Southern Redswire edge,
To farthest Rosse's rocky ledge :
From west to east, from south to north,
Scotland sent all her warriors forth.
Marmion might hear the mingled hum
Of myriads up the mountain come ;
The horses' tramp, and tingling clank,
Where chiefs review'd their vassal rank,
    And charger's shrilling neigh ;
And see the shifting lines advance,
While frequent flash'd from shield and lance,
    The sun's reflected ray.

XXVII.

Thin curling in the morning air,
The wreaths of failing smoke declare
To embers now the brands decay'd,
Where the night-watch their fires had made.
They saw, slow rolling on the plain,
Full many a baggage cart and wain,
And dire artillery's clumsy car,
By sluggish oxen tugg'd to war ;
And there were Borthwick's Sisters seven,
And culverins which France had given.
Ill-omen'd gift ! the guns remain
The conqueror's spoil on Flodden plain.

XXVIII.

Nor mark'd they less, where in the air
A thousand streamers flaunted fair;
  Various in shape, device, and hue,
Green, sanguine, purple, red, and blue,
Broad, narrow, swallow-tail'd, and square,
Scroll, pennon, pensil, bandrol, there
  O'er the pavilions flew.
Highest and midmost, was descried
The royal banner floating wide;
  The staff, a pine-tree, strong and straight,
Pitch'd deeply in a massive stone,
Which still in memory is shown,
  Yet bent beneath the standard's weight
    Whene'er the western wind unroll'd,
    With toil, the huge and cumbrous fold,
And gave to view the dazzling field,
Where, in proud Scotland's royal shield,
    The ruddy lion ramp'd in gold.

XXIX.

Lord Marmion view'd the landscape bright, —
He view'd it with a chief's delight, —
  Until within him burn'd his heart,
  And lightning from his eye did part,
    As on the battle-day;
  Such glance did falcon never dart,
    When stooping on his prey.
"Oh! well, Lord-Lion, hast thou said,
Thy King from warfare to dissuade
  Were but a vain essay:
For, by St. George, were that host mine,
Not power infernal nor divine,

Should once to peace my soul incline,
Till I had dimm'd their armour's shine
  In glorious battle-fray ! "
Answer'd the Bard, of milder mood :
" Fair is the sight, — and yet 'twere good,
  That kings would think withal,
When peace and wealth their land has bless'd,
'Tis better to sit still at rest,
  Than rise, perchance to fall."

XXX.

Still on the spot Lord Marmion stay'd,
For fairer scene he ne'er survey'd.
  When sated with the martial show
  That peopled all the plain below,
  The wandering eye could o'er it go,
  And mark the distant city glow
    With gloomy splendour red ;
  For on the smoke-wreaths, huge and slow,
  That round her sable turrets flow,
    The morning beams were shed,
  And tinged them with a lustre proud,
  Like that which streaks a thunder-cloud.
Such dusky grandeur clothed the height,
Where the huge Castle holds its state,
  And all the deep slope down,
Whose ridgy back heaves to the sky,
Piled deep and massy, close and high,
  Mine own romantic town !
But northward far, with purer blaze,
On Ochil mountains fell the rays,
And as each heathy top they kissed,
It gleam'd a purple amethyst.

Yonder the shores of Fife you saw;
Here Preston-Bay and Berwick-Law:
   And, broad between them roll'd
The gallant Frith the eye might note,
Whose islands on its bosom float,
   Like emeralds chased in gold.
Fitz-Eustace' heart felt closely pent;
As if to give his rapture vent,
The spur he to his charger lent,
   And raised his bridle hand,
And, making demi-volte in air,
Cried, " Where's the coward that would not dare
   To fight for such a land?"
The Lindesay smiled his joy to see;
Nor Marmion's frown repress'd his glee.

XXXI.

Thus, while they look'd, a flourish proud,
Where mingled trump and clarion loud,
   And fife, and kettle-drum,
And sackbut deep, and psaltery,
And war-pipe with discordant cry,
And cymbal clattering to the sky,
Making wild music bold and high,
   Did up the mountain come;
The whilst the bells, with distant chime,
Merrily told the hour of prime,
And thus the Lindesay spoke:
" Thus clamour still the war-notes when
The king to mass his way has ta'en,
Or to St. Katharine's of Sienne,
   Or Chapel of St. Rocque.

To you they speak of martial fame,
But me remind of peaceful game,
 When blither was their cheer,
Thrilling in Falkland-woods the air,
In signal none his steed should spare,
But strive which foremost might repair
 To the downfall of the deer.

XXXII.

" Nor less," he said, — " when looking forth,
I view yon Empress of the North
 Sit on her hilly throne;
Her palace's imperial bowers,
Her castle, proof to hostile powers,
Her stately halls and holy towers —
 Nor less," he said, " I moan,
To think what woe mischance may bring,
And how these merry bells may ring
The death-dirge of our gallant king;
 Or with the larum call
The burghers forth to watch and ward,
'Gainst Southern sack and fires to guard
 Dun-Edin's leaguer'd wall. —
But not for my presaging thought,
Dream conquest sure, or cheaply bought '
 Lord Marmion, I say nay:
God is the guider of the field,
He breaks the champion's spear and shield, —
 But thou thyself shalt say,
When joins yon host in deadly stowre,
That England's dames must weep in bower,
 Her monks the death-mass sing;
For never saw'st thou such a power
 Led on by such a King." —

And now, down winding to the plain,
The barriers of the camp they gain,
 And there they made a stay. —
There stays the Minstrel, till he fling
His hand o'er every Border string,
And fit his harp the pomp to sing,
Of Scotland's ancient Court and King,
 In the succeeding lay.

CANTO FIFTH.

The Court.

I.

THE train has left the hills of Braid;
The barrier guard have open made
(So Lindesay bade) the palisade,
　　That closed the tented ground;
Their men the warders backward drew,
And carried pikes as they rode through,
　　Into its ample bound.
Fast ran the Scottish warriors there,
Upon the Southern band to stare,
And envy with their wonder rose,
To see such well-appointed foes;
Such length of shafts, such mighty bows,
So huge, that many simply thought,
But for a vaunt such weapons wrought;
And little deem'd their force to feel,
Through links of mail, and plates of steel,
When rattling upon Flodden vale,
The cloth-yard arrows flew like hail.

II.

Nor less did Marmion's skilful view
Glance every line and squadron through;
And much he marvell'd one small land
Could marshal forth such various band:
　　For men-at-arms were here,

Heavily sheathed in mail and plate,
Like iron towers for strength and weight,
On Flemish steeds of bone and height,
   With battle-axe and spear.
Young knights and squires, a lighter train,
Practised their chargers on the plain,
By aid of leg, of hand, and rein,
   Each warlike feat to show,
To pass, to wheel, the croupe to gain,
And high curvett, that not in vain
The sword sway might descend amain
   On foeman's casque below.
He saw the hardy burghers there
March arm'd, on foot, with faces bare,
   For vizor they wore none,
Nor waving plume, nor crest of knight;
But burnished were their corslets bright,
Their brigantines, and gorgets light,
   Like very silver shone.
Long pikes they had for standing fight,
   Two-handed swords they wore,
And many wielded mace of weight,
   And bucklers bright they bore.

III.

On foot the yeoman too, but dress'd
In his steel-jack, a swarthy vest,
   With iron quilted well;
Each at his back (a slender store)
His forty days' provision bore,
   As feudal statutes tell.
His arms were halbert, axe, or spear,
A crossbow there, a hagbut here,
   A dagger-knife, and brand.

Sober he seem'd, and sad of cheer,
As loth to leave his cottage dear,
And march to foreign strand;
Or musing, who would guide his steer,
   To till the fallow land.
Yet deem not in his thoughtful eye
Did aught of dastard terror lie;
   More dreadful far his ire,
Than theirs, who, scorning danger's name,
In eager mood to battle came,
Their valour like light straw on flame,
   A fierce but fading fire.

IV.

Not so the Borderer: — bred to war,
He knew the battle's din afar,
   And joy'd to hear it swell.
His peaceful day was slothful ease;
Nor harp, nor pipe, his ear could please
   Like the loud slogan yell.
On active steed, with lance and blade,
The light-arm'd pricker plied his trade, —
   Let nobles fight for fame;
Let vassals follow where they lead,
Burghers to guard their townships bleed,
   But war's the Borderer's game.
Their game, their glory, their delight,
To sleep the day, maraud the night,
   O'er mountain, moss, and moor;
Joyful to fight they took their way,
Scarce caring who might win the day,
   Their booty was secure.

These, as Lord Marmion's train pass'd by,
Look'd on at first with careless eye,
Nor marvell'd aught, well taught to know
The form and force of English bow.
But when they saw the Lord array'd
In splendid arms and rich brocade,
Each Borderer to his kinsman said, —
    "Hist, Ringan! seest thou there!
Canst guess which road they'll homeward ride? —
O! could we but on Border side,
By Eusedale glen, or Liddell's tide,
    Beset a prize so fair!
That fangless Lion, too, their guide,
Might chance to lose his glistering hide;
Brown Maudlin, of that doublet pied,
    Could make a kirtle rare."

V.

Next, Marmion mark'd the Celtic race,
Of different language, form, and face,
    A various race of man;
Just then the Chiefs their tribes array'd,
And wild and garish semblance made,
The chequer'd trews, and belted plaid,
And varying notes the war-pipes bray'd,
    To every varying clan;
Wild through their red or sable hair
Look'd out their eyes with savage stare,
    On Marmion as he pass'd;
Their legs above the knee were bare;
Their frame was sinewy, short, and spare,
    And harden'd to the blast;

Of taller race, the chiefs they own
Were by the eagle's plumage known.
The hunted red-deer's undress'd hide
Their hairy buskins well supplied;
The graceful bonnet deck'd their head:
Back from their shoulders hung the plaid;
A broadsword of unwieldy length,
A dagger proved for edge and strength,
    A studded targe they wore,
And quivers, bows, and shafts, — but, O !
Short was the shaft, and weak the bow,
    To that which England bore.
The Isles-men carried at their backs
The ancient Danish battle-axe.
They raised a wild and wondering cry,
As with his guide rode Marmion by.
Loud were their clamouring tongues as when
The clanging sea-fowl leave the fen,
And, with their cries discordant mix'd,
Grumbled and yell'd the pipes betwixt.

VI.

Thus through the Scottish camp they pass'd,
And reach'd the City gate at last,
Where all around, a wakeful guard,
Arm'd burghers kept their watch and ward.
Well had they cause of jealous fear,
When lay encamp'd, in field so near,
The Borderer and the Mountaineer.
As through the bustling streets they go,
All was alive with martial show:
At every turn, with dinning clang,
The armourer's anvil clash'd and rang;

Or toil'd the swarthy smith, to wheel
The bar that arms the charger's heel ;
Or axe, or falchion, to the side
Of jarring grindstone was applied.
Page, groom, and squire, with hurrying pace,
Through street, and lane, and market-place,
   Bore lance, or casque, or sword ;
While burghers, with important face,
   Described each new-come lord,
Discuss'd his lineage, told his name,
His following, and his warlike fame.
The Lion led to lodging meet,
Which high o'erlook'd the crowded street ;
   There must the Baron rest,
Till past the hour of vesper tide,
And then to Holy-Rood must ride, —
   Such was the King's behest.
Meanwhile the Lion's care assigns
A banquet rich, and costly wines,
   To Marmion and his train ;
And when the appointed hour succeeds,
The Baron dons his peaceful weeds,
And following Lindesay as he leads,
   The palace-halls they gain.

VII.

Old Holy-Rood rung merrily,
That night, with wassell, mirth, and glee ; ·
King James within her princely bower,
Feasted the Chiefs of Scotland's power,
Summon'd to spend the parting hour ;
For he had charged, that his array

Should southward march by break of day.
Well loved that splendid monarch aye
  The banquet and the song,
By day the tourney, and by night
The merry dance, traced fast and light,
The maskers quaint, the pageant bright,
  The revel loud and long.
This feast outshone his banquets past,
It was his blithest — and his last.
The dazzling lamps, from gallery gay,
Cast on the Court a dancing ray;
Here to the harp did minstrels sing;
There ladies touch'd a softer string;
With long-ear'd cap, and motley vest,
The licensed fool retail'd his jest;
His magic tricks the juggler plied;
At dice and draughts the gallants vied;
While some, in close recess apart,
Courted the ladies of their heart,
  Nor courted them in vain;
For often, in the parting hour,
Victorious Love asserts his power
  O'er coldness and disdain;
And flinty is her heart, can view
To battle march a lover true —
Can hear, perchance, his last adieu,
  Nor own her share of pain.

VIII.

Through this mix'd crowd of glee and game,
The King to greet Lord Marmion came,
  While, reverent, all made room.

An easy task it was, I trow,
King James's manly form to know.
Although, his courtesy to show,
He doff'd to Marmion bending low,
  His broider'd cap and plume.
For royal was his garb and mien,
  His cloak, of crimson velvet piled,
    Trimm'd with the fur of martin wild;
His vest of changeful satin sheen,
  The dazzled eye beguiled;
His gorgeous collar hung adown,
Wrought with the badge of Scotland's crown,
The thistle brave, of old renown:
His trusty blade, Toledo right,
Descended from a baldric bright;
White were his buskins, on the heel
His spurs inlaid of gold and steel;
His bonnet, all of crimson fair,
Was button'd with a ruby rare:
And Marmion deem'd he ne'er had seen
A prince of such a noble mien.

IX.

The monarch's form was middle size;
For feat of strength, or exercise,
  Shaped in proportion fair;
And hazel was his eagle eye,
And auburn of the darkest dye,
  His short curl'd beard and hair.
Light was his footstep in the dance,
  And firm his stirrup in the lists;
And, oh! he had that merry glance,
  That seldom lady's heart resists.

Lightly from fair to fair he flew,
And loved to plead, lament, and sue; —
Suit lightly won, and short-lived pain,
For monarchs seldom sigh in vain.
   I said he joy'd in banquet bower;
But, 'mid his mirth, 'twas often strange,
How suddenly his cheer would change,
   His look o'ercast and lower,
If, in a sudden turn, he felt
The pressure of his iron belt,
That bound his breast in penance pain,
In memory of his father slain.
Even so 'twas strange how, evermore,
Soon as the passing pang was o'er
Forward he rush'd, with double glee,
Into the stream of revelry:
Thus, dim-seen object of affright
Startles the courser in his flight,
And half he halts, half springs aside;
But feels the quickening spur applied,
And, straining on the tighten'd rein,
Scours doubly swift o'er hill and plain.

X.

O'er James's heart, the courtiers say,
Sir Hugh the Heron's wife held sway;
   To Scotland's Court she came,
To be a hostage for her lord,
Who Cessford's gallant heart had gored,
And with the King to make accord,
   Had sent his lovely dame.
Nor to that lady free alone
Did the gay King allegiance own;
   For the fair Queen of France

Sent him a turquois ring and glove,
And charged him, as her knight and love,
　　For her to break a lance ;
And strike three strokes with Scottish brand,
And march three miles on Southron land,
And bid the banners of his band
　　In English breezes dance.
And thus, for France's Queen he drest
His manly limbs in mailed vest ;
And thus admitted English fair
His inmost counsels still to share ;
And thus for both, he madly plann'd
The ruin of himself and land !
　　And yet, the sooth to tell,
Nor England's fair, nor France's Queen,
Were worth one pearl drop, bright and sheen,
　　From Margaret's eyes that fell, —
His own Queen Margaret, who, in Lithgow's bower,
All lonely sat, and wept the weary hour.

XI.

The Queen sits lone in Lithgow pile,
　　And weeps the weary day,
The war against her native soil,
Her Monarch's risk in battle broil : —
And in gay Holy-Rood, the while
Dame Heron rises with a smile
　　Upon the harp to play.
Fair was her rounded arm, as o'er
　　The strings her fingers flew ;
And as she touch'd and tuned them all,
Even her bosom's rise and fall
　　Was plainer given to view ;

For, all for heat, was laid aside
Her wimple, and her hood untied.
And first she pitch'd her voice to sing,
Then glanced her dark eye on the King,
And then around the silent ring;
And laugh'd, and blush'd, and oft did say,
Her pretty oath, by Yea, and Nay,
She could not, would not, durst not play!
At length, upon the harp, with glee,
Mingled with arch simplicity,
A soft, yet lively air she rung,
While thus the wily lady sung: —

XII.

LOCHINVAR.

Lady Heron's Song.

O, young Lochinvar is come out of the west,
Through all the wide Border his steed was the best;
And save his good broadsword he weapons had none,
He rode all unarm'd, and he rode all alone.
So faithful in love, and so dauntless in war,
There never was knight like the young Lochinvar.

He staid not for brake, and he stopp'd not for stone,
He swam the Eske river where ford there was none;
But ere he alighted at Netherby gate,
The bride had consented, the gallant came late;
For a laggard in love, and a dastard in war,
Was to wed the fair Ellen of brave Lochinvar.

So boldly he enter'd the Netherby Hall,
Among bride's-men, and kinsmen, and brothers, and all:

Then spoke the bride's father, his hand on his **sword**,
(For the poor craven bridegroom said never a word,)
" O come ye in peace here, or come ye in war,
Or to dance at our bridal, young Lord Lochinvar?"—

" I long **woo'd** your daughter, my suit you denied;—
Love swells like the Solway, but ebbs like its tide—
And now am I come, with this lost love of mine,
To lead but one measure, drink one cup of wine.
There are maidens in Scotland more lovely by far,
That would gladly be bride to the young Lochinvar.

The bride kiss'd the goblet: the knight took it up,
He quaff'd off the wine, and he threw down the cup.
She look'd down to blush, and she look'd up to sigh,
With a smile on her lips, and a tear in her eye.
He took her soft hand, ere her mother could bar, —
"Now tread we a measure!" said young Lochinvar.

So stately his form, and so lovely her face,
That never a hall such a galliard did grace;
While her mother did fret, and her father did fume,
And the bridegroom stood dangling his bonnet and plume;
And the bride-maidens whisper'd, " 'Twere better by far,
To have match'd our fair cousin with young Lochinvar."

One touch to her hand, and one word in her ear,
When they reach'd the hall-door, and the charger stood near;
So light to the croupe the fair lady he swung,
So light to the saddle before her he sprung!
"She is won! we are gone, over bank, bush, and scaur;
They'll have fleet steeds that follow," quoth young Lochinvar.

There was mounting 'mong Græmes of the Netherby clan;
Forsters, Fenwicks, and Musgraves, they rode and they ran:
There was racing and chasing, on Cannobie Lee,
But the lost bride of Netherby ne'er did they see.
So daring in love, and so dauntless in war,
Have ye e'er heard of gallant like young Lochinvar?

XIII.

The Monarch o'er the siren hung
And beat the measure as she sung;
And, pressing closer, and more near,
He whisper'd praises in her ear.
In loud applause the courtiers vied;
And ladies wink'd and spoke aside.
  The witching dame to Marmion threw
    A glance, where seem'd to reign
  The pride that claims applauses due,
  And of her royal conquest too,
    A real or feign'd disdain:
Familiar was the look, and told,
Marmion and she were friends of old.
The King observed their meeting eyes,
With something like displeased surprise;
For monarchs ill can rivals brook,
Even in a word, or smile, or look.
Straight took he forth the parchment broad,
Which Marmion's high commission show'd:
" Our Borders sack'd by many a raid,
Our peaceful liege-men robb'd," he said:
" On day of truce our Warden slain,
Stout Barton kill'd, his vassals ta'en —

Unworthy were we here to reign,
Should these for vengeance cry in vain ;
Our full defiance, hate, and scorn,
Our herald has to Henry borne."

XIV.

He paused, and led where Douglas stood,
And with stern eye the pageant view'd :
I mean that Douglas, sixth of yore,
Who coronet of Angus bore,
And, when his blood and heart were high,
Did the third James in camp defy,
And all his minions led to die
 On Lauder's dreary flat ;
Princes and favourites long grew tame,
And trembled at the homely name
 Of Archibald Bell-the-Cat ;
The same who left the dusky vale
Of Hermitage in Liddisdale,
 Its dungeons, and its towers,
Where Bothwell's turrets brave the air,
And Bothwell bank is blooming fair,
 To fix his princely bowers.
Though now, in age, he had laid down
His armour for the peaceful gown
 And for a staff his brand,
Yet often would flash forth the fire,
That could, in youth, a monarch's ire
 And minion's pride withstand ;
And even that day, at council board,
 Unapt to soothe his sovereign's mood,
 Against the war had Angus stood,
And chafed his royal lord.

XV.

His giant-form, like ruin'd tower,
Though fall'n its muscles' brawny vaunt,
Huge-boned, and tall, and grim, and gaunt,
    Seem'd o'er the gaudy scene to lower:
His locks and beard in silver grew;
His eyebrows kept their sable hue.
Near Douglas when the Monarch stood
His bitter speech he thus pursued:
" Lord Marmion, since these letters say
That in the North you needs must stay,
    While slightest hopes of peace remain,
Uncourteous speech it were, and stern,
To say — Return to Lindisfarne,
    Until my herald come again. —
Then rest you in Tantallon Hold;
Your host shall be the Douglas bold, —
A chief unlike his sires of old.
He wears their motto on his blade,
Their blazon o'er his towers display'd;
Yet loves his sovereign to oppose,
More than to face his country's foes.
And, I bethink me, by St. Stephen,
    But e'en this morn to me was given
A prize, the first fruits of the war,
Ta'en by a galley from Dunbar,
    A bevy of the maids of Heaven.
Under your guard, these holy maids
Shall safe return to cloister shades,
And, while they at Tantallon stay,
Requiem for Cochran's soul may say."
And, with the slaughter'd favourite's name,
Across the Monarch's brow there came
A cloud of ire, remorse and shame.

XVI.

In answer nought could Angus speak;
His proud heart swell'd well nigh to break;
He turn'd aside, and down his cheek
    A burning tear there stole.
His hand the Monarch sudden took,
That sight his kind heart could not brook.
    "Now, by the Bruce's soul,
Angus, my hasty speech forgive!
For sure as doth his spirit live,
As he said of the Douglas old,
    I well may say of you, —
That never king did subject hold,
In speech more free, in war more bold,
    More tender and more true:
Forgive me, Douglas, once again." —
And, while the King his hand did strain,
The old man's tears fell down like rain.
To seize the moment Marmion tried,
And whisper'd to the King aside:
    "Oh! let such tears unwonted plead
For respite short from dubious deed!
A child will weep a bramble's smart,
A maid to see her sparrow part,
A stripling for a woman's heart:
But woe awaits a country, when
She sees the tears of bearded men.
Then, oh! what omen, dark and high,
When Douglas wets his manly eye!"

XVII.

Displeased was James, that stranger view'd
And tamper'd with his changing mood.

"Laugh those that can, weep those that may,"
Thus did the fiery Monarch say,
"Southward I march by break of day;
And if within Tantallon strong,
The good Lord Marmion tarries long,
Perchance our meeting next may fall
At Tamworth, in his castle-hall."—
The haughty Marmion felt the taunt,
And answer'd, grave, the royal vaunt:
"Much honour'd were my humble home,
If in its halls King James should come;
But Nottingham has archers good,
And Yorkshiremen are stern of mood;
Northumbrian prickers wild and rude.
On Derby hills the paths are steep;
In Ouse and Tyne the fords are deep;
And many a banner will be torn,
And many a knight to earth be borne,
And many a sheaf of arrows spent,
Ere Scotland's King shall cross the Trent.
Yet pause, brave Prince, while yet you may!"—
The Monarch lightly turn'd away,
And to his nobles loud did call,—
"Lords, to the dance,— a hall! a hall"
Himself his cloak and sword flung by,
And led Dame Heron gallantly;
And minstrels, at the royal order,
Rung out— "Blue Bonnets o'er the Border."

XVIII.

Leave we these revels now, to tell
What to St. Hilda's maids befell,
Whose galley as they sail'd again
To Whitby, by a Scot was ta'en.

Now at Dun-Edin did they bide,
Till James should of their fate decide;
   And soon, by his command,
Were gently summon'd to prepare
To journey under Marmion's care,
As escort honour'd, safe, and fair,
   Again to English land.
The Abbess told her chaplet o'er,
Nor knew which saint she should implore;
For, when she thought of Constance, sore
   She fear'd Lord Marmion's mood.
And judge what Clara must have felt!
The sword, that hung in Marmion's belt,
   Had drunk De Wilton's blood.
Unwittingly, King James had given,
   As guard to Whitby's shades,
The man most dreaded under Heaven
By these defenceless maids:
Yet what petition could avail,
Or who would listen to the tale
Of woman, prisoner, and nun,
'Mid bustle of a war begun?
They deem'd it hopeless to avoid
The convoy of their dangerous guide.

XIX.

Their lodging, so the King assign'd,
To Marmion's, as their guardian, join'd;
And thus it fell, that, passing nigh,
The Palmer caught the Abbess' eye,
   Who warn'd him by a scroll,
She had a secret to reveal,
That much concern'd the Church's weal,
   And health of sinner's soul,

And, with deep charge of secrecy,
　She nam'd a place to meet,
Within an open balcony,
That hung from dizzy pitch and high,
　Above the stately street;
To which, as common to each home,
At night they might in secret come.

XX.

At night, in secret, there they came,
The Palmer and the holy Dame.
The moon among the clouds rose high,
And all the city hum was by.
Upon the street, where late before
Did din of war and warriors roar,
　You might have heard a pebble fall,
A beetle hum, a cricket sing,
An owlet flap his boding wing
　On Giles's steeple tall.
The antique buildings, climbing high,
Whose Gothic frontlets sought the sky,
　Were here wrapt deep in shade;
There on their brows the moonbeam broke,
Through the faint wreaths of silvery smoke,
　And on the casements play'd.
　And other light was none to see,
　　Save torches gliding far,
　Before some chieftain of degree,
　Who left the royal revelry
　　To bowne him for the war. —
A solemn scene the Abbess chose;
A solemn hour, her secret to disclose.

XXI.

" O, holy Palmer ! " she began, —
" For sure he must be sainted man,
Whose blessed feet have trod the ground
Where the Redeemer's tomb is found, —
For His dear Church's sake, my tale
Attend, nor deem of light avail,
Though I must speak of worldly love, —
How vain to those who wed above ! —
De Wilton and Lord Marmion woo'd
Clara de Clare, of Gloster's blood ;
(Idle it were of Whitby's dame,
To say of that same blood I came ;)
And once, when jealous rage was high,
Lord Marmion said despiteously,
Wilton was traitor in his heart,
And had made league with Martin Swart,
When he came here on Simnel's part ;
And only cowardice did restrain
His rebel aid on Stokefield's plain, —
And down he threw his glove : — the thing
Was tried, as wont, before the King ;
Where frankly did De Wilton own,
That Swart in Gueldres he had known ;
And that between them then there went
Some scroll of courteous compliment.
For this he to his castle sent ;
But when his messenger return'd,
Judge how De Wilton's fury burn'd !
For in his packet there were laid
Letters that claim'd disloyal aid,
And proved King Henry's cause betray'd.

His fame, thus blighted, in the field
He strove to clear, by spear and shield; —
To clear his fame in vain he strove,
For wondrous are His ways above!
Perchance some form was unobserved;
Perchance in prayer, or faith, he swerved;
Else how could guiltless champion quail,
Or how the blessed ordeal fail?

XXII.

"His squire, who now De Wilton saw
As recreant doom'd to suffer law,
  Repentant, own'd in vain,
That, while he had the scrolls in care,
A stranger maiden, passing fair,
Had drench'd him with a beverage rare;
  His words no faith could gain.
With Clare alone he credence won,
Who, rather than wed Marmion,
Did to Saint Hilda's shrine repair,
To give our house her livings fair
And die a vestal vot'ress there.
The impulse from the earth was given,
But bent her to the paths of heaven.
A purer heart, a lovelier maid,
Ne'er shelter'd her in Whitby's shade,
No, not since Saxon Edelfled;
  Only one trace of earthly strain,
    That for her lover's loss
  She cherishes a sorrow vain,
    And murmurs at the cross. —
  And then her heritage; — it goes
    Along the bank of Tame;

Deep fields of grain the reaper mows,
In meadows rich the heifer lows;
The falconer and huntsman knows
   Its woodlands for the game.
Shame were it to Saint Hilda dear,
And I, her humble vot'ress here,
   Should do a deadly sin,
Her temple spoil'd before mine eyes,
If this false Marmion such a prize
   By my consent should win;
Yet hath our boisterous monarch sworn
That Clare shall from our house be torn,
And grievous cause have I to fear
Such mandate doth Lord Marmion bear.

XXIII.

"Now, prisoner, helpless, and betray'd
To evil power, I claim thine aid,
   By every step that thou hast trod
To holy shrine and grotto dim,
By every martyr's tortured limb,
By angel, saint, and seraphim,
   And by the Church of God!
For mark: — when Wilton was betray'd,
And with his squire forged letters laid,
She was, alas! that sinful maid,
   By whom the deed was done, —
O! shame and horror to be said!
   She was a perjured nun!
No clerk in all the land, like her,
Traced quaint and varying character.

Perchance you may a marvel deem,
   That Marmion's paramour
(For such vile thing she was) should scheme
   Her lover's nuptial hour;
But o'er him thus she hoped to gain,
As privy to his honour's stain,
   Illimitable power:
For this she secretly retain'd
   Each proof that might the plot reveal,
   Instructions with his hand and seal;
And thus Saint Hilda deign'd,
   Through sinner's perfidy impure,
   Her house's glory to secure,
And Clare's immortal weal.

XXIV.

" 'Twere long, and needless, here to tell,
How to my hand these papers fell;
   With me they must not stay.
Saint Hilda keep her Abbess true!
Who knows what outrage he might do
   While journeying by the way? —
O, blessed Saint, if e'er again
I venturous leave thy calm domain,
To travel or by land or main,
   Deep penance may I pay! —
Now, saintly Palmer, mark my prayer:
I give this packet to thy care,
For thee to stop they will not dare;
   And O! with cautious speed,
To Wolsey's hand the papers bring,
That he may show them to the King:
   And, for thy well-earn'd meed,

Thou holy man, at Whitby's shrine
A weekly mass shall still be thine,
   While priests can sing and read. —
What ail'st thou? — Speak!" for as he took
The charge, a strong emotion shook
   His frame; and, ere reply,
They heard a faint, yet shrilly tone,
Like distant clarion feebly blown,
   That on the breeze did die;
And loud the Abbess shriek'd in fear,
".Saint Withold, save us! What is here?
   Look at yon City Cross!
See on its battled tower appear
Phantoms, that scutcheons seem to rear,
   And blazon'd banners toss!"

XXV.

Dun-Edin's Cross, a pillar'd stone,
Rose on a turret octagon;
(But now is razed that monument,
   Whence royal edict rang,
And voice of Scotland's law was sent
   In glorious trumpet-clang,
O! be his tomb as lead to lead,
Upon its dull destroyer's head!
A minstrel's malison is said.)
Then on its battlements they saw
A vision, passing nature's law,
   Strange, wild, and dimly seen;
Figures that seem'd to rise and die,
Gibber and sign, advance and fly,
While nought confirm'd could ear or eye
   Discern of sound or mien.

Yet darkly did it seem, as there
Heralds and Pursuivants prepare,
With trumpet sound and blazon fair,
   A summons to proclaim;
But indistinct the pageant proud,
As fancy forms of midnight cloud,
When flings the moon upon her shroud
   A wavering tinge of flame;
It flits, expands, and shifts, till loud,
From midmost of the spectre crowd,
   This awful summons came: —

XXVI.

" Prince, prelate, potentate, and peer,
   Whose names I now shall call,
Scottish or foreigner, give ear;
Subjects of him who sent me here,
At his tribunal to appear,
   I summon one and all:
I cite you by each deadly sin,
That e'er hath soil'd your hearts within:
I cite you by each brutal lust,
That e'er defil'd your earthly dust, —
   By wrath, by pride, by fear,
By each o'er-mastering passion's tone,
By the dark grave, and dying groan!
When forty days are pass'd and gone,
I cite you, at your Monarch's throne,
   To answer and appear."
Then thunder'd forth a roll of names:
The first was thine, unhappy James!
   Then all thy nobles came;

Crawford, Glencairn, Montrose, Argyle,
Ross, Bothwell, Forbes, Lennox, Lyle, —
Why should I tell their separate style?
　　Each chief of birth and fame,
Of Lowland, Highland, Border, Isle,
Fore-doom'd to Flodden's carnage pile,
　　Was cited there by name;
And Marmion, Lord of Fontenaye,
Of Lutterward, and Scrivelbaye;
De Wilton, erst of Aberley,
The self-same thundering voice did say. —
　　But then another spoke:
" Thy fatal summons I deny,
And thine infernal Lord defy,
Appealing me to Him on High,
　　Who burst the sinner's yoke."
At that dread accent, with a scream,
Parted the pageant like a dream,
　　The summoner was gone.
Prone on her face the Abbess fell,
And fast, and fast, her beads did tell;
Her nuns came, startled by the yell,
　　And found her there alone.
She mark'd not, at the scene aghast,
What time, or how, the Palmer pass'd.

XXVII.

Shift we the scene. — The camp doth move,
　　Dun-Edin's streets are empty now,
Save when, for weal of those they love,
　　To pray the prayer, and vow the vow,
The tottering child, the anxious fair,

The grey-hair'd sire, with pious care,
To chapels and to shrines repair —
Where is the Palmer now? and where
The Abbess, Marmion, and Clare? —
Bold Douglas! to Tantallon fair
  They journey in thy charge:
Lord Marmion rode on his right hand,
The Palmer still was with the band;
Angus, like Lindesay, did command,
  That none should roam at large.
But in that Palmer's altered mien,
A wondrous change might now be seen.
  Freely he spoke of war,
Of marvels wrought by single hand,
When lifted for a native land;
And still look'd high, as if he plann'd
  Some desperate deed afar.
His courser would he feed and stroke,
And, tucking up his sable frocke,
Would first his mettle bold provoke,
  Then soothe or quell his pride.
Old Hubert said, that never one
He saw, except Lord Marmion,
  A steed so fairly ride.

XXVIII.

Some half-hour's march behind, there came,
  By Eustace govern'd fair,
A troop escorting Hilda's Dame,
  With all her nuns, and Clare.
No audience had Lord Marmion sought;
  Ever he fear'd to aggravate
  Clara de Clare's suspicious hate;

And safer 'twas, he thought,
  To wait till, from the nuns removed,
  The influence of kinsmen loved,
  And suit by Henry's self approved,
Her slow consent had wrought.
  His was no flickering flame, that dies
  Unless when fann'd by looks and sighs,
  And lighted oft at lady's eyes;
  He long'd to stretch his wide command
  O'er luckless Clara's ample land:
  Besides, when Wilton with him vied,
  Although the pang of humbled pride
  The place of jealousy supplied,
Yet conquest by that meanness won
He almost loath'd to think upon,
Led him, at times, to hate the cause,
Which made him burst through honour's laws.
If e'er he loved, 'twas her alone,
Who died within that vault of stone.

XXIX.

And now, when close at hand they saw
North Berwick's town, and lofty Law,
Fitz-Eustace bade them pause awhile,
Before a venerable pile,
  Whose turrets view'd, afar,
The lofty Bass, the Lambie Isle,
  The ocean's peace or war.
At tolling of a bell, forth came
The convent's venerable Dame,
And pray'd Saint Hilda's Abbess rest
With her, a loved and honour'd guest,

Till Douglas should a bark prepare
To waft her back to Whitby fair.
Glad was the Abbess, you may guess,
And thank'd the Scottish Prioress;
And tedious were to tell, I ween,
The courteous speech that pass'd between.
 O'erjoy'd the nuns their palfreys leave;
But when fair Clara did intend,
Like them, from horseback to descend,
 Fitz-Eustace said, — "I grieve,
Fair lady, grieve e'en from my heart,
Such gentle company to part; —
 Think not discourtesy,
But lords' commands must be obey'd;
And Marmion and the Douglas said,
 That you must wend with me.
Lord Marmion hath a letter broad,
Which to the Scottish Earl he show'd,
Commanding that, beneath his care,
Without delay, you shall repair
To your good kinsman, Lord Fitz-Clare."

XXX.

The startled Abbess loud exclaim'd;
But she, at whom the blow was aim'd,
Grew pale as death, and cold as lead, —
She deem'd she heard her death-doom read.
"Cheer thee, my child!" the Abbess said,
"They dare not tear thee from my hand,
To ride alone with armed band."
 "Nay, holy mother, nay,"
Fitz-Eustace said, "the lovely Clare
Will be in Lady Angus' care,
 In Scotland while we stay;

And, when we move, an easy ride
Will bring us to the English side,
Female attendance to provide
   Befitting Gloster's heir:
Nor thinks nor dreams my noble lord,
By slightest look, or act, or word,
   To harass Lady Clare.
Her faithful guardian he will be,
Nor sue for slightest courtesy
   That e'en to stranger falls,
Till he shall place her, safe and free,
   Within her kinsman's halls."
He spoke, and blush'd with earnest grace;
His faith was painted on his face,
   And Clare's worst fear relieved.
The Lady Abbess loud exclaim'd
On Henry, and the Douglas blamed,
   Entreated, threaten'd, grieved;
To martyr, saint, and prophet pray'd,
Against Lord Marmion inveigh'd,
And call'd the Prioress to aid,
To curse with candle, bell, and book.
Her head the grave Cistertian shook:
"The Douglas, and the King," she said,
"In their commands will be obey'd;
Grieve not, nor dream that harm can fall
The maiden in Tantallon Hall."

XXXI.

The Abbess, seeing strife was vain,
Assumed her wonted state again, —
   For much of state she had, —

Composed her veil, and raised her head,
And — " Bid," in solemn voice she said,
  "Thy master, bold and bad,
The records of his house turn o'er,
  And, when he shall there written see,
  That one of his own ancestry
  Drove the monks forth of Coventry,
Bid him his fate explore !
  Prancing in pride of earthly trust,
  His charger hurl'd him to the dust,
  And, by a base plebeian thrust,
He died his band before.
  God judge 'twixt Marmion and me;
  He is a Chief of high degree,
And I a poor recluse :
  Yet oft, in holy writ, we see
  Even such weak minister as me
May the oppressor bruise :
  For thus, inspired, did Judith slay
    The mighty in his sin,
And Jael thus, and Deborah," —
  Here hasty Blount broke in :
"Fitz-Eustace, we must march our band,
St. Anton' fire thee! wilt thou stand
All day, with bonnet in thy hand,
  To hear the lady preach?
By this good light! if thus we stay,
Lord Marmion, for our fond delay,
  Will sharper sermon teach.
Come, don thy cap, and mount thy horse;
The Dame must patience take perforce." —

XXXII.

"Submit we then to force," said Clare,
"But let this barbarous lord despair
　His purposed aim to win;
Let him take living, land, and life:
But to be Marmion's wedded wife
　In me were deadly sin:
And if it be the King's decree
That I must find no sanctuary,
In that inviolable dome,
Where even a homicide might come,
　And safely rest his head,
Though at its open portals stood,
Thirsting to pour forth blood for blood,
　The kinsmen of the dead;
Yet one asylum is my own
　Against the dreaded hour;
A low, a silent, and a lone,
　Where kings have little power.
One victim is before me there.—
Mother, your blessing, and in prayer,
Remember your unhappy Clare!"
Loud weeps the Abbess, and bestows
　Kind blessings many a one:
Weeping and wailing loud arose,
Round patient Clare, the clamourous woes
　Of every simple nun.
His eyes the gentle Eustace dried,
And scarce rude Blount the sight could bide.
　Then took the squire her rein,
And gently led away her steed,
And, by each courteous word and deed,
　To cheer her strove in vain.

XXXIII.

But scant three miles the band had rode,
  When o'er a height they pass'd,
And, sudden, close before them show'd
  His towers, Tantallon vast;
Broad, massive, high, and stretching far,
And held impregnable in war.
On a projecting rock they rose,
And round three sides the ocean flows,
The fourth did battled walls enclose,
  And double mound and fosse.
By narrow drawbridge, outworks strong,
Through studded gates, an entrance long,
  To the main court they cross.
It was a wide and stately square:
Around were lodgings, fit and fair,
  And towers of various form,
Which on the court projected far,
And broke its lines quadrangular.
Here was square keep, there turret high,
Or pinnacle that sought the sky,
Whence oft the warder could descry
  The gathering ocean storm.

XXXIV.

Here did they rest, — the princely care
Of Douglas, why should I declare,
Or say they met reception fair?
  Or why the tidings say,

Which, varying, to Tantallon came,
By hurrying posts or fleeter fame,
  With every varying day?
And, first they heard King James had won
  Etall, and Wark, and Ford; and then,
  That Norham Castle strong was ta'en.
At that sore marvell'd Marmion; —
And Douglas hoped his monarch's hand
Would soon subdue Northumberland:
  But whisper'd news there came,
That, while his host inactive lay,
And melted by degrees away,
King James was dallying off the day
  With Heron's wily dame. —
Such acts to chronicles I yield;
  Go seek them there, and see:
Mine is a tale of Flodden Field,
  And not a history. —
At length they heard the Scottish host
On that high ridge had made their post,
  Which frowns o'er Millfield Plain;
And that brave Surrey many a band
Had gather'd in the southern land,
And march'd into Northumberland,
  And camp at Wooler ta'en.
Marmion, like charger in the stall,
That hears, without, the trumpet-call,
  Began to chafe, and swear: —
" A sorry thing to hide my head
In castle, like a fearful maid,
  When such a field is near!
Needs must I see this battle-day:
Death to my fame if such a fray

Were fought, and Marmion away!
The Douglas, too, I wot not why,
Hath 'bated of his courtesy :
No longer in his halls I'll stay."
Then bade his band they should array
For march against the dawning day.

CANTO SIXTH.

The Battle.

I.

WHILE great events were on the gale,
And each hour brought a varying tale,
And the demeanour, changed and cold,
Of Douglas, fretted Marmion bold,
And, like the impatient steed of war,
He snuff'd the battle from afar;
And hopes were none, that back again
Herald should come from Terouenne,
Where England's King in leaguer lay,
Before decisive battle-day;
Whilst these things were, the mournful Clare
Did in the Dame's devotions share:
For the good Countess ceaseless pray'd
To Heaven and Saints, her sons to aid,
And, with short interval, did pass
From prayer to book, from book to mass,
And all in high Baronial pride, —
A life both dull and dignified; —
Yet as Lord Marmion nothing press'd
Upon her intervals of rest,
Dejected Clara well could bear
The formal state, the lengthen'd prayer,
Though dearest to her wounded heart
The hours that she might spend apart.

II.

I said, Tantallon's dizzy steep
Hung o'er the margin of the deep.
Many a rude tower and rampart there
Repell'd the insult of the air,
Which, when the tempest vex'd the sky,
Half breeze, half spray, came whistling by.
Above the rest, a turret square
Did o'er its Gothic entrance bear,
Of sculpture rude, a stony shield ;
The Bloody Heart was in the Field,
And in the chief three mullets stood,
The cognizance of Douglas blood.
The turret held a narrow stair,
Which, mounted, gave you access where
A parapet's embattled row
Did seaward round the castle go.
Sometimes in dizzy steps descending,
Sometimes in narrow circuit bending,
Sometimes in platform broad extending,
Its varying circle did combine
Bulwark, and bartizan, and line,
And bastion, tower, and vantage-coign ;
Above the booming ocean leant
The far-projecting battlement ;
The billows burst, in ceaseless flow,
Upon the precipice below.
Where'er Tantallon faced the land,
Gate-works, and walls, were strongly mann'd ;
No need upon the sea-girt side ;
The steepy rock, and frantic tide,
Approach of human step denied ;
And thus these lines and ramparts rude,
Were left in deepest solitude.

III.

And, for they were so lonely, Clare
Would to these battlements repair,
And muse upon her sorrows there,
    And list the sea-birds cry;
Or slow, like noontide ghost, would glide
Along the dark-grey bulwarks' side,
And ever on the heaving tide
    Look down with weary eye.
Oft did the cliff and swelling main,
Recall the thoughts of Whitby's fane,
A home she ne'er might see again;
    For she had laid adown,
So Douglas bade, the hood and veil,
And frontlet of the cloister pale,
    And Benedictine gown:
It were unseemly sight, he said,
A novice out of convent shade. —
Now her bright locks, with sunny glow,
Again adorn'd her brow of snow;
Her mantle rich, whose borders, round,
A deep and fretted broidery bound,
In golden foldings sought the ground;
Of holy ornament, alone
Remain'd a cross with ruby stone;
    And often did she look
On that which in her hand she bore,
With velvet bound, and broider'd o'er,
    Her breviary book.
In such a place, so lone, so grim,
At dawning pale, or twilight dim,
    It fearful would have been

To meet a form so richly dress'd,
With book in hand, and cross on breast,
   And such a woeful mien.
Fitz-Eustace, loitering with his bow,
To practise on the gull and crow,
Saw her, at distance, gliding slow,
   And did by Mary swear, —
Some love-lorn Fay she might have been,
Or, in Romance, some spell-bound Queen;
For ne'er, in work-day world, was seen
   A form so witching fair.

IV.

Once walking thus, at evening tide,
It chanced a gliding sail she spied,
And, sighing, thought — "The Abbess, there,
Perchance, does to her home repair;
Her peaceful rule, where Duty, free,
Walks hand in hand with Charity;
Where oft Devotion's tranced glow
Can such a glimpse of heaven bestow,
That the enraptured sisters see
High vision and deep mystery;
The very form of Hilda fair,
Hovering upon the sunny air,
And smiling on her votaries' prayer.
O! wherefore, to my duller eye,
Did still the Saint her form deny!
Was it, that, sear'd by sinful scorn,
My heart could neither melt nor burn?
Or lie my warm affections low,
With him, that taught them first to glow?

Yet, gentle Abbess, well I knew,
To pay thy kindness grateful due,
And well could brook the mild command,
That ruled thy simple maiden band.
How different now ! condemn'd to bide
My doom from this dark tyrant's pride. —
But Marmion has to learn, ere long,
That constant mind, and hate of wrong,
Descended to a feeble girl,
From Red De Clare, stout Gloster's Earl:
Of such a stem, a sapling weak,
He ne'er shall bend, although he break.

V.

"But see! what makes this armour here?"—
    For in her path there lay
Targe, corslet, helm;—she view'd them near. —
"The breast-plate pierced!—Ay, much I fear,
Weak fence wert thou 'gainst foeman's spear,
That hath made fatal entrance here,
    As these dark blood-gouts say. —
Thus Wilton!—Oh! not corslet's ward,
Not truth, as diamond pure and hard,
Could be thy manly bosom's guard,
    On yon disastrous day!"—
She raised her eyes in mournful mood, —
WILTON himself before her stood!
It might have seem'd his passing ghost,
For every youthful grace was lost;
And joy unwonted, and surprise,   .
Gave their strange wildness to his eyes. —
Expect not, noble dames and lords,
That I can tell such scene in words:

What skilful limner e'er would choose
To paint the rainbow's varying hues,
Unless to mortal it were given
To dip his brush in dyes of heaven ?
Far less can my weak line declare
  Each changing passion's shade ;
Brightening to rapture from despair,
Sorrow, surprise, and pity there,
And joy, with her angelic air,
And hope, that paints the future fair,
  Their varying hues display'd :
Each o'er its rival's ground extending,
Alternate conquering, shifting, blending,
Till all, fatigued, the conflict yield,
And mighty Love retains the field.
Shortly I tell what then he said,
By many a tender word delay'd,
And modest blush, and bursting sigh,
And question kind, and fond reply : —

VI.

De Wilton's History.

" Forget we that disastrous day,
When senseless in the lists I lay.
  Thence dragg'd, — but how I cannot know,
    For sense and recollection fled, —
  I found me on a pallet low,
    Within my ancient beadsman's shed.
  Austin, — remember'st thou, my Clare,
How thou didst blush, when the old man,
When first our infant love began,
  Said we would make a matchless pair ? —

Menials, and friends, and kinsmen fled
From the degraded traitor's bed, —
He only held my burning head,
And tended me for many a day,
While wounds and fever held their sway.
But far more needful was his care,
When sense return'd to wake despair;
 For I did tear the closing wound,
 And dash me frantic on the ground,
If e'er I heard the name of Clare.
At length, to calmer reason brought,
Much by his kind attendance wrought,
 With him I left my native strand,
And, in a palmer's weeds array'd,
My hated name and form to shade,
 I journey'd many a land;
No more a lord of rank and birth,
But mingled with the dregs of earth.
 Oft Austin for my reason fear'd,
When I would sit, and deeply brood
On dark revenge, and deeds of blood,
 Or wild mad schemes uprear'd.
My friend at length fell sick, and said,
 God would remove him soon:
And, while upon his dying bed,
 He begg'd of me a boon —
If e'er my deadliest enemy
Beneath my brand should conquer'd lie,
Even then my mercy should awake,
And spare his life for Austin's sake.

VII.

"Still restless as a second Cain,
To Scotland next my route was ta'en,
  Full well the paths I knew.
Fame of my fate made various sound,
That death in pilgrimage I found,
That I had perish'd of my wound,
  None cared which tale was true;
And living eye could never guess
De Wilton in his Palmer's dress;
For now that sable slough is shed,
And trimm'd my shaggy beard and head,
I scarcely know me in the glass.
A chance most wondrous did provide,
That I should be that Baron's guide —
  I will not name his name! —
Vengeance to God alone belongs;
But, when I think on all my wrongs,
  My blood is liquid flame!
And ne'er the time shall I forget,
When, in a Scottish hostel set,
  Dark looks we did exchange:
What were his thoughts I cannot tell;
But in my bosom muster'd Hell
  Its plans of dark revenge.

VIII.

"A word of vulgar augury,
That broke from me, I scarce knew why,
  Brought on a village tale;
Which wrought upon his moody sprite,
And sent him armed forth by night.
  I borrow'd steed and mail,

And weapons, from his sleeping band ;
  And, passing from a postern door,
We met, and 'counter'd hand to hand, —
  He fell on Gifford moor.
For the death-stroke my brand I drew,
(O then my helmed head he knew,
  The Palmer's cowl was gone,)
Then had three inches of my blade
The heavy debt of vengeance paid, —
My hand the thought of Austin staid,
  I left him there alone. —
O good old man! even from the grave
Thy spirit could thy master save :
If I had slain my foeman, ne'er
Had Whitby's Abbess, in her fear,
Given to my hand this packet dear,
Of power to clear my injured fame,
And vindicate De Wilton's name. —
Perchance you heard the Abbess tell
Of the strange pageantry of Hell,
  That broke our secret speech —
It rose from the infernal shade,
Or featly was some juggle play'd
  A tale of peace to teach.
Appeal to Heaven I judged was best,
When my name came among the rest.

IX.

"Now here, within Tantallon Hold,
To Douglas late my tale I told,
To whom my house was known of old.
Won by my proofs, his falchion bright
This eve anew shall dub me knight.

These were the arms that once did turn
The tide of fight on Otterburne,
And Harry Hotspur forced to yield,
When the Dead Douglas won the field.
These Angus gave — his armourer's care,
Ere morn shall every breach repair;
For nought, he said, was in his halls,
But ancient armour on the walls,
And aged chargers in the stalls,
And women, priests, and grey-hair'd men;
The rest were all in Twisel glen.
And now I watch my armour here,
By law of arms, till midnight's near;
Then, once again a belted knight,
Seek Surrey's camp with dawn of light.

X.

" There soon again we meet, my Clare!
This Baron means to guide thee there:
Douglas reveres his King's command,
Else would he take thee from his band.
And there thy kinsman, Surrey, too,
Will give De Wilton justice due.
Now meeter far for martial broil,
Firmer my limbs, and strung by toil,
Once more " — "O Wilton! must we then
Risk new-found happiness again,
    Trust fate of arms once more?
And is there not an humble glen,
    Where we, content and poor,
Might build a cottage in the shade,
A shepherd thou, and I to aid
    Thy task on dale and moor? —

That reddening brow ! — too well I know,
Not even thy Clare can peace bestow,
　　While falsehood stains thy name ;
Go then to fight! Clare bids thee go!
Clare can a warrior's feelings know,
　　And weep a warrior's shame :
Can Red Earl Gilbert's spirit feel,
Buckle the spurs upon thy heel,
And belt thee with thy brand of steel,
　　And send thee forth to fame! "

XI.

That night, upon the rocks and bay,
The midnight moon-beam slumbering lay,
And pour'd its silver light, and pure,
Through loop-hole, and through embrazure,
　　Upon Tantallon tower and hall ;
But chief where arched windows wide
Illuminate the chapel's pride,
　　The sober glances fall.
Much was their need ; though scam'd with scars,
Two veterans of the Douglas' wars,
　　Though two grey priests were there,
And each a blazing torch held high,
You could not by their blaze descry
　　The chapel's carving fair.
Amid that dim and smoky light,
Chequering the silver moon-shine bright,
　　A bishop by the altar stood,
　　A noble lord of Douglas blood,
With mitre sheen, and rocquet white.
Yet show'd his meek and thoughtful eye
But little pride of prelacy ;

More pleased that, in a barbarous age,
He gave rude Scotland Virgil's page,
Than that beneath his rule he held
The bishopric of fair Dunkeld.
Beside him ancient Angus stood,
Doff'd his furr'd gown, and sable hood;
O'er his huge form and visage pale,
He wore a cap and shirt of mail;
And lean'd his large and wrinkled hand
Upon the huge and sweeping brand
Which wont of yore, in battle fray,
His foeman's limbs to shred away,
As wood-knife lops the sapling spray.
  He seem'd as, from the tombs around
    Rising at judgment-day,
  Some giant Douglas may be found
    In all his old array;
So pale his face, so huge his limb,
So old his arms, his look so grim.

XII.

Then at the altar Wilton kneels,
And Clare the spurs bound on his heels;
And think what next he must have felt,
At buckling of the falchion belt!
  And judge how Clara changed her hue,
While fastening to her lover's side
A friend, which, though in danger tried,
  He once had found untrue!
Then Douglas struck him with his blade:
" St. Michael and St. Andrew aid,
  I dub thee knight.

Arise, Sir Ralph, De Wilton's heir!
For King, for Church, for Lady fair,
  See that thou fight."—
And Bishop Gawain, as he rose,
Said—"Wilton! grieve not for thy woes,
  Disgrace, and trouble:
For He, who honour best bestows,
  May give thee double."
De Wilton sobb'd, for sob he must—
"Where'er I meet a Douglas, trust
  That Douglas is my brother!"
"Nay, nay," old Angus said, "not so;
To Surrey's camp thou now must go,
  Thy wrongs no longer smother.
I have two sons in yonder field,
And, if thou meet'st them under shield,
Upon them bravely—do thy worst;
And foul fall him that blenches first!"

XIII.

Not far advanced was morning day,
When Marmion did his troop array
  To Surrey's camp to ride;
He had safe conduct for his band,
Beneath the royal seal and hand,
  And Douglas gave a guide:
The ancient Earl, with stately grace,
Would Clara on her palfrey place,
And whisper'd in an under tone,
"Let the hawk stoop, his prey is flown."·
The train from out the castle drew,
But Marmion stopp'd to bid adieu:—
  "Though something I might plain," he said,

"Of cold respect to stranger guest,
Sent hither by your King's behest,
   While in Tantallon's towers I staid;
Part we in friendship from your land,
And, noble Earl, receive my hand."—
But Douglas round him drew his cloak,
Folded his arms, and thus he spoke:—
"My manors, halls, and bowers, shall still
Be open, at my Sovereign's will,
To each one whom he lists, howe'er
Unmeet to be the owner's peer.
My castles are my King's alone,
From turret to foundation-stone—
The hand of Douglas is his own;
And never shall in friendly grasp
The hand of such as Marmion clasp."—

XIV.

Burn'd Marmion's swarthy cheek like fire,
And shook his very frame for ire,
   And—"This to me!" he said,—
"An 'twere not for thy hoary beard,
Such hand as Marmion's had not spared
   To cleave the Douglas' head!
And, first, I tell thee, haughty Peer,
He, who does England's message here,
Although the meanest in her state,
May well, proud Angus, be thy mate:
And, Douglas, more I tell thee here,
   Even in thy pitch of pride,
Here in thy hold, thy vassals near,
(Nay, never look upon your lord,
And lay your hands upon your sword,)
   I tell thee, thou'rt defied!

And if thou said'st I am not peer
To any lord in Scotland here,
Lowland or Highland, far or near,
   Lord Angus, thou hast lied!"
On the Earl's cheek the flush of rage
O'ercame the ashen hue of age:
Fierce he broke forth, — "And darest thou, then,
To beard the lion in his den,
   The Douglas in his hall?
And hopest thou hence unscathed to go?—
No, by Saint Bride of Bothwell, no!
Up drawbridge, grooms — What, Warder, ho!
   Let the portcullis fall."
Lord Marmion turn'd, — well was his need,
And dash'd the rowels in his steed,
Like arrow through the archway sprung,
The ponderous grate behind him rung:
To pass there was such scanty room,
The bars, descending, razed his plume.

XV.

The steed along the drawbridge flies,
Just as it trembled on the rise;
Nor lighter does the swallow skim
Along the smooth lake's level brim:
And when Lord Marmion reach'd his band,
He halts, and turns with clenched hand,
   And shout of loud defiance pours,
And shook his gauntlet at the towers.
"Horse! horse!" the Douglas cried, "and chase!"
But soon he rein'd his fury's pace:
"A royal messenger he came,
Though most unworthy of the name. —

A letter forged! Saint Jude to speed!
Did ever knight so foul a deed!
At first in heart it liked me ill,
When the King praised his clerkly skill.
Thanks to Saint Bothan, son of mine,
Save Gawain, ne'er could pen a line.
So swore I, and I swear it still,
Let my boy-bishop fret his fill. —
Saint Mary mend my fiery mood!
Old age ne'er cools the Douglas blood,
I thought to slay him where he stood.
'Tis pity of him too," he cried:
"Bold can he speak, and fairly ride,
I warrant him a warrior tried."
With this his mandate he recalls,
And slowly seeks his castle halls.

XVI.

The day in Marmion's journey wore;
Yet, ere his passion's gust was o'er,
They cross'd the heights of Stanrigmoor.
His troop more closely there he scann'd,
And missed the Palmer from the band. —
"Palmer or not," young Blount did say,
"He parted at the peep of day;
Good sooth, it was in strange array." —
"In what array?" said Marmion, quick.
"My lord, I ill can spell the trick;
But all night long, with clink and bang,
Close to my couch did hammers clang;
At dawn the falling drawbridge rang,
And from a loop-hole while I peep,
Old Bell-the-Cat came from the Keep,

Wrapped in a gown of sables fair,
As fearful of the morning air;
Beneath, when that was blown aside,
A rusty shirt of mail I spied,
By Archibald won in bloody work,
Against the Saracen and Turk:
Last night it hung not in the hall;
I thought some marvel would befall.
And next I saw them saddled lead
Old Cheviot forth, the Earl's best steed;
A matchless horse, though something old,
Prompt in his paces, cool and bold.
I heard the Sheriff Sholto say,
The Earl did much the Master pray
To use him on the battle-day;
But he preferr'd —" " Nay, Henry, cease!
Thou sworn horse-courser, hold thy peace. —
Eustace, thou bear'st a brain — I pray
What did Blount see at break of day?"—

XVII.

" In brief, my lord, we both descried
(For then I stood by Henry's side)
The Palmer mount, and outwards ride,

  Upon the Earl's own favourite steed:
All sheathed he was in armour bright,
And much resembled that same knight,
Subdued by you in Cotswold fight:

  Lord Angus wished him speed."—
The instant that Fitz-Eustace spoke,
A sudden light on Marmion broke; —
" Ah! dastard fool, to reason lost!"
He mutter'd; " 'Twas not fay nor ghost

I met upon the moonlight wold,
But living man of earthly mould. —
   O dotage blind and gross!
Had I but fought as wont, one thrust
Had laid De Wilton in the dust,
   My path no more to cross. —
How stand we now? — he told his tale
To Douglas; and with some avail;
   'Twas therefore gloom'd his rugged brow. —
Will Surrey dare to entertain
'Gainst Marmion, charge disproved and vain?
   Small risk of that, I trow.
Yet Clare's sharp questions must I shun;
Must separate Constance from the Nun —
O, what a tangled web we weave,
When first we practise to deceive!
A Palmer too! — no wonder why
I felt rebuked beneath his eye:
I might have known there was but one
Whose look could quell Lord Marmion."

XVIII.

Stung with these thoughts, he urged to speed
His troop, and reach'd, at eve, the Tweed,
Where Lennel's convent closed their march;
(There now is left but one frail arch;
   Yet mourn thou not its cells;
Our time a fair exchange has made;
Hard by, in hospitable shade,
   A reverend pilgrim dwells,
Well worth the whole Bernardine brood,
That e'er wore sandal, frock, or hood.)

Yet did Saint Bernard's Abbot there
Give Marmion entertainment fair,
And lodging for his train and Clare.
Next morn the Baron climb'd the tower,
To view afar the Scottish power,
 Encamp'd on Flodden edge:
The white pavilions made a show,
Like remnants of the winter snow,
 Along the dusky ridge.
Long Marmion look'd: — at length his eye
Unusual movement might descry
 Amid the shifting lines:
The Scottish host drawn out appears,
For, flashing on the hedge of spears
 The eastern sunbeam shines.
Their front now deepening, now extending;
Their flank inclining, wheeling, bending,
Now drawing back, and now descending,
The skilful Marmion well could know,
They watch'd the motions of some foe,
Who traversed on the plain below.

XIX.

Even so it was. From Flodden ridge
 The Scots beheld the English host
 Leave Barmore-wood, their evening post,
 And heedful watch'd them as they cross'd
The Till by Twisel Bridge.
 High sight it is, and haughty, while
 They dive into the deep defile;
 Beneath the cavern'd cliff they fall,
 Beneath the castle's airy wall.

By rock, by oak, by hawthorn-tree,
 Troop after troop are disappearing ;
 Troop after troop their banners rearing,
Upon the eastern bank you see.
Still pouring down the rocky den,
 Where flows the sullen Till,
And rising from the dim-wood glen,
Standards on standards, men on men,
 In slow succession still,
And, sweeping o'er the Gothic arch,
And pressing on, in ceaseless march,
 To gain the opposing hill.
That morn, to many a trumpet clang,
Twisel ! thy rock's deep echo rang ;
And many a chief of birth and rank,
Saint Helen ! at thy fountain drank.
Thy hawthorn glade, which now we see
In spring-time bloom so lavishly,
Had then from many an axe its doom,
To give the marching columns room.

XX.

And why stands Scotland idly now,
Dark Flodden ! on thy airy brow,
Since England gains the pass the while,
And struggles through the deep defile ?
What checks the fiery soul of James ?
Why sits that champion of the dames
 Inactive on his steed,
And sees, between him and his land,
Between him and Tweed's southern strand,
 His host Lord Surrey lead ?

What 'vails the vain knight-errant's brand?
— O, Douglas, for thy leading wand!
　Fierce Randolph, for thy speed!
O for one hour of Wallace wight,
Or well-skill'd Bruce, to rule the fight,
And cry — " Saint Andrew and our right! "
Another sight had seen that morn,
From Fate's dark book a leaf been torn,
And Flodden had been Bannockbourne! —
The precious hour has pass'd in vain,
And England's host had gain'd the plain;
Wheeling their march, and circling still,
Around the base of Flodden hill.

XXI.

Ere yet the bands met Marmion's eye,
Fitz-Eustace shouted loud and high,
"Hark! hark! my lord, an English drum!
And see ascending squadrons come
　Between Tweed's river and the hill,
Foot, horse, and cannon: — hap what hap,
My basnet to a prentice cap,
　Lord Surrey's o'er the Till!
Yet more! yet more! — how far array'd
They file from out the hawthorn shade,
　And sweep so gallant by:
With all their banners bravely spread,
　And all their armour flashing high,
St. George might waken from the dead,
　To see fair England's standards fly."—
" Stint in thy prate," quoth Blount, " thou'dst best,
And listen to our lord's behest."—

With kindling brow Lord Marmion said, —
" This instant be our band array'd ;
The river must be quickly cross'd,
That we may join Lord Surrey's host.
If fight King James, — as well I trust,
That fight he will, and fight he must, —
The Lady Clare behind our lines
Shall tarry, while the battle joins."

XXII.

Himself he swift on horseback threw,
Scarce to the Abbot bade adieu ;
Far less would listen to his prayer,
To leave behind the helpless Clare.
Down to the Tweed his band he drew,
And mutter'd as the flood they view,
" The pheasant in the falcon's claw,
He scarce will yield to please a daw.
Lord Angus may the Abbot awe,
    So Clare shall bide with me."
Then on that dangerous ford, and deep,
Where to the Tweed Leat's eddies creep,
    He ventured desperately :
And not a moment will he bide,
Till squire, or groom, before him ride ;
Headmost of . all he stems the tide ;
    And stems it gallantly.
Eustace held Clare upon her horse,
    Old Hubert led her rein,
Stoutly they braved the current's course,
And, though far downward driven per force,
    The southern bank they gain ;

Behind them straggling, came to shore,
  As best they might, the train:
Each o'er his head his yew-bow bore,
  A caution not in vain;
Deep need that day that every string,
By wet unharm'd, should sharply ring.
A moment then Lord Marmion staid,
And breathed his steed, his men array'd,
  Then forward mov'd his band,
Until, Lord Surrey's rear-guard won,
He halted by a Cross of Stone,
That, on a hillock standing lone,
  Did all the field command.

XXIII.

Hence might they see the full array
Of either host, for deadly fray;
Their marshall'd lines stretch'd east and west,
  And fronted north and south,
And distant salutation pass'd
  From the loud cannon mouth;
Not in the close successive rattle,
That breathes the voice of modern battle,
  But slow and far between. —
The hillock gain'd, Lord Marmion staid:
"Here, by this Cross," he gently said,
  "You well may view the scene.
Here shalt thou tarry, lovely Clare:
O! think of Marmion in thy prayer! —
Thou wilt not? — well, — no less my care
Shall, watchful, for thy weal prepare. —

You, Blount and Eustace, are her guard,
  With ten pick'd archers of my train;
With England if the day go hard,
  To Berwick speed amain. —
But if we conquer, cruel maid,
My spoils shall at your feet be laid,
  When here we meet again."
He waited not for answer there,
And would not mark the maid's despair,
  Nor heed the discontented look
From either squire; but spurr'd amain,
And dashing through the battle plain,
  His way to Surrey took.

XXIV.

" ——The good Lord Marmion, by my life!
  Welcome to danger's hour! —
Short greeting serves in time of strife!
  Thus have I ranged my power: —
Myself will rule this central host,
  Stout Stanley fronts their right,
My sons command the vaward post,
  With Brian Tunstall, stainless knight,
  Lord Dacre, with his horsemen light,
  Shall be in rear-ward of the fight,
And succour those that need it most.
  Now, gallant Marmion, well I know,
  Would gladly to the vanguard go;
Edmund, the Admiral, Tunstall there,
With thee their charge will blithely share;
There fight thine own retainers too,
Beneath De Burg, thy steward true."

"Thanks, noble Surrey!" Marmion said,
Nor farther greeting there he paid;
But, parting like a thunderbolt,
First in the vanguard made a halt,
    Where such a shout there rose
Of "Marmion! Marmion!" that the cry,
Up Flodden mountain shrilling high,
    Startled the Scottish foes.

XXV.

Blount and Fitz-Eustace rested still
With Lady Clare upon the hill!
On which (for far the day was spent)
The western sunbeams now were bent.
The cry they heard, its meaning knew,
Could plain their distant comrades view;
Sadly to Blount did Eustace say,
"Unworthy office here to stay!
No hope of gilded spurs to-day. —
But see! look up — on Flodden bent
The Scottish foe has fired his tent."
    And sudden, as he spoke,
From the sharp ridges of the hill,
All downward to the banks of Till,
    Was wreathed in sable smoke.
Volumed and fast, and rolling far,
The cloud enveloped Scotland's war,
    As down the hill they broke;
Nor martial shout, nor minstrel tone,
Announced their march; their tread alone,
At times one warning trumpet blown,
    At times a stifled hum,

Told England, from his mountain-throne
  King James did rushing come. —
Scarce could they hear or see their foes,
  Until at weapon-point they close. —
They close, in clouds of smoke and dust,
With sword-sway, and with lance's thrust;
  And such a yell was there,
Of sudden and portentous birth,
As if men fought upon the earth,
And fiends in upper air;
O life and death were in the shout,
Recoil and rally, charge and rout,
  And triumph and despair.
Long look'd the anxious squires; their eye
Could in the darkness nought descry.

XXVI.

At length the freshening western blast
Aside the shroud of battle cast;
And, first, the ridge of mingled spears
Above the brightening cloud appears;
And in the smoke the pennons flew,
As in the storm the white seamew.
Then mark'd they, dashing broad and far,
The broken billows of the war,
And plumed crests of chieftains brave,
Floating like foam upon the wave;
  But nought distinct they see:
Wide raged the battle on the plain;
Spears shook, and falchions flash'd amain;
Fell England's arrow-flight like rain;
Crests rose, and stoop'd, and rose again,
  Wild and disorderly.

Amid the scene of tumult, high
They saw Lord Marmion's falcon fly:
And stainless Tunstall's banner white,
And Edmund Howard's lion bright,
Still bear them bravely in the fight:
    Although against them come,
Of gallant Gordons many a one,
And many a stubborn Highlandman,
And many a rugged Border clan,
    With Huntly, and with Home.

XXVII.

Far on the left, unseen the while,
Stanley broke Lennox and Argyle;
Though there the western mountaineer
Rush'd with bare bosom on the spear,
And flung the feeble targe aside,
And with both hands the broadsword plied.
'Twas vain: — but Fortune, on the right,
With fickle smile, cheer'd Scotland's fight.
Then fell that spotless banner white,
    The Howard's lion fell;
Yet still Lord Marmion's falcon flew
With wavering flight, while fiercer grew
    Around the battle-yell.
The Border slogan rent the sky!
A Home! a Gordon! was the cry:
    Loud were the clanging blows;
Advanced, — forced back, — now low, now high,
    The pennon sunk and rose;
As bends the bark's mast in the gale,
When rent are rigging, shrouds, and sail,
    It waver'd 'mid the foes.

No longer Blount the view could bear:
" By Heaven, and all its saints ! I swear
   I will not see it lost!
Fitz-Eustace, you with Lady Clare
May bid your beads, and patter prayer, —
   I gallop to the host."
And to the fray he rode amain,
Follow'd by all the archer train.
The fiery youth, with desperate charge,
Made, for a space, an opening large, —
   The rescued banner rose, —
But darkly closed the war around,
Like pine-tree, rooted from the ground,
   It sunk among the foes.
Then Eustace mounted too : — yet staid
As loath to leave the helpless maid,
   When, fast as shaft can fly,
Blood-shot his eyes, his nostrils spread,
The loose rein dangling from his head,
Housing and saddle bloody red,
   Lord Marmion's steed rush'd by ;
And Eustace, maddening at the sight,
   A look and sign to Clara cast
   To mark he would return in haste,
Then plunged into the fight.

XXVIII.

Ask me not what the maiden feels,
   Left in that dreadful hour alone :
Perchance her reason stoops, or reels ;
   Perchance a courage, not her own,
   Braces her mind to desperate tone. —
The scatter'd van of England wheels : —

She only said, as loud in air
The tumult roar'd, "Is Wilton there?"—
They fly, or, madden'd by despair,
Fight but to die,—"Is Wilton there?"
With that, straight up the hill there rode
Two horsemen drench'd with gore,
And in their arms, a helpless load,
   A wounded knight they bore.
His hand still strain'd the broken brand;
His arms were smear'd with blood and sand.
Dragg'd from among the horses' feet,
With dinted shield, and helmet beat,
The falcon-crest and plumage gone,
Can that be haughty Marmion! . . .
Young Blount his armour did unlace,
And, gazing on his ghastly face,
   Said—"By Saint George, he's gone!
That spear-wound has our master sped,
And see the deep cut on his head!
   Good-night to Marmion."—
"Unnurtured Blount! thy brawling cease,
He opes his eyes," said Eustace; "peace!"

XXIX.

When, doff'd his casque, he felt free air,
Around 'gan Marmion wildly stare:—
"Where's Harry Blount? Fitz-Eustace where?
Linger ye here, ye hearts of hare!
Redeem my pennon,—charge again!
Cry—'Marmion to the rescue!'—Vain!
Last of my race, on battle-plain
That shout shall ne'er be heard again!—

Yet my last thought is England's — fly,
  To Dacre bear my signet-ring :
  Tell him his squadrons up to bring. —
Fitz-Eustace, to Lord Surrey hie ;
  Tunstall lies dead upon the field,
  His life-blood stains the spotless shield :
  Edmund is down : — my life is reft ;
  The Admiral alone is left.
  Let Stanley charge with spur of fire, —
  With Chester charge, and Lancashire,
  Full upon Scotland's central host,
  Or Victory and England's lost. —
  Must I bid twice? — hence, varlets! fly!
  Leave Marmion here alone — to die."
  They parted, and alone he lay ;
  Clare drew her from the sight away,
Till pain wrung forth a lowly moan,
And half he murmur'd, — " Is there none,
  Of all my halls have nurst,
Page, squire, or groom, one cup to bring
Of blessed water from the spring,
  To slake my dying thirst ! "

XXX.

O, Woman ! in our hours of ease,
Uncertain, coy, and hard to please,
And variable as the shade
By the light quivering aspen made ;
When pain and anguish wring the brow,
A ministering angel thou ! —
Scarce were the piteous accents said,
When, with the Baron's casque, the maid
  To the nigh streamlet ran :

Forgot were hatred, wrongs, and fears;
The plaintive voice alone she hears,
   Sees but the dying man.
She stoop'd her by the runnel's side,
   But in abhorrence backward drew;
For, oozing from the mountain's side,
Where raged the war, a dark-red tide
   Was curdling in the streamlet blue.
Where shall she turn ? — behold her mark
   A little fountain cell,
Where water, clear as diamond-spark,
   In a stone basin fell.
Above, some half-worn letters say,
𝔇rink. wearp. pilgrim. 𝔡rink. an𝔡. prap.
𝔉or. t𝔥e. kin𝔡. soul. of. 𝔖pbil. ℭrep.
   𝔚𝔥o. built. t𝔥is. cross. an𝔡. well.
She fill'd the helm, and back she hied,
And with surprise and joy espied
   A monk supporting Marmion's head:
A pious man, whom duty brought
To dubious verge of battle fought,
   To shrieve the dying, bless the dead.

XXXI.

Deep drank Lord Marmion of the wave,
And, as she stoop'd his brow to lave —
" Is it the hand of Clare," he said,
" Or injured Constance, bathes my head?"
   Then, as remembrance rose, —
" Speak not to me of shrift or prayer!
   I must redress her woes.

Short space, few words, are mine to spare;
Forgive and listen, gentle Clare!"—
  "Alas!" she said, "the while,—
O, think of your immortal weal!
In vain for Constance is your zeal;
  She —— died at Holy Isle."—
Lord Marmion started from the ground,
As light as if he felt no wound;
Though in the action burst the tide,
In torrents, from his wounded side.
"Then it was truth,"—he said—"I knew
That the dark presage must be true.—
I would the Fiend, to whom belongs
The vengeance due to all her wrongs,
  Would spare me but a day!
For wasting fire, and dying groan,
And priests slain on the altar-stone,
  Might bribe him for delay.
It may not be!—this dizzy trance—
Curse on yon base marauder's lance,
And doubly cursed my failing brand!
A sinful heart makes feeble hand."
Then, fainting, down on earth he sunk,
Supported by the trembling Monk.

XXXII.

With fruitless labour, Clara bound,
And strove to staunch the gushing wound:
The Monk, with unavailing cares,
Exhausted all the Church's prayers.
Ever, he said, that, close and near,
A lady's voice was in his ear,
And that the priest he could not hear,
  For that she ever sung,

" In the lost battle, borne down by the flying,
Where mingles war's rattle with groans of the dying!"
    So the notes rang ; —
"Avoid thee, Fiend! — with cruel hand,
Shake not the dying sinner's sand! —
O, look, my son, upon yon sign
Of the Redeemer's grace divine ;
    O, think on faith and bliss ! —
By many a death-bed I have been,
And many a sinner's parting seen,
    But never aught like this." —
The war, that for a space did fail,
Now trebly thundering swell'd the gale,
    And — STANLEY! was the cry ;
A light on Marmion's visage spread,
    And fired his glazing eye ;
With dying hand, above his head,
He shook the fragment of his blade,
    And shouted " Victory ! —
Charge, Chester, charge! On, Stanley, on!"
Were the last words of Marmion.

XXXIII.

By this, though deep the evening fell,
Still rose the battle's deadly swell,
For still the Scots, around their King,
Unbroken, fought in desperate ring.
Where's now their victor vaward wing,
Where Huntly, and where Home?" —
O, for a blast of that dread horn,
On Fontarabian echoes borne,
    That to King Charles did come,

When Rowland brave, and Olivier,
And every paladin and peer,
   On Roncesvalles died!
Such blast might warn them, not in vain,
To quit the plunder of the slain,
And turn the doubtful day again,
   While yet on Flodden side,
Afar, the Royal Standard flies,
And round it toils, and bleeds, and dies,
   Our Caledonian pride!
In vain the wish — for far away,
While spoil and havoc mark their way,
Near Sybil's Cross the plunderers stray. —
" O, Lady," cried the Monk, " away!"
   And placed her on her steed,
And led her to the chapel fair,
   Of Tillmouth upon Tweed.
There all the night they spent in prayer,
And at the dawn of morning, there
She met her kinsman, Lord Fitz-Clare.

XXXIV.

But as they left the dark'ning heath,
More desperate grew the strife of death.
The English shafts in volleys hail'd,
In headlong charge their horse assail'd;
Front, flank, and rear, the squadrons sweep
To break the Scottish circle deep,
   That fought around their King.
But yet, though thick the shafts as snow,
Though charging knights like whirlwinds go,
Though bill-men ply the ghastly blow,
   Unbroken was the ring;

The stubborn spear-men still made good
Their dark impenetrable wood,
Each stepping where his comrade stood,
   The instant that he fell.
No thought was there of dastard flight,
Link'd in the serried phalanx tight,
Groom fought like noble, squire like knight,
   As fearlessly and well;
Till utter darkness closed her wing
O'er their thin host and wounded King.
Then skilful Surrey's sage commands
Led back from strife his shatter'd bands;
And from the charge they drew,
As mountain-waves, from wasted lands,
   Sweep back to ocean blue.
Then did their loss his foemen know;
Their King, their Lords, their mightiest low,
They melted from the field as snow,
When streams are swoln and south winds blow,
   Dissolves in silent dew.
Tweed's echoes heard the ceaseless plash,
   While many a broken band,
Disorder'd, through her currents dash,
   To gain the Scottish land;
To town and tower, to down and dale,
To tell red Flodden's dismal tale,
And raise the universal wail.
Tradition, legend, tune, and song,
Shall many an age that wail prolong:
Still from the sire the son shall hear
Of the stern strife, and carnage drear,
   Of Flodden's fatal field,
Where shiver'd was fair Scotland's spear,
   And broken was her shield.

XXXV.

Day dawns upon the mountain's side : —
There, Scotland! lay thy bravest pride,
Chiefs, knights, and nobles, many a one:
The sad survivors all are gone. —
View not that corpse mistrustfully —
Defaced and mangled though it be ;
Nor to yon Border Castle high,
Look northward with upbraiding eye ;
   Nor cherish hope in vain,
That, journeying far on foreign strand
The Royal Pilgrim to his land
   May yet return again.
He saw the wreck his rashness wrought ;
Reckless of life, he desperate fought,
   And fell on Flodden plain ;
And well in death his trusty brand,
Firm clench'd within his manly hand,
   Beseem'd the monarch slain.
But, O! how changed since yon blithe night ! —
Gladly I turn me from the sight,
   Unto my tale again.

XXXVI.

Short is my tale : — Fitz-Eustace' care
A pierced and mangled body bare
To moated Lichfield's lofty pile ;
And there, beneath the southern aisle,
A tomb, with Gothic sculpture fair,
Did long Lord Marmion's image bear,
(Now vainly for its sight you look ;

'Twas levell'd when fanatic Brook
The fair cathedral storm'd and took;
But, thanks to Heaven and good Saint Chad,
A guerdon meet the spoiler had!)
There erst was martial Marmion found,
His feet upon a couchant hound,
   His hands to heaven upraised;
And all around, on scutcheon rich,
And tablet carved, and fretted niche,
   His arms and feats were blazed.
And yet, though all was carved so fair,
And priest for Marmion breathed the prayer,
The last Lord Marmion lay not there.
From Ettrick woods a peasant swain
Follow'd his lord to Flodden plain, —
One of those flowers, whom plaintive lay
In Scotland mourns as " wede away:"
Sore wounded, Sybil's Cross he spied,
And dragg'd him to its foot, and died,
Close by the noble Marmion's side.
The spoilers stripp'd and gash'd the slain,
And thus their corpses were mista'en;
And thus, in the proud Baron's tomb,
The lowly woodsman took the room.

XXXVII.

Less easy task it were, to show
Lord Marmion's nameless grave, and low.
   They dug his grave e'en where he lay,
     But every mark is gone;
   Time's wasting hand has done away
   The simple Cross of Sybil Grey,
     And broke her font of stone.

But yet from out the little hill
Oozes the slender springlet still.
  Oft halts the stranger there,
For thence may best his curious eye
The memorable field descry;
  And shepherd boys repair
To seek the water-flag and rush,
And rest them by the hazel bush,
  And plait their garlands fair;
Nor dream they sit upon the grave,
That holds the bones of Marmion brave. —
When thou shalt find the little hill,
With thy heart commune, and be still.
If ever, in temptation strong,
Thou left'st the right path for the wrong;
If every devious step, thus trod,
Still lead thee farther from the road;
Dread thou to speak presumptuous doom
On noble Marmion's lowly tomb;
But say, "He died a gallant knight,
With sword in hand, for England's right."

XXXVIII.

I do not rhyme to that dull elf,
Who cannot image to himself,
That all through Flodden's dismal night,
Wilton was foremost in the fight;
That, when brave Surrey's steed was slain,
'Twas Wilton mounted him again;
'Twas Wilton's brand that deepest hew'd,
Amid the spearmen's stubborn wood;
Unnamed by Hollinshed or Hall,
He was the living soul of all:

That, after fight, his faith made plain,
He won his rank and lands again ;
And charged his old paternal shield
With bearings won on Flodden field.
Nor sing I to that simple maid,
To whom it must in terms be said,
That King and kinsman did agree,
To bless fair Clara's constancy ;
Who cannot, unless I relate,
Paint to her mind the bridal state ;
That Wolsey's voice the blessing spoke,
More, Sands, and Denny, pass'd the joke ;
That bluff King Hal the curtain drew,
And Catherine's hand the stocking threw :
And afterwards, for many a day,
That it was held enough to say,
In blessing to a wedded pair,
" Love they like Wilton and like Clare ! "

L'Envoy.

TO THE READER.

WHY then a final note prolong,
Or lengthen out a closing song,
Unless to bid the gentles speed,
Who long have listed to my rede ?
To Statesmen grave, if such may deign
To read the Minstrel's idle strain,
Sound head, clean hand, and piercing wit,
And patriotic heart — as PITT !
A garland for the hero's crest,
And twined by her he loves the best ;

To every lovely lady bright,
What can I wish but faithful knight?
To every faithful lover too,
What can I wish but lady true?
And knowledge to the studious sage;
And pillow to the head of age.
To thee, dear school-boy, whom my lay
Has cheated of thy hour of play,
Light task, and merry holiday!
To all, to each, a fair good night,
And pleasing dreams, and slumbers light!

INTRODUCTION TO CANTO FIRST.

TO WILLIAM STEWART ROSE, ESQ.

Ashestiel, Ettrick Forest.

I.

NOVEMBER's sky is chill and drear,
November's leaf is red and sear:
Late, gazing down the steepy linn,
That hems our little garden in,
Low in its dark and narrow glen,
You scarce the rivulet might ken,
So thick the tangled greenwood grew,
So feeble trill'd the streamlet through:
Now murmuring hoarse, and frequent seen
Through bush and briar, no longer green,
An angry brook, it sweeps the glade,
Brawls over rock and wild cascade,
And, foaming brown with doubled speed,
Hurries its waters to the Tweed.

II.

No longer Autumn's glowing red
Upon our Forest hills is shed;
No more, beneath the evening beam,
Fair Tweed reflects their purple gleam;
Away hath pass'd the heather-bell
That bloom'd so rich on Needpathfell;

Sallow his brow, and russet bare
Are now the sister-heights of Yair.
The sheep, before the pinching heaven,
To shelter'd dale and down are driven,
Where yet some faded herbage pines,
And yet a watery sunbeam shines:
In meek despondency they eye
The wither'd sward and wintry sky,
And far beneath their summer hill,
Stray sadly by Glenkinnon's rill:
The shepherd shifts his mantle's fold,
And wraps him closer from the cold;
'His dogs, no merry circles wheel,
But, shivering, follow at his heel;
A cowering glance they often cast,
As deeper moans the gathering blast.

III.

My imps, though hardy, bold, and wild,
As best befits the mountain child,
Feel the sad influence of the hour,
And wail the daisy's vanished flower;
Their summer gambols tell, and mourn,
And anxious ask, — Will spring return,
And birds and lambs again be gay,
And blossoms clothe the hawthorn spray?

IV.

Yes, prattlers, yes. The daisy's flower
Again shall paint your summer bower;
Again the hawthorn shall supply
The garlands you delight to tie;

The lambs upon the lea shall bound,
The wild birds carol to the round,
And while you frolic light as they,
Too short shall seem the summer day.

V.

To mute and to material things
New life revolving summer brings;
The genial call dead nature hears,
And in her glory reappears.
But oh! my country's wintry state
What second spring shall renovate?
What powerful call shall bid arise
The buried warlike and the wise;
The mind that thought for Britain's weal,
The hand that grasp'd the victor steel?
The vernal sun new life bestows
Even on the meanest flower that blows;
But vainly, vainly may he shine,
Where glory weeps o'er NELSON's shrine;
And vainly pierce the solemn gloom,
That shrouds, O PITT, thy hallowed tomb!

VI.

Deep graved in every British heart,
O never let those names depart!
Say to your sons, — Lo, here his grave,
Who victor died on Gadite wave;
To him, as to the burning levin,
Short, bright, resistless course was given.
Where'er his country's foes were found,
Was heard the fated thunder's sound,
Till burst the bolt on yonder shore,
Roll'd, blazed, destroy'd, — and was no more.

VII.

Nor mourn ye less his perish'd worth,
Who bade the conqueror go forth,
And launch'd that thunderbolt of war
On Egypt, Hafnia, Trafalgar;
Who, born to guide such high emprize,
For Britain's weal was early wise;
Alas! to whom the Almighty gave,
For Britain's sins an early grave!
His worth, who, in his mightiest hour
A bauble held the pride of power,
Spurn'd at the sordid lust of pelf,
And served his Albion for herself;
Who, when the frantic crowd amain
Strain'd at subjection's bursting rein,
O'er their wild mood full conquest gain'd,
The pride, he would not crush, restrain'd,
Show'd their fierce zeal a worthier cause,
And brought the freeman's arm, to aid the freeman's laws.

VIII.

Had'st thou but lived, though stripp'd of power,
A watchman on the lonely tower,
Thy thrilling trump had roused the land,
When fraud or danger were at hand;
By thee, as by the beacon-light,
Our pilots had kept course aright;
As some proud column, though alone,
Thy strength had propp'd the tottering throne:
Now is the stately column broke,
The beacon-light is quench'd in smoke,
The trumpet's silver sound is still,
The warder silent on the hill!

IX.

Oh think, how to his latest day,
When Death, just hovering, claim'd his prey,
With Palinure's unalter'd mood,
Firm at his dangerous post he stood;
Each call for needful rest repell'd,
With dying hand the rudder held,
Till, in his fall, with fateful sway,
The steerage of the realm gave way!
Then, while on Britain's thousand plains,
One unpolluted church remains,
Whose peaceful bells ne'er sent around
The bloody tocsin's maddening sound,
But still, upon the hallow'd day,
Convoke the swains to praise and pray;
While faith and civil peace are dear,
Grace this cold marble with a tear, —
He, who preserved them, PITT, lies here!

X.

Nor yet suppress the generous sigh,
Because his rival slumbers nigh;
Nor be thy *requiescat* dumb,
Lest it be said o'er Fox's tomb.
For talents mourn, untimely lost,
When best employ'd, and wanted most,
Mourn genius high, and lore profound,
And wit that loved to play, not wound;
And all the reasoning powers divine,
To penetrate, resolve, combine;
And feelings keen, and fancy's glow, —
They sleep with him who sleeps below:

And, if thou mourn'st they could not save
From error him who owns this grave,
Be every harsher thought suppress'd,
And sacred be the last long rest.
Here, where the end of earthly things
Lays heroes, patriots, bards, and kings ;
Where stiff the hand, and still the tongue,
Of those who fought, and spoke, and sung ;
Here, where the fretted aisles prolong
The distant notes of holy song,
As if some angel spoke agen,
" All peace on earth, good-will to men ; "
If ever from an English heart,
O, *here* let prejudice depart,
And, partial feeling cast aside,
Record, that Fox a Briton died !
When Europe crouch'd to France's yoke,
And Austria bent, and Prussia broke,
And the firm Russian's purpose brave,
Was barter'd by a timorous slave,
Even then dishonour's peace he spurn'd,
The sullied olive-branch return'd,
Stood for his country's glory fast,
And nail'd her colours to the mast !
Heaven, to reward his firmness, gave
A portion in his honour'd grave,
And ne'er held marble in its trust
Of two such wondrous men the dust.

XI.

With more than mortal powers endow'd,
How high they soar'd above the crowd !
Theirs was no common party race,
Jostling by dark intrigue for place ;

Like fabled Gods, their mighty war
Shook realms and nations in its jar;
Beneath each banner proud to stand,
Look'd up the noblest of the land,
Till through the British world were known
The names of PITT and FOX alone.
Spells of such force no wizard grave
E'er framed in dark Thessalian cave,
Though his could drain the ocean dry,
And force the planets from the sky.
These spells are spent, and, spent with these,
The wine of life is on the lees.
Genius, and taste, and talent gone,
For ever tomb'd beneath the stone,
Where — taming thought to human pride! —
The mighty chiefs sleep side by side.
Drop upon Fox's grave the tear,
'Twill trickle to his rival's bier;
O'er PITT's the mournful requiem sound,
And Fox's shall the notes rebound.
The solemn echo seems to cry, —
" Here let their discord with them die.
Speak not for those a separate doom,
Whom Fate made Brothers in the tomb;
But search the land of living men,
Where wilt thou find their like agen?"

XII.

Rest, ardent Spirits! till the cries
Of dying Nature bid you rise;
Not even your Britain's groans can pierce
The leaden silence of your hearse;

Then, O, how impotent and vain
This grateful tributary strain!
Though not unmark'd from northern clime,
Ye heard the Border Minstrel's rhyme ;
His Gothic harp has o'er you rung ;
The Bard you deign'd to praise, your deathless names
  has sung.

XIII.

 Stay yet, illusion, stay a while,
My wilder'd fancy still beguile!
From this high theme how can I part,
Ere half unloaded is my heart!
For all the tears e'er sorrow drew,
And all the raptures fancy knew,
And all the keener rush of blood,
That throbs through bard in bard-like mood,
Were here a tribute mean and low,
Though all their mingled streams could flow —
Woe, wonder, and sensation high,
In one spring-tide of ecstasy ! —
It will not be — it may not last —
The vision of enchantment's past:
Like frostwork in the morning ray,
The fancied fabric melts away ;
Each Gothic arch, memorial-stone,
And long, dim, lofty aisle, are gone ;
And, lingering last, deception dear,
The choir's high sounds die on my ear.
Now slow return the lonely down,
The silent pastures bleak and brown,
The farm begirt with copsewood wild,
The gambols of each frolic child,
Mixing their shrill cries with the tone
Of Tweed's dark waters rushing on.

XIV.

Prompt on unequal tasks to run,
Thus Nature disciplines her son:
Meeter, she says, for me to stray,
And waste the solitary day,
In plucking from yon fen the reed,
And watch it floating down the Tweed;
Or idly list the shrilling lay,
With which the milkmaid cheers her way,
Marking its cadence rise and fail,
As from the field, beneath her pail,
She trips it down the uneven dale:
Meeter for me, by yonder cairn,
The ancient shepherd's tale to learn;
Though oft he stop in rustic fear,
Lest his old legends tire the ear
Of one, who, in his simple mind,
May boast of book-learn'd taste refined.

XV.

But thou, my friend, canst fitly tell,
(For few have read romance so well),
How still the legendary lay
O'er poet's bosom holds its sway;
How on the ancient minstrel strain
Time lays his palsied hand in vain;
And how our hearts at doughty deeds,
By warriors wrought in steely weeds,
Still throb for fear and pity's sake;
As when the champion of the Lake
Enters Morgana's fated house,
Or in the Chapel Perilous,

Despising spells and demons' force,
Holds converse with the unburied corse ;
Or when, Dame Ganore's grace to move,
(Alas, that lawless was their love !)
He sought proud Tarquin in his den,
And freed full sixty knights ; or when,
A sinful man, and unconfess'd,
He took the Sangreal's holy quest,
And, slumbering, saw the vision high,
He might not view with waking eye.

XVI.

The mightiest chiefs of British song
Scorn'd not such legends to prolong :
They gleam through Spenser's elfin dream,
And mix in Milton's heavenly theme ;
And Dryden, in immortal strain,
Had raised the Table Round again,
But that a ribald king and court
Bade him toil on, to make them sport ;
Demanded for their niggard pay,
Fit for their souls, a looser lay,
Licentious satire, song, and play ;
The world defrauded of the high design,
Profaned the God-given strength, and marr'd the
    lofty line.

XVII.

Warm'd by such names well may we then,
Though dwindled sons of little men,
Essay to break a feeble lance
In the fair fields of old romance ;

Or seek the moated castle's cell,
Where long through talisman and spell,
While tyrants ruled, and damsels wept,
Thy Genius, Chivalry, hath slept:
There sound the harpings of the North,
Till he awake and sally forth,
On venturous quest to prick again,
In all his arms, with all his train,
Shield, lance, and brand, and plume, and scarf,
Fay, giant, dragon, squire, and dwarf,
And wizard with his wand of might,
And errant maid on palfrey white.
Around the Genius weave their spells,
Pure Love, who scarce his passion tells;
Mystery, half-veil'd and half-reveal'd;
And Honour, with his spotless shield;
Attention, with fix'd eye; and Fear,
That loves the tale she shrinks to hear;
And gentle Courtesy; and Faith,
Unchanged by sufferings, time, or death:
And Valour, lion-mettled lord,
Leaning upon his own good sword.

XVIII.

Well has thy fair achievement shown,
A worthy meed may thus be won;
Ytene's oaks — beneath whose shade
Their theme the merry minstrels made,
Of Ascapart, and Bevis bold,
And that Red King, who, while of old,
Through Boldrewood the chase he led,
By his loved huntsman's arrow bled —

Ytene's oaks have heard again
Renewed such legendary strain;
For thou hast sung, how He of Gaul,
That Amadis so famed in hall,
For Oriana, foil'd in fight
The Necromancer's felon might;
And well in modern verse hast wove
Partenopex's mystic love:
Hear, then, attentive to my lay,
A knightly tale of Albion's elder day.

INTRODUCTION TO CANTO SECOND.

TO THE REV. JOHN MARRIOTT, A.M.

Ashestiel, Ettrick Forest.

I.

THE scenes are desert now, and bare,
Where flourish'd once a forest fair,
When these waste glens with copse were lined,
And peopled with the heart and hind.
Yon Thorn — perchance whose prickly spears
Have fenced him for three hundred years,
While fell around his green compeers —
Yon lonely Thorn, would he could tell
The changes of his parent dell,
Since he, so grey and stubborn now,
Waved in each breeze a sapling bough;
Would he could tell how deep the shade
A thousand mingled branches made;
How broad the shadows of the oak,
How clung the rowan to the rock,
And through the foliage showed his head,
With narrow leaves and berries red;
What pines on every mountain sprung,
O'er every dell what birches hung,
In every breeze what aspens shook,
What alders shaded every brook!
"Here, in my shade," methinks he'd say,
"The mighty stag at noon-tide lay:

The wolf I've seen, a fiercer game,
(The neighbouring dingle bears his name,)
With lurching step around me prowl,
And stop, against the moon to howl;
The mountain-boar, on battle set,
His tusks upon my stem would whet;
While doe, and roe, and red-deer good,
Have bounded by, through gay greenwood.
Then oft, from Newark's riven tower,
Sallied a Scottish monarch's power:
A thousand vassals muster'd round,
With horse, and hawk, and horn, and hound;
And I might see the youth intent,
Guard every pass with crossbow bent;
And through the brake the rangers stalk,
And falc'ners hold the ready hawk;
And foresters, in greenwood trim,
Lead in the leash the gazehounds grim,
Attentive, as the bratchet's bay
From the dark covert drove the prey,
To slip them as he broke away.
The startled quarry bounds amain,
As fast the startled greyhounds strain
Whistles the arrow from the bow,
Answers the harquebuss below;
While all the rocking hills reply,
To hoof-clang, hound, and hunters' cry,
And bugles ringing lightsomely."

II.

Of such proud huntings many tales
Yet linger in our lonely dales,
Up pathless Ettrick and on Yarrow,
Where erst the outlaw drew his arrow.

But not more blithe that silvan court,
Than we have been at humbler sport;
Though small our pomp, and mean our game,
Our mirth, dear Marriott, was the same.
Remember'st thou my greyhounds true?
O'er holt or hill there never flew,
From slip or leash there never sprang,
More fleet of foot, or sure of fang.
Nor dull, between each merry chase,
Pass'd by the intermitted space;
For we had fair resource in store,
In Classic and in Gothic lore:
We mark'd each memorable scene,
And held poetic talk between;
Nor hill, nor brook, we paced along,
But had its legend or its song.
All silent now — for now are still
Thy bowers, untenanted Bowhill!
No longer, from thy mountains dun,
The yeoman hears the well-known gun,
And while his honest heart glows warm,
At thought of his paternal farm,
Round to his mates a brimmer fills,
And drinks, "The Chieftain of the Hills!"
No fairy forms, in Yarrow's bowers,
Trip o'er the walks, or tend the flowers,
Fair as the elves whom Janet saw
By moonlight dance on Carterhaugh;
No youthful Baron's left to grace
The Forest-Sheriff's lonely chase,
And ape, in manly step and tone,
The majesty of Oberon:
And she is gone, whose lovely face
Is but her least and lowest grace;

Though if to Sylphid Queen 'twere given,
To show our earth the charms of Heaven,
She could not glide along the air,
With form more light, or face more fair.
No more the widow's deafen'd ear
Grows quick that lady's step to hear:
At noontide she expects her not,
Nor busies her to trim the cot;
Pensive she turns her humming-wheel,
Or pensive cooks her orphan's meal;
Yet blesses, ere she deals their bread,
The gentle hand by which they're fed.

III.

From Yair, — which hills so closely bind,
Scarce can the Tweed his passage find,
Though much he fret, and chafe, and toil,
Till all his eddying currents boil, —
Her long-descended lord is gone,
And left us by the stream alone.
And much I miss those sportive boys,
Companions of my mountain joys,
Just at the age 'twixt boy and youth,
When thought is speech, and speech is truth.
Close to my side, with what delight
They press'd to hear of Wallace wight,
When, pointing to his airy mound,
I call'd his ramparts holy ground!
Kindled their brows to hear me speak;
And I have smiled, to feel my cheek,
Despite the difference of our years,
Return again the glow of theirs.

Ah, happy boys! such feelings pure,
They will not, cannot, long endure;
Condemn'd to stem the world's rude tide,
You may not linger by the side;
For Fate shall thrust you from the shore,
And Passion ply the sail and oar.
Yet cherish the remembrance still,
Of the lone mountain, and the rill;
For trust, dear boys, the time will come,
When fiercer transport shall be dumb,
And you will think right frequently,
But, well, I hope, without a sigh,
On the free hours that we have spent
Together, on the brown hill's bent.

IV.

When, musing on companions gone,
We doubly feel ourselves alone,
Something, my friend, we yet may gain;
There is a pleasure in this pain:
It soothes the love of lonely rest,
Deep in each gentler heart impress'd.
'Tis silent amid worldly toils,
And stifled soon by mental broils;
But in a bosom thus prepared,
Its still small voice is often heard,
Whispering a mingled sentiment,
'Twixt resignation and content.
Oft in my mind such thoughts awake,
By lone St. Mary's silent lake;
Thou know'st it well, — nor fen, nor sedge,
Pollute the pure lake's crystal edge;

Abrupt and sheer, the mountains sink
At once upon the level brink;
And just a trace of silver sand
Marks where the water meets the land.
Far in the mirror, bright and blue,
Each hill's huge outline you may view;
Shaggy with heath, but lonely bare,
Nor tree, nor bush, nor brake is there,
Save where, of land, yon slender line
Bears thwart the lake the scatter'd pine.
Yet even this nakedness has power,
And aids the feeling of the hour:
Nor thicket, dell, nor copse you spy,
Where living thing conceal'd might lie;
Nor point, retiring, hides a dell,
Where swain, or woodman lone, might dwell;
There's nothing left to fancy's guess,
You see that all is loneliness:
And silence aids — though the steep hills
Send to the lake a thousand rills;
In summer tide, so soft they weep,
The sound but lulls the ear asleep;
Your horse's hoof-tread sounds too rude,
So stilly is the solitude.

V.

Nought living meets the eye or ear,
But well I ween the dead are near;
For though, in feudal strife, a foe
Hath laid Our Lady's chapel low,
Yet still, beneath the hallow'd soil,
The peasant rests him from his toil,
And, dying, bids his bones be laid,
Where erst his simple fathers pray'd.

VI.

If age had tamed the passions' strife,
And Fate had cut my ties to life,
Here, have I thought, 'twere sweet to dwell,
And rear again the chaplain's cell,
Like that same peaceful hermitage,
Where Milton long'd to spend his age.
'Twere sweet to mark the setting day,   .
On Bourhope's lonely top decay;
And, as it faint and feeble died
On the broad lake, and mountain's side,
To say, " Thus pleasures fade away;
Youth, talents, beauty, thus decay,
And leave us dark, forlorn, and grey; "
Then gaze on Dryhope's ruin'd tower,
And think on Yarrow's faded Flower:
And when that mountain-sound I heard,
Which bids us be for storm prepared,
The distant rustling of his wings,   ·
As up his force the Tempest brings,
'Twere sweet, ere yet his terrors rave,
To sit upon the Wizard's grave;
That Wizard Priest's, whose bones are thrust
From company of holy dust;
On which no sunbeam ever shines —
(So superstition's creed divines) —
Thence view the lake with sullen roar,
Heave her broad billows to the shore;
And mark the wild swans mount the gale,
Spread wide through mist their snowy sail,
And ever stoop again, to lave
Their bosoms on the surging wave:

Then, when against the driving hail
No longer might my plaid avail,
Back to my lonely home retire,
And light my lamp, and trim my fire ;
There ponder o'er some mystic lay,
Till the wild tale had all its sway.
And, in the bittern's distant shriek,
I heard unearthly voices speak,
And thought the Wizard Priest was come,
To claim again his ancient home !
And bade my busy fancy range,
To frame him fitting shape and strange,
Till from the task my brow I clear'd,
And smiled to think that I had fear'd.

VII.

But chief, 'twere sweet to think such life,
(Though but escape from fortune's strife,)
Something most matchless good and wise,
A great and grateful sacrifice ;
And deem each hour to musing given,
A step upon the road to heaven.

VIII.

Yet him, whose heart is ill at ease,
Such peaceful solitudes displease :
He loves to drown his bosom's jar
Amid the elemental war :
And my black Palmer's choice had been
Some ruder and more savage scene,
Like that which frowns round dark Lochskene.
There eagles scream from isle to shore ;
Down all the rocks the torrents roar ;

O'er the black waves incessant driven,
Dark mists infect the summer heaven;
Through the rude barriers of the lake,
Away its hurrying waters break,
Faster and whiter dash and curl,
Till down yon dark abyss they hurl.
Rises the fog-smoke, white as snow,
Thunders the viewless stream below,
Diving, as if condemned to lave
Some demon's subterranean cave,
Who, prison'd by enchanter's spell,
Shakes the dark rock with groan and yell.
And well that Palmer's form and mien
Had suited with the stormy scene,
Just on the edge, straining his ken
To view the bottom of the den,
Where, deep deep down, and far within,
Toils with the rocks the roaring linn;
Then, issuing forth one foamy wave,
And wheeling round the Giant's Grave,
White as the snowy charger's tail,
Drives down the pass of Moffatdale.

IX.

Marriott, thy harp, on Isis strung,
To many a Border theme has rung!
Then list to me, and thou shalt know
Of this mysterious Man of Woe.

INTRODUCTION TO CANTO THIRD.

TO WILLIAM ERSKINE, ESQ.

Ashestiel, Ettrick Forest.

I.

LIKE April morning clouds, that pass,
With varying shadow, o'er the grass,
And imitate, on field and furrow,
Life's chequer'd scene of joy and sorrow;
Like streamlet of the mountain north,
Now in a torrent racing forth,
Now winding slow its silver train,
And almost slumbering on the plain;
Like breezes of the autumn day,
Whose voice inconstant dies away,
And ever swells again as fast,
When the ear deems its murmur past;
Thus various, my romantic theme
Flits, winds, or sinks, a morning dream.
Yet pleased, our eye pursues the trace
Of Light and Shade's inconstant race;
Pleased, views the rivulet afar,
Weaving its maze irregular;
And pleased, we listen as the breeze
Heaves its wild sigh through autumn trees;
Then, wild as cloud, or stream, or gale,
Flow on, flow unconfined, my Tale!

II.

Need I to thee, dear Erskine, tell
I love the license all too well,
In sounds now lowly, and now strong,
To raise the desultory song? —
Oft, when 'mid such capricious chime,
Some transient fit of lofty rhyme
To thy kind judgment seem'd excuse
For many an error of the muse,
Oft hast thou said, " If, still misspent,
Thine hours to poetry are lent,
Go, and to tame thy wandering course,
Quaff from the fountain at the source;
Approach those masters, o'er whose tomb
Immortal laurels ever bloom:
Instructive of the feebler bard,
Still from the grave their voice is heard;
From them, and from the paths they show'd,
Choose honour'd guide and practised road;
Nor ramble on through brake and maze,
With harpers rude, of barbarous days.

III.

" Or deem'st thou not our later time
Yields topic meet for classic rhyme?
Hast thou no elegiac verse
For Brunswick's venerable hearse?
What, not a line, a tear, a sigh,
When valour bleeds for liberty? —
Oh, hero of that glorious time,
When, with unrivall'd light sublime, —

Though martial Austria, and though all
The might of Russia, and the Gaul,
Though banded Europe stood her foes —
The star of Brandenburgh arose!
Thou could'st not live to see her beam
For ever quench'd in Jena's stream.
Lamented chief! — it was not given
To thee to change the doom of Heaven,
And crush that dragon in its birth,
Predestined scourge of guilty earth.
Lamented chief! — not thine the power,
To save in that presumptuous hour,
When Prussia hurried to the field,
And snatch'd the spear, but left the shield;
Valour and skill 'twas thine to try,
And, tried in vain, 'twas thine to die.
Ill had it seem'd thy silver hair
The last, the bitterest pang to share,
For princedoms reft, and scutcheons riven,
And birthrights to usurpers given;
Thy land's, thy children's wrongs to feel,
And witness woes thou couldst not heal!
On thee relenting Heaven bestows
For honour'd life an honour'd close;
And when revolves, in time's sure change,
The hour of Germany's revenge,
When, breathing fury for her sake,
Some new Arminius shall awake,
Her champion, ere he strike, shall come,
To whet his sword on BRUNSWICK'S tomb.

IV.

"Or of the Red-Cross hero teach,
Dauntless in dungeon as on breach:
Alike to him, the sea, the shore,
The brand, the bridle, or the oar:
Alike to him the war that calls
Its votaries to the shatter'd walls, ·
Which the grim Turk, besmear'd with blood,
Against the Invincible made good;
Or that, whose thundering voice could wake
The silence of the polar lake,
When stubborn Russ, and metal'd Swede,
On the warp'd wave their death-game play'd;
Or that, where Vengeance and Affright
Howl'd round the father of the fight,
Who snatch'd, on Alexandria's sand,
The conqueror's wreath with dying hand.

V.

"Or, if to touch such chord be thine,
Restore the ancient tragic line,
And emulate the notes that rung
From the wild harp, which silent hung
By silver Avon's holy shore,
Till twice an hundred years roll'd o'er;
When she, the bold Enchantress, came,
With fearless hand and heart on flame!
From the pale willow snatch'd the treasure,
And swept it with a kindred measure,
Till Avon's swans, while rung the grove
With Montfort's hate and Basil's love,
Awakening at the inspired strain,
Deem'd their own Shakspeare lived again."

VI.

Thy friendship thus thy judgment wronging,
With praises not to me belonging,
In task more meet for mightiest powers,
Wouldst thou engage my thriftless hours.
But say, my Erskine, hast thou weigh'd
That secret power by all obey'd,
Which warps not less the passive mind,
Its source conceal'd or undefined;
Whether an impulse, that has birth
Soon as the infant wakes on earth,
One with our feelings and our powers,
And rather part of us than ours;
Or whether fitlier term'd the sway
Of habit form'd in early day?
Howe'er derived, its force confest
Rules with despotic sway the breast,
And drags us on by viewless chain,
While taste and reason plead in vain.
Look east, and ask the Belgian why,
Beneath Batavia's sultry sky,
He seeks not eager to inhale
The freshness of the mountain gale,
Content to rear his whiten'd wall
Beside the dank and dull canal?
He'll say, from youth he loved to see
The white sail gliding by the tree.
Or see yon weather-beaten hind,
Whose sluggish herds before him wind,
Whose tatter'd plaid and rugged cheek
His northern clime and kindred speak;
Through England's laughing meads he goes,
And England's wealth around him flows;

Ask, if it would content him well,
At ease in those gay plains to dwell,
Where hedge-rows spread a verdant screen,
And spires and forests intervene,
And the neat cottage peeps between?
No! not for these will he exchange
His dark Lochaber's boundless range:
Not for fair Devon's meads forsake
Bennevis grey, and Garry's lake.

VII. ·

  Thus, while I ape the measure wild
Of tales that charmed me yet a child,
Rude though they be, still with the chime
Return the thoughts of early time;
And feelings, roused in life's first day,
Glow in the line, and prompt the lay.
Then rise those crags, that mountain tower,
Which charm'd my fancy's wakening hour.
Though no broad river swept along,
To claim, perchance, heroic song;
Though sigh'd no groves in summer gale,
To prompt of love a softer tale;
Though scarce a puny streamlet's speed
Claim'd homage from a shepherd's reed;
Yet was poetic impulse given,
By the green hill and clear blue heaven.
It was a barren scene, and wild,
Where naked cliffs were rudely piled;
But ever and anon between
Lay velvet tufts of loveliest green;
And well the lonely infant knew
Recesses where the wall-flower grew,

And honey-suckle loved to crawl
Up the low crag and ruin'd wall.
I deem'd such nooks the sweetest shade
The sun in all its round survey'd;
And still I thought that shatter'd tower
The mightiest work of human power;
And marvell'd as the aged hind
With some strange tale bewitch'd my mind,
Of forayers, who, with headlong force,
Down from that strength had spurr'd their horse,
Their southern rapine to renew,
Far in the distant Cheviots blue,
And, home returning, fill'd the hall
With revel, wassail-rout, and brawl.
Methought that still with trump and clang,
The gateway's broken arches rang;
Methought grim features, seam'd with scars,
Glared through the window's rusty bars,
And ever, by the winter hearth,
Old tales I heard of woe or mirth,
Of lovers' slights, of ladies' charms,
Of witches' spells, of warriors' arms;
Of patriot battles, won of old
By Wallace wight and Bruce the bold;
Of later fields of feud and fight,
When, pouring from their Highland height,
The Scottish clans, in headlong sway,
Had swept the scarlet ranks away.
While stretch'd at length upon the floor,
Again I fought each combat o'er,
Pebbles and shells, in order laid,
The mimic ranks of war display'd;
And onward still the Scottish Lion bore,
And still the scatter'd Southron fled before.

VIII.

Still, with vain fondness, could I trace,
Anew, each kind familiar face,
That brighten'd at our evening fire!
From the thatch'd mansion's grey-hair'd Sire,
Wise without learning, plain and good,
And sprung of Scotland's gentler blood;
Whose eye, in age, quick, clear, and keen,
Show'd what in youth its glance had been;
Whose doom discording neighbours sought,
Content with equity unbought;
To him the venerable Priest,
Our frequent and familiar guest,
Whose life and manners well could paint
Alike the student and the saint;
Alas! whose speech too oft I broke
With gambol rude and timeless joke:
For I was wayward, bold, and wild,
A self-will'd imp, a grandame's child,
But half a plague, and half a jest,
Was still endured, beloved, caress'd.

IX.

For me, thus nurtured, dost thou ask
The classic poet's well-conn'd task?
Nay, Erskine, nay — On the wild hill
Let the wild heath-bell flourish still;
Cherish the tulip, prune the vine,
But freely let the woodbine twine,
And leave untrimm'd the eglantine:
Nay, my friend, nay — Since oft thy praise
Hath given fresh vigour to my lays;

Since oft thy judgment could refine
My flatten'd thought, or cumbrous line;
Still kind, as is thy wont, attend,
And in the minstrel spare the friend.
Though wild as cloud, as stream, as gale,
Flow forth, flow unrestrain'd, my Tale!

INTRODUCTION TO CANTO FOURTH.

TO JAMES SKENE, ESQ.

Ashestiel, Ettrick Forest.

I.

An ancient Minstrel sagely said,
" Where is the life which late we led ? "
That motley clown in Arden wood,
Whom humourous Jacques with envy view'd,
Not even that clown could amplify,
On this trite text, so long as I.
Eleven years we now may tell,
Since we have known each other well;
Since, riding side by side, our hand
First drew the voluntary brand,
And sure, through many a varied scene,
Unkindness never came between.
Away these winged years have flown,
To join the mass of ages gone;
And though deep-mark'd, like all below,
With chequer'd shades of joy and woe;
Though thou o'er realms and seas hast ranged,
Mark'd cities lost, and empires changed,
While here, at home, my narrower ken
Somewhat of manners saw, and men;
Though varying wishes, hopes, and fears,
Fever'd the progress of these years,

Yet now, days, weeks, and months but seem
The recollection of a dream,
So still we glide down to the sea
Of fathomless eternity.

II.

Even now it scarcely seems a day,
Since first I tuned this idle lay;
A task so often thrown aside,
When leisure graver cares denied,
That now, November's dreary gale,
Whose voice inspired my opening tale,
That same November gale once more
Whirls the dry leaves on Yarrow shore.
Their vex'd boughs streaming to the sky,
Once more our naked birches sigh,
And Blackhouse heights, and Ettrick Pen,
Have donn'd their wintry shrouds again:
And mountain dark, and flooded mead,
Bid us forsake the banks of Tweed.
Earlier than wont along the sky,
Mix'd with the rack, the snow mists fly;
The shepherd, who in summer sun,
Had something of our envy won,
As thou with pencil, I with pen,
The features traced of hill and glen; —
He who, outstretch'd the livelong day,
At ease among the heath-flowers lay,
View'd the light clouds with vacant look,
Or slumber'd o'er his tatter'd book,
Or idly busied him to guide
His angle o'er the lessen'd tide; —
At midnight now, the snowy plain
Finds sterner labour for the swain.

III.

When red hath set the beamless sun,
Through heavy vapours dark and dun ;
When the tired ploughman, dry and warm,
Hears, half asleep, the rising storm
Hurling the hail, and sleeted rain,
Against the casement's tinkling pane ;
The sounds that drive wild deer, and fox,
To shelter in the brake and rocks,
Are warnings which the shepherd ask
To dismal and to dangerous task.
Oft he looks forth, and hopes, in vain,
The blast may sink in mellowing rain ;
Till, dark above, and white below,
Decided drives the flaky snow,
And forth the hardy swain must go.
Long, with dejected look and whine,
To leave the hearth his dogs repine ;
Whistling and cheering them to aid,
Around his back he wreathes the plaid :
His flock he gathers, and he guides,
To open downs, and mountain-sides,
Where fiercest though the tempest blow,
Least deeply lies the drift below.
The blast, that whistles o'er the fells,
Stiffens his locks to icicles ;
Oft he looks back, while streaming far,
His cottage window seems a star, —
Loses its feeble gleam, — and then
Turns patient to the blast again,
And, facing to the tempest's sweep,
Drives through the gloom his lagging sheep.

If fails his heart, if his limbs fail,
Benumbing death is in the gale:
His paths, his landmarks, all unknown,
Close to the hut, no more his own,
Close to the aid he sought in vain,
The morn may find the stiffen'd swain:
The widow sees, at dawning pale,
His orphans raise their feeble wail;
And, close beside him, in the snow,
Poor Yarrow, partner of their woe,
Couches upon his master's breast,
And licks his cheek to break his rest.

IV.

Who envies now the shepherd's lot,
His healthy fare, his rural cot,
His summer couch by greenwood tree,
His rustic kirn's loud revelry,
His native hill-notes, tuned on high,
To Marion of the blithesome eye;
His crook, his scrip, his oaten reed,
And all Arcadia's golden creed?

V.

Changes not so with us, my Skene,
Of human life the varying scene?
Our youthful summer oft we see
Dance by on wings of game and glee,
While the dark storm reserves its rage,
Against the winter of our age:
As he, the ancient Chief of Troy,
His manhood spent in peace and joy;

But Grecian fires, and loud alarms,
Call'd ancient Priam forth to arms.
Then happy those, since each must drain
His share of pleasure, share of pain, —
Then happy those, beloved of Heaven,
To whom the mingled cup is given;
Whose lenient sorrows find relief,
Whose joys are chasten'd by their grief.
And such a lot, my Skene, was thine,
When thou of late, wert doom'd to twine, —
Just when thy bridal hour was by, —
The cypress with the myrtle tie.
Just on thy bride her Sire had smiled,
And bless'd the union of his child,
When love must change its joyous cheer,
And wipe affection's filial tear.
Nor did the actions next his end,
Speak more the father than the friend.
Scarce had lamented Forbes paid
The tribute to his Minstrel's shade;
The tale of friendship scarce was told,
Ere the narrator's heart was cold —
Far may we search before we find
A heart so manly and so kind!
But not around his honour'd urn,
Shall friends alone and kindred mourn;
The thousand eyes his care had dried,
Pour at his name a bitter tide;
And frequent falls the grateful dew,
For benefits the world ne'er knew.
If mortal charity dare claim
The Almighty's attributed name,
Inscribe above his mouldering clay,
"The widow's shield, the orphan's stay."

Nor, though it wake thy sorrow, deem
My verse intrudes on this sad theme;
For sacred was the pen that wrote,
" Thy father's friend forget thou not : "
And grateful title may I plead,
For many a kindly word and deed,
To bring my tribute to his grave : —
'Tis little — but 'tis all I have

VI.

To thee, perchance, this rambling strain
Recalls our summer walks again;
When, doing nought, — and, to speak true,
Not anxious to find aught to do, —
The wild unbounded hills we ranged,
While oft our talk its topic changed,
And, desultory as our way,
Ranged, unconfined, from grave to gay.
Even when it flagg'd, as oft will chance,
No effort made to break its trance,
We could right pleasantly pursue
Our sports in social silence too;
Thou bravely labouring to portray
The blighted oak's fantastic spray;
I spelling o'er, with much delight,
The legend of that antique knight,
Tirante by name, yclep'd the White.
At either's feet a trusty squire,
Pandour and Camp, with eyes of fire,
Jealous, each other's motions view'd,
And scarce suppress'd their ancient feud.
The laverock whistled from the cloud;
The stream was lively, but not loud;

From the white thorn the May-flower shed
Its dewy fragrance round our head:
Not Ariel lived more merrily
Under the blossom'd bough, than we.

VII.

And blithesome nights, too, have been ours,
When Winter stript the summer's bowers.
Careless we heard, what now I hear,
The wild blast sighing deep and drear,
When fires were bright, and lamps beam'd gay,
And ladies tuned the lovely lay;
And he was held a laggard soul,
Who shunn'd to quaff the sparkling bowl.
Then he, whose absence we deplore,
Who breathes the gales of Devon's shore,
The longer miss'd, bewail'd the more;
And thou, and I, and dear loved R——,
And one whose name I may not say, —
For not Mimosa's tender tree
Shrinks sooner from the touch than he, —
In merry chorus well combined,
With laughter drown'd the whistling wind.
Mirth was within; and Care without
Might gnaw her nails to hear our shout.
Not but amid the buxom scene
Some grave discourse might intervene —
Of the good horse that bore him best,
His shoulder, hoof, and arching crest:
For, like mad Tom's, our chiefest care
Was horse to ride, and weapon wear.
Such nights we've had; and, though the game
Of manhood be more sober tame,

And though the field-day, or the drill,
Seem less important now — yet still
Such may we hope to share again.
The sprightly thought inspires my strain!
And mark, how, like a horseman true,
Lord Marmion's march I thus renew.

INTRODUCTION TO CANTO FIFTH.

TO GEORGE ELLIS, ESQ.

Edinburgh.

I.

When dark December glooms the day,
And takes our autumn joys away;
When short and scant the sunbeam throws,
Upon the weary waste of snows,
A cold and profitless regard,
Like patron on a needy bard;
When silvan occupation's done,
And o'er the chimney rests the gun,
And hang, in idle trophy, near,
The game-pouch, fishing-rod, and spear;
When wiry terrier, rough and grim,
And greyhound, with his length of limb,
And pointer, now employ'd no more,
Cumber our parlour's narrow floor:
When in his stall the impatient steed
Is long condemn'd to rest and feed;
When from our snow-encircled home,
Scarce cares the hardiest step to roam,
Since path is none, save that to bring
The needful water from the spring;
When wrinkled news-page, thrice conn'd o'er,
Beguiles the dreary hour no more,

And darkling politician, cross'd,
Inveighs against the lingering post,
And answering housewife sore complains
Of carriers' snow-impeded wains;
When such the country cheer, I come,
Well pleased, to seek our city home;
For converse, and for books, to change
The Forest's melancholy range,
And welcome, with renew'd delight,
The busy day and social night.

II.

Not here need my desponding rhyme
Lament the ravages of time,
As erst by Newark's riven towers,
And Ettrick stripp'd of forest bowers.
True, — Caledonia's Queen is changed,
Since on her dusky summit ranged,
Within its steepy limits pent,
By bulwark, line, and battlement,
And flanking towers, and laky flood,
Guarded and garrison'd she stood,
Denying entrance or resort,
Save at each tall embattled port;
Above whose arch, suspended, hung
Portcullis spiked with iron prong.
That long is gone, — but not so long
Since, early closed, and opening late,
Jealous revolved the studded gate,
Whose task, from eve to morning tide,
A wicket churlishly supplied.
Stern then, and steel-girt was thy brow,
Dun-Edin! O, how alter'd now,

When safe amid thy mountain court
Thou sit'st, like Empress at her sport,
And liberal, unconfined, and free,
Flinging thy white arms to the sea.
For thy dark cloud, with umber'd lower,
That hung o'er cliff, and lake, and tower,
Thou gleam'st against the western ray
Ten thousand lines of brighter day.

III.

Not she, the Championess of old,
In Spenser's magic tale enroll'd,
She, for the charmed spear renown'd,
Which forced each night to kiss the ground, —
Not she more changed, when placed at rest,
What time she was Malbecco's guest,
She gave to flow her maiden vest;
When from the corslet's grasp relieved,
Free to the sight her bosom heaved;
Sweet was her blue eye's modest smile,
Erst hidden by the aventayle;
And down her shoulders graceful roll'd
Her locks profuse, of paly gold.
They who whilom, in midnight fight,
Had marvell'd at her matchless might,
No less her maiden charms approved,
But looking liked, and liking loved.
The sight could jealous pangs beguile,
And charm Malbecco's cares a while;
And he, the wandering Squire of Dames,
Forgot his Columbella's claims,
And passion, erst unknown, could gain
The breast of blunt Sir Satyrane;

Nor durst light Paridel advance,
Bold as he was, a looser glance.
She charm'd, at once, and tamed the heart,
Incomparable Britomarte!

IV.

So thou, fair City! disarray'd
Of battled wall, and rampart's aid,
As stately seem'st, but lovelier far
Than in that panoply of war.
Nor deem that from thy fenceless throne
Strength and security are flown;
Still, as of yore, Queen of the North!
Still canst thou send thy children forth.
Ne'er readier at alarm-bell's call
Thy burghers rose to man thy wall,
Than now, in danger, shall be thine,
Thy dauntless voluntary line,
For fosse and turret proud to stand,
Their breasts the bulwarks of the land,
Thy thousands, train'd to martial toil,
Full red would stain their native soil,
Ere from thy mural crown there fell
The slightest knosp, or pinnacle.
And if it come, — as come it may,
Dun-Edin! that eventful day, —
Renown'd for hospitable deed,
That virtue much with Heaven may plead,
In patriarchal times whose care
Descending angels deign'd to share;
That claim may wrestle blessings down
On those who fight for The Good Town,

Destined in every age to be
Refuge of injured royalty;
Since first, when conquering York arose,
To Henry meek she gave repose,
Till late, with wonder, grief, and awe,
Great Bourbon's relics, sad she saw.

V.

Truce to these thoughts!—for, as they rise,
How gladly I avert mine eyes,
Bodings, or true or false, to change,
For Fiction's fair romantic range,
Or for tradition's dubious light,
That hovers 'twixt the day and night:
Dazzling alternately and dim,
Her wavering lamp I'd rather trim,
Knights, squires, and lovely dames to see,
Creation of my fantasy,
Than gaze abroad on reeky fen,
And make of mists invading men.
Who loves not more the night of June
Than dull December's gloomy noon?
The moonlight than the fog of frost?
And can we say, which cheats the most?

VI.

But who shall teach my harp to gain
A sound of the romantic strain,
Whose Anglo-Norman tones whilere
Could win the royal Henry's ear,
Famed Beauclerc call'd, for that he loved
The minstrel and his lay approved?

Who shall these lingering notes redeem,
Decaying on Oblivion's stream;
Such notes as from the Breton tongue
Marie translated, Blondel sung?
O! born, Time's ravage to repair,
And make the dying muse thy care;
Who, when his scythe her hoary foe
Was poising for the final blow,
The weapon from his hand could wring,
And break his glass, and shear his wing,
And bid, reviving in his strain,
The gentle poet live again;
Thou, who canst give to lightest lay
An unpedantic moral gay,
Nor less the dullest theme bid flit
On wings of unexpected wit;
In letters as in life approved,
Example honour'd, and beloved, —
Dear ELLIS! to the bard impart
A lesson of thy magic art,
To win at once the head and heart, —
At once to charm, instruct and mend,
My guide, my pattern, and my friend!

VII.

Such minstrel lesson to bestow
Be long thy pleasing task, — but, O!
No more by thy example teach,
— What few can practice, all can preach, —
With even patience to endure
Lingering disease, and painful cure,

And boast affliction's pangs subdued
By mild and manly fortitude,
Enough, the lesson has been given:
Forbid the repetition, Heaven!

VIII.

Come listen, then! for thou hast known,
And loved the Minstrel's varying tone,
Who, like his Border sires of old,
Waked a wild measure rude and bold,
Till Windsor's oaks, and Ascot plain,
With wonder heard the northern strain.
Come listen! bold in thy applause,
The bard shall scorn pedantic laws;
And, as the ancient art could stain
Achievements on the storied pane,
Irregularly traced and plann'd,
But yet so glowing and so grand, —
So shall he strive, in changeful hue,
Field, feast, and combat, to renew,
And loves, and arms, and harpers' glee,
And all the pomp of chivalry.

INTRODUCTION TO CANTO SIXTH.

TO RICHARD HEBER, ESQ.

Mertoun-House, Christmas.

I.

HEAP on more wood! the wind is chill;
But let it whistle as it will,
We'll keep our Christmas merry still.
Each age has deem'd the new-born year
The fittest time for festal cheer:
Even, heathen yet, the savage Dane
At Iol more deep the mead did drain;
High on the beach his galleys drew,
And feasted all his pirate crew;
Then in his low and pine-built hall,
Where shields and axes deck'd the wall,
They gorged upon the half dress'd steer;
Caroused in seas of sable beer;
While round, in brutal jest, were thrown
The half-gnaw'd rib and marrow-bone:
Or listen'd all, in grim delight,
While Scalds yell'd out the joys of fight.
Then forth, in frenzy, would they hie,
While, wildly-loose their red locks fly,
And dancing round the blazing pile,
They make such barbarous mirth the while,
As best might to the mind recall
The boisterous joys of Odin's hall.

II.

And well our Christian sires of old
Loved when the year its course had roll'd,
And brought blithe Christmas back again,
With all his hospitable train.
Domestic and religious rite
Gave honour to the holy night;
On Christmas-eve the bells were rung;
On Christmas-eve the mass was sung:
That only night in all the year,
Saw the stoled priest the chalice rear.
The damsel donn'd her kirtle sheen;
The hall was dress'd with holly green;
Forth to the wood did merry-men go,
To gather in the mistletoe.
Then open'd wide the Baron's hall
To vassal, tenant, serf, and all;
Power laid his rod of rule aside,
And Ceremony doff'd his pride.
The heir, with roses in his shoes,
That night might village partner choose;
The lord, underogating, share
The vulgar game of " post and pair."
All hail'd, with uncontroll'd delight,
And general voice, the happy night,
That to the cottage, as the crown,
Brought tidings of salvation down.

III.

The fire, with well-dried logs supplied,
Went roaring up the chimney wide;
The huge hall-table's oaken face,
Scrubb'd till it shone, the day to grace,

Bore then upon its massive board
No mark to part the squire and lord.
Then was brought in the lusty brawn,
By old blue-coated serving-man;
Then the grim boar's head frown'd on high,
Crested with bays and rosemary.
Well can the green-garb'd ranger tell,
How, when, and where, the monster fell;
What dogs before his death he tore,
And all the baiting of the boar.
The wassail round, in good brown bowls,
Garnish'd with ribbons, blithely trowls.
There the huge sirloin reek'd; hard by
Plum-porridge stood, and Christmas pie;
Nor fail'd old Scotland to produce,
At such high-tide, her savoury goose.
Then came the merry maskers in,
And carols roar'd with blithesome din;
If unmelodious was the song,
It was a hearty note, and strong.
Who lists may in their mumming see
Traces of ancient mystery;
White shirts supplied the masquerade,
And smutted cheeks the visors made;
But, O! what maskers, richly dight,
Can boast of bosoms half so light!
England was merry England, when
Old Christmas brought his sports again.
'Twas Christmas broach'd the mightiest ale;
'Twas Christmas told the merriest tale;
A Christmas gambol oft could cheer
The poor man's heart through half the year.

IV.

Still linger, in our northern clime,
Some remnants of the good old time;
And still, within our valleys here,
We hold the kindred title dear,
Even when, perchance, its far-fetch'd claim
To Southron ear sounds empty name:
For course of blood, our proverbs deem,
Is warmer than the mountain-stream.
And thus, my Christmas still I hold
Where my great-grandsire came of old,
With amber beard, and flaxen hair,
And reverend apostolic air —
The feast and holy-tide to share,
And mix sobriety with wine,
And honest mirth with thoughts divine:
Small thought was his, in after time
E'er to be hitch'd into a rhyme.
The simple sire could only boast,
That he was loyal to his cost;
The banish'd race of kings revered,
And lost his land, — but kept his beard.

V.

In these dear halls, where welcome kind
Is with fair liberty combined;
Where cordial friendship gives the hand,
And flies constraint the magic wand
Of the fair dame that rules the land,
Little we heed the tempest drear,
While music, mirth, and social cheer,
Speed on their wings the passing year.
And Mertoun's halls are fair e'en now,
When not a leaf is on the bough.

Tweed loves them well, and turns again,
As loath to leave the sweet domain,
And holds his mirror to her face,
And clips her with a close embrace: —
Gladly as he, we seek the dome,
And as reluctant turn us home.

VI.

How just that, at this time of glee,
My thoughts should, Heber, turn to thee!
For many a merry hour we've known,
And heard the chimes of midnight's tone.
Cease, then, my friend! a moment cease,
And leave these classic tomes in peace!
Of Roman and of Grecian lore,
Sure mortal brain can hold no more.
These ancients, as Noll Bluff might say,
" Were pretty fellows in their day ; "
But time and tide o'er all prevail —
On Christmas eve a Christmas tale —
Of wonder and of war — " Profane!
What! leave the lofty Latian strain,
Her stately prose, her verse's charms,
To hear the clash of rusty arms :
In Fairy Land or Limbo lost,
To jostle conjurer and ghost,
Goblin and witch ! " — Nay, Heber dear,
Before you touch my charter, hear :
Though Leyden aids, alas ! no more,
My cause with many-languaged lore,
This may I say : — in realms of death
Ulysses meets Alcides' *wraith ;*
Æneas, upon Thracia's shore,
The ghost of murder'd Polydore ;

For omens, we in Livy cross,
At every turn, *locutus Bos.*
As grave and duly speaks that ox,
As if he told the price of stocks;
Or held, in Rome republican,
The place of common-councilman.

VII.

All nations have their omens drear,
Their legends wild of woe and fear.
To Cambria look — the peasant see,
Bethink him of Glendowerdy,
And shun " the spirit's Blasted Tree."
The Highlander, whose red claymore
The battle turn'd on Maida's shore,
Will, on a Friday morn, look pale,
If ask'd to tell a fairy tale:
He fears the vengeful Elfin King,
Who leaves that day his grassy ring:
Invisible to human ken,
He walks among the sons of men.

VIII.

Didst e'er, dear Heber, pass along
Beneath the towers of Franchémont,
Which, like an eagle's nest in air,
Hang o'er the stream and hamlet fair?
Deep in their vaults, the peasants say,
A mighty treasure buried lay,
Amass'd through rapine and through wrong
By the last Lord of Franchémont.
The iron chest is bolted hard,
A huntsman sits, its constant guard;

Around his neck his horn is hung,
His hanger in his belt is slung;
Before his feet his blood-hounds lie.
And 'twere not for his gloomy eye,
Whose withering glance no heart can brook,
As true a huntsman doth he look,
As bugle e'er in brake did sound,
Or ever holloo'd to a hound.
To chase the fiend, and win the prize
In that same dungeon ever tries
An aged necromantic priest;
It is an hundred years at least,
Since 'twixt them first the strife begun,
And neither yet has lost nor won.
And oft the Conjurer's words will make
The stubborn Demon groan and quake;
And oft the bands of iron break,
Or bursts one lock, that still amain,
Fast as 'tis open'd, shuts again.
That magic strife within the tomb
May last until the day of doom,
Unless the adept shall learn to tell
The very word that clench'd the spell,
When Franch'mont lock'd the treasure cell.
An hundred years are pass'd and gone,
And scarce three letters has he won.

IX.

Such general superstition may
Excuse for old Pitscottie say;
Whose gossip history has given
My song the messenger from Heaven,

That warn'd, in Lithgow, Scotland's King,
Nor less the infernal summoning ;
May pass the Monk of Durham's tale,
Whose demon fought in Gothic mail ;
May pardon plead for Fordun grave,
Who told of Gifford's Goblin-Cave.
But why such instances to you,
Who, in an instant, can renew
Your treasured hoards of various lore,
And furnish twenty thousand more ;
Hoards, not like theirs whose volumes rest
Like treasures in the Franch'mont chest,
While gripple owners still refuse
To others what they cannot use ;
Give them the priest's whole century,
They shall not spell you letters three ;
Their pleasure in the books the same
The magpie takes in pilfer'd gem.
Thy volumes, open as thy heart,
Delight, amusement, science, art,
To every ear and eye impart ;
Yet who of all who thus employ them,
Can like the owner's self enjoy them ? —
But, hark ! I hear the distant drum !
The day of Flodden Field is come. —
Adieu, dear Heber ! life and health,
And store of literary wealth.

NOTES ON MARMION.

CANTO FIRST.

The Castle.

STANZA 1. **Norham.** A ruined castle on south bank of the Tweed, not far from Berwick, and where the Tweed marks the boundary between Scotland and England. Edward I. lived at Norham while umpire concerning the Scottish succession. The donjon, or keep, or prison, was added in 1164 by the Bishop of Durham. The ruins of Norham "consist of a large shattered tower with many vaults and fragments of other edifices enclosed within an outward wall of great circuit."

ST. 2. **Donjon.** The donjon of a feudal castle was the strongest part, and was placed in the centre of the other buildings. The donjon contained the great hall, principal staterooms, and the prison: hence the modern word dungeon.

ST. 2. **Saint George.** Patron saint of England.

ST. 3. **Plump of spears.** Body of men-at-arms.

ST. 3. **Server.** An ancient officer who served up a feast.

ST. 3. **Squire.** "The shield-bearer of a knight."

ST. 3. **Seneschal.** Principal officer of the household. A euphuistic word limited to poetry.

ST. 4. **Pipe.** Large cask for liquors.

ST. 4. **Malvoisie.** Malmsey. A delicious white wine prepared in Madeira. It came originally from Malvoisia in the Morea.

ST. 4. **Salvo.** A salute by firing guns. A military salvo.

ST. 4. **Portcullis.** Framework of timbers pointed with iron, hung in grooves in the chief gateway of a fortress, and let down to stop passage when there is not time to shut the gates.

ST. 5. **Stalworth.** Stalwart.

STANZA 5. **Bosworth Field.** A moor in Leicestershire, England, where was fought the battle in which Richard III. was slain, and which terminated the War of the Roses, in 1485.

ST. 5. **Carpet-knight.** One made a knight at court and honoring some service other than military.

ST. 6. **Milan steel.** "The artists of the Middle Ages were famous for their skill in armory."

ST. 6. **Plate.** "Armor composed of flat pieces of metal; distinguished from mail."

ST. 6. **Mail.** "Defensive armour formed of iron rings or round meshes."

ST. 6. **Checks.** (Falconry.) A forsaking of game by a hawk to follow other prey.

ST. 6. **Dight.** Prepared; made ready. — *Chambers.*

ST. 6. **Housing.** A saddle-cloth.

ST. 6. **Trap** (trapp'd). Decorated.

ST. 7. **Spurs.** The title of knight in the Middle Ages was conferred by binding the sword and spurs on the candidate as the first step in the investiture of this new dignity.

ST. 8. **Halberd.** Ancient military weapon intended for both cutting and thrusting. A combination of spear and battle-axe. It is rarely used now except in Scotland. — *Ogilvie.*

ST. 8. **Bill.** Sword.

ST. 8. **Sumpter.** An animal, particularly a horse or mule, carrying loads on its back. — *Shakspeare.*

ST. 8. **Listed.** From Anglo-Saxon, lystan, listan — to desire, to be disposed.

ST. 8. **Jerkin.** A jacket; a close waistcoat. — *Shakespeare.*

ST. 8. **Palfrey.** Horse for the road or for state occasions, opposed to steed; a horse for the battle. — *Worcester.*

ST. 9. **Morion.** A helmet without a visor.

ST. 9. **Linstock.** A pike or staff having branches at one end, to which were affixed pieces of slow-match used for firing cannon. — *Mil. Ency.*

ST. 9. **Yare.** Ready.

ST. 10. **Morrice-pike.** Moorish pike.

ST. 10. **"Angel.** "A gold coin of the period, value about ten shillings."

ST. 10. **Brook.** Manage.

S_T. 11. **Pursuivants.** Followers; heralds.

S_TANZA 11. **Tabarts.** A light, embroidered garment worn over armor.

S_T. 11. **Scutcheon.** Escutcheon; shield of a family on which coats-of-arms are emblazoned.

S_T. 11. **Lord Marmion.** "The principal character of the present romance is entirely a fictitious personage. In earlier times, indeed, the family of Marmion, Lords of Fontenay, in Normandy, was highly distinguished. Robert de Marmion, Lord of Fontenay, a distinguished follower of the Conqueror, obtained a grant of the castle and town of Tamworth, and also of the manor of Scrivelby in Lincolnshire. One or both of these noble possessions was held by the honourable service of being the royal champion, as the ancestors of Marmion had formerly been to the Dukes of Normandy. But after the castle and demesne of Tamworth had passed through four successive barons from Robert, the family became extinct in the person of Philip de Marmion, who died in 29th Edward I. without issue male. . . . I have not, therefore, created a new family, but only revived the titles of an old one in an imaginary personage." — *Walter Scott.*

S_T. 11. **Marks.** An old English coin, value 13*s*. 4*d*. sterling (about $3.22). — *Brande.*

S_T. 11. **Largesse.** The cry by which the bounty of knights and nobles was thanked.

S_T. 12. **With the crest and helm of gold.** In the reign of Edward II., one of the Marmion family wore a helmet with a crest of gold.

S_T. 13. **Sir Hugh the Heron.** "Were accuracy of any consequence in a fictitious narrative, this castellan's name ought to have been William; for William Heron of Ford was husband to the famous Lady Ford, whose siren charms are said to have cost our James IV. so dear. Moreover, the said William Heron was, at the time supposed, a prisoner in Scotland, being surrendered by Henry VIII. on account of his share in the slaughter of Sir Robert Ker of Cessford." — *Walter Scott.*

S_T. 13. **Hold.** A fort; a castle.

S_T. 13. **Deas.** Dais.

S_T. 13. **Scantly.** With difficulty.

S_T. 13. **Brook.** Endure.

St. 14. **Giust.** Joust.

Stanza 15. **Wassail.** Anglo-Saxon, waes-hael: health be with you; anciently, a salutation in drinking. — *Ritson.*

St. 15. **Brand.** Sword (used in poetry).

St. 15. **Russet.** Coarse homespun.

St. 16. **Lindisfarn.** An island peninsula off the north-east coast of England. The monastery established here in the seventh century by Aidan, gave the peninsula, which is an island at low tide, the name of Holy Island.

St. 17. **Unrecked.** Unheeded.

St. 18. **Warbeck.** "The story of Perkin Warbeck, or Richard, Duke of York, is well known. In 1496 he was received honourably in Scotland; and James IV., after conferring upon him in marriage his own relation, the Lady Catherine Gordon, made war on England in behalf of his pretensions. To retaliate an invasion of England, Surrey advanced into Berwickshire at the head of considerable forces, but retreated after taking the inconsiderable fortress of Ayton." — *Scott.*

St. 19. "The garrisons of the English castles of Wark, Norham, and Berwick, were, as may be easily supposed, very troublesome neighbors to Scotland." — *Walter Scott.*

St. 19. **Harry.** To lay waste; to pillage.

St. 20. **Forayer.** One who makes an invasion; a plunderer.

St. 20. **Pardoner.** A seller of indulgences granted by the Pope.

St. 21. **Ween.** An archaic word; think.

St. 21. **Durham** was farther south than Norham. The sarcasm in this stanza is true to the disrepute into which priests, monks, etc., had fallen in the fourteenth, fifteenth, and sixteenth centuries.

St. 22. **Carved to his uncle and that lord.** Marmion.

St. 22. **Tables.** Backgammon or draughts.

St. 23. **Levin.** Lightning.

St. 23. **Salem.** Jerusalem.

St. 23. **Cockle-shells** were used by pilgrims to Jerusalem for drinking-cups.

St. 23. **Montserrat.** Mountain in north-east of Spain. The pious Catalonians believe that its fantastic outline was caused by its being riven and shattered at the time of the Crucifixion. The mountain is celebrated because of its Benedictine Abbey, built at an elevation of twelve hundred feet, and for its thirteen hermitages "formerly perched like eagles' nests on inaccessible pinnacles."

STANZA 23. **And of that Grot where olives nod.** On northern coast of Sicily, near Palermo.

ST. 24. **To stout Saint George of Norwich merry.** At the shrines of St. George, etc.

ST. 25. **Gramercy.** French, *grand merci;* many thanks.

ST. 25. **Holy-Rood** (Castle).

ST. 25. **Like his good saint, I'll pay his meed.** Recompense him.

This stanza is a fair specimen of the manner in which Scott often qualifies the faults of mankind with a kindly, gentle humor that finds a proper use for every one and every thing.

ST. 26. **Howe'er.** Although.

ST. 26. **Aves — Ave — Hail!** First part of salutation used by Roman Catholics to Virgin Mary; prayers.

ST. 27. **By my fay.** Faith.

ST. 27. **Palmer.** "A palmer, opposed to a pilgrim, was one who made it his sole business to visit different holy shrines." — *Walter Scott.*

ST. 27. **Loretto.** In Italy.

ST. 27. **Scrip.** Bag; wallet.

ST. 28. This stanza is full of direct, simple pathos.

ST. 29.   "To fair St. Andrew's bound,
          Within the ocean-cave to pray,
          Where good Saint Rule his holy lay."

"Saint Regulus (Scottice, St. Rule), a monk of Patrae, in Achaia, warned by a vision, is said, A.D. 370, to have sailed westward until he landed at St. Andrews in Scotland, where he founded a chapel and tower. The latter is still standing, and, though we may doubt the precise date of its foundation, is certainly one of the most ancient edifices in Scotland. A cave, nearly fronting the ruinous castle of the archbishops of St. Andrews, bears the name of this religious person. It is difficult of access; and the rock in which it is hewn is washed by the German Ocean. It is nearly round, about ten feet in diameter, and the same in height. On one side is a sort of stone altar; on the other an aperture into an inner den, where the miserable ascetic, who inhabited this dwelling, probably slept. At full tide, egress and regress are hardly practicable. As Regulus first colonized the metropolitan see of Scotland, and converted the inhabitants in the vicinity, he has some reason to complain that the ancient name of Killrule (Cella Reguli) should have been superseded, even in favor of the tutelar saint of Scotland. The reason of the change was, that St. Rule is said to have brought to Scotland the relics of St. Andrew." — *Walter Scott.*

STANZA 29.   "Saint Fillan's blessed well,
    Whose spring can frensied dreams dispel,
    And the crazed brain restore."

"St. Fillan was a Scottish saint of some reputation. Although Popery is, with us, matter of abomination, yet the common people still retain some of the superstitions connected with it. There are in Perthshire several wells and springs dedicated to St. Fillan, which are still places of pilgrimages and offerings, even among the Protestants. They are held powerful in cases of madness, and, in some of very late occurrence, lunatics have been left all night bound to the holy stone, in confidence that the saint would cure and unloose them before morning." — *Walter Scott.*

ST. 30.   **Wassel.** This word here means merry-making.

ST. 31.   **Stirrup-cup.** A parting cup, taken on horseback. — *Halliwell.*

CANTO SECOND.

The Convent.

STANZA 1.   "The breeze which swept away the smoke" [that].

ST. 1.   **Northumbria** was the north-east division of the Saxon Heptarchy; the ancient name is still retained in Northumberland.

ST. 1.   "**Holy Island** was the Episcopal seat of the See of Durham during the early ages of British Christianity." — *Walter Scott.*

ST. 1.   **St. Cuthbert** was the sixth bishop of Durham.

"The ruins of the monastery betoken great antiquity. The arches are, in general, strictly Saxon, and the pillars which support them, short, strong, and massy." — *Walter Scott.*

ST. 1.   The Abbey of **Whitby** was reared by the Abbess Hild, in the seventh century. Here it was that Cædmon sang "The beginning of created things."

Notice the iambic tetrameter of the last ten verses of the first stanza of Canto II. Observe how well this measure serves to develop the idea conveyed.

Stanza 2. The fourth verse is really parenthetical. All the thoughts in this stanza have the loose association of descriptive conversation.

How dexterously and briefly the poet indicates in 15–20 the subtle intermixture of super-conscientiousness and vanity!

St. 4. The Benedictine order was founded in the sixth century by St. Benedict. This order was a powerful agent in the spread of Christianity and learning in the West. At one time there were thirty-seven thousand Benedictine monasteries. The rule of St. Benedict was not as severe as those of some other orders. "Compared with the ascetic orders, [this one], both in dress and manners, may be styled the gentlemanly order of monks." Convents for Benedictine nuns cannot be traced earlier than the seventh century.

St. 4. "Summon'd to Lindisfarne, she *came*."

" Came" should be " went," were it not for the rhyme.

St. 6. What grammatical error exists in lines 8 and 9? What rhetorical figure is embodied in lines 8, 9, and 10 ?

What word is crudely added in the last verse of this stanza to complete the prescribed number of feet?

St. 7. Una and the lion are here alluded to.

St. 7. **Bowl.** Cup of poison.

Notice the confusion of tenses in this stanza.

St. 8. **Alne.** A small river of Northumberland.

St. 8. For story of Percys see " Ballad of Chevy Chase."

St. 8. **Bamborough** was the royal city, the rocky fortress of Northumberland at the time of the Saxon Heptarchy. Bamborough is now a small village. The castle founded about 554 still stands.

St. 8. **Ida** was king of Deira, a section of Northumbria, in 547. He probably founded Bamborough Castle. See " Green's History of the English People," vol. i., p. 37.

St. 10. " And needful was such strength to these," [walls].

St. 10. " Open to rovers fierce as they," [the Danes].

Sts. 11, 12, etc. Notice the confusion of tenses. Scott's careless style often veils the otherwise clear and limpid flow of his description.

St. 13. " And monks cry Fye upon your name! "

[The names of Herbert, Bruce, and Percy.]

St. 13.
            In their convent cell
     A Saxon princess once did dwell,
     The lovely Edelfled."

"She was the daughter of King Oswy, who, in gratitude to Heaven for the great victory which he won in 655 against Penda, the Pagan king of Mercia, dedicated Edelfleda, then but a year old, to the service of God, in the monastery of Whitby, of which St. Hilda was then abbess. She afterwards adorned the place of her education with great magnificence." — *Walter Scott.*

Lines 14–22. "These two miracles are much insisted upon by all ancient writers who have occasion to mention either Whitby or St. Hilda. The relics of the snakes which infested the precincts of the convent, and were, at the abbess's prayer, not only beheaded, but petrified, are still found about the rocks, and are termed by Protestant fossilists, Ammonitæ.

"The other miracle is thus mentioned by Camden: 'It is also ascribed to the power of her sanctity, that these wild geese which, in the winter, fly in great flocks to the lakes and rivers unfrozen in the southern parts, to the great amazement of every one, fall down suddenly upon the ground, when they are in their flight over certain neighbouring fields hereabouts, — a relation I should not have made, if I had not received it from several credible men. But those who are less inclined to heed superstition attribute it to some occult quality in the ground, and to somewhat of antipathy between it and the geese, such as they say is betwixt wolves and scylla roots; for that such hidden tendencies and aversions, as we call sympathies and antipathies, are implanted in many things by provident nature for the preservation of them, is a thing so evident that everybody grants it.' Mr. Charlton, in his 'History of Whitby,' points out the true origin of the fable from the number of sea-gulls that, when flying from a storm, often alight near Whitby; and from the woodcocks and other birds of passage who do the same upon their arrival on shore after a long flight." — *Walter Scott.*

STANZA 14. **Melrose** is on the Tweed, in sight of Abbotsford, Walter Scott's home.

ST. 14. **Tilmouth** is in Northumberland.

ST. 14. **Wear.** A river of Durham county, south of Northumberland.

ST. 14. **St. Cuthbert.** "The resting-place of the remains of this saint is not now matter of uncertainty. So recently as 17th May, 1827, eleven hundred and thirty-nine years after his death, their discovery and disinterment were effected. Under a blue stone, in the middle of the shrine of St. Cuthbert, at the eastern extremity of the choir of Durham Cathedral, there was then found a walled grave, containing the coffins of the Saint. The first, or outer one, was ascertained to be that of 1541, the second of 1041; the third, or inner one, answering in every particular to the description of that of 698, was found to contain, not, indeed, as had been averred then, and even till 1539, the incorruptible body, but the entire skeleton of the Saint, the bottom of the grave being perfectly dry, free from offensive smell, and without the slightest symptom that a human body had ever undergone decomposition within its walls. The skeleton was found swathed in five silk robes of emblematic embroidery, the ornamental parts laid with gold leaf, and these again covered with a robe of linen. Beside the skeleton were also deposited several gold and silver insignia, and other relics of the Saint." — *History of Northumberland.*

See on St. Cuthbert, " Early Monasticism," by Odell Travers Hill.

St. 15. " Even Scotland's dauntless king, and heir."

" Every one has heard that when David I., with his son Henry, invaded Northumberland in 1136, the English host marched against them under the holy banner of St. Cuthbert; to the efficacy of which was imputed the great victory which they obtained in the bloody battle of Northallerton, or Cutonmoor. The conquerors were at least as much indebted to the jealousy and intractability of the different tribes who composed David's army." — *Walter Scott.*

Stanza 15. " 'Twas he, to vindicate his reign,
      Edged Alfred's falchion on the Dane,
      And turned the Conqueror back again, " etc.

St. Cuthbert "appeared in a vision to Alfred, when lurking in the marshes of Glastonbury, and promised him assistance and victory over his heathen enemies, — a consolation which, as was reasonable, Alfred, after the victory of Ashendown, rewarded by a royal offering at the shrine of the Saint. As to William the Conqueror, the terror which spread before his army when he marched to punish the revolt of the Northumbrians, in 1096, had forced the Monks to fly once more to Holy Island with the body of the Saint. It was, however, replaced before William left the North; and, to balance accounts, the conqueror, having intimated an indiscreet curiosity to view the Saint's body, he was, while in the act of commanding the shrine to be opened, seized with heat and sickness, accompanied with such a panic terror that, notwithstanding there was such a sumptuous dinner prepared for him,

he fled without eating a morsel (which the monkish historian seems to
have thought no small part both of the miracle and the penance), and
never drew his bridle till he got to the river Tees." — *Walter Scott.*

STANZA 17.   "Old Colwulf built it, for his fault."

"Ceowulf, or Colwulf, King of Northumberland, flourished in the
eighth century. He was a man of some learning, for the venerable
Bede dedicates to him his "Ecclesiastical History. He abdicated the
throne about 738, and retired to Holy Island, where he died in the
odor of sanctity. Saint as Colwulf was, however, I fear the foundation of the penance vault does not correspond with his character;
for it is recorded among his *memorabilia* that, finding the air of the
island raw and cold, he indulged the monks, whose rule had hitherto
confined them to milk or water, with the comfortable privilege of using
wine or ale. If any rigid antiquary insists on this objection, he is
welcome to suppose the penance vault was intended by the founder
for the more genial purposes of a cellar."— *Walter Scott.*

ST. 17. **Colwulf's fault.** It must have been one of ordinary
human nature, for his historical record is an unusually fair one.

STS. 18-26 inclusive. A beautiful piece of descriptive writing, if
we except the confusion of tenses.

ST. 18. **Cresset.** Antique chandelier.

ST. 19.   "Tynemouth's haughty prioress."

"That there was an ancient priory at Tynemouth is certain. Its
ruins are situated on a high, rocky point; and, doubtless, many a vow
was made to the shrine by the distressed mariners who drove towards
the iron-bound coast of Northumberland in stormy weather. It was
anciently a nunnery; for Virca, abbess of Tynemouth, presented St.
Cuthbert (yet alive) with a rare winding-sheet, in emulation of a holy
lady called Tuda, who had sent him a coffin. But, as in the case of
Whitby, and of Holy Island, the introduction of nuns at Tynemouth
in the reign of Henry VIII. is an anachronism. The nunnery at Holy
Island is altogether fictitious. Indeed, St. Cuthbert was unlikely to
permit such an establishment; for, notwithstanding his accepting the
mortuary gifts above mentioned, and his carrying on a visiting acquaintance with the Abbess of Coldingham, he certainly hated the
whole female sex; and, in revenge of a slippery trick played to him
by an Irish princess, he, after death, inflicted severe penances on
such as presumed to approach within a certain distance of his shrine."
— *Walter Scott.*

Stanza 19. The second foot in verse twenty-four must be treated as a pyrrhic, in order to read the line rhythmically.

St. 20. **Doublet.** A waist garment under the cloak; a man's waistcoat.

St. 20. **Fontevraud.** There was a celebrated abbey at Fontevrault, in France, in the department of Maine-et-Loire. The abbey is now a prison.

Sts. 22 and 24. Verses 8–13 inclusive in Stanza 22, and verses 9–13 inclusive in Stanza 24, are the only digressions — for the teaching in Stanza 22 of a moral lesson, and in Stanza 24 for the purpose of analysis — which break the flow of the description from Stanzas 18–26 inclusive.

In Stanza 26 notice the beauty of the simile.

St. 27. " Successless *might* I sue."

" Might " equals " should."

Notice the lofty pride and reticence of Constance in the last four verses.

St. 28. The alternation of verses of four, three, and two feet in this stanza gives to Constance's speech an impassioned effect.

St. 29. **King Henry.** Henry VIII. of England.

St. 29. **Cowardice** should be scanned as a word of two syllables.

St. 30. A picture of the blending of revenge, despair, and love.

The last two verses are a good example of those numerous passages in Scott which persist in clinging to the memory.

St. 31. A prophecy, introduced with fine effect, of Henry VIII.'s withdrawal from Roman Catholicism.

St. 32. The trochaic effect of lines 16 and 17, and the iambic effect of lines 18–24 inclusive, give the stanza a solemn and dignified rhythmical ending.

St. 32. How much more tragically Constance's dreadful fate impresses the reader, because the fine art of the poet leaves the act of incarceration to the reader's imagination!

St. 33. " *As* hurrying, tottering on." While, etc.

Notice the artistic contrast between the hermit and peasant, lines 16 and 17.

St. 33. **Fell.** Local and English.

CANTO THIRD.

The Hostel, or Inn.

Stanza 1. "The mountain path the Palmer show'd." [which, etc.]

St. 1. **Merse.** District in Berwickshire.

St. 1. **Black-cock and ptarmigan.** Varieties of grouse.

St. 1. **Gifford.** Knox the reformer was born at Gifford, which is but a few miles from Edinburgh.

St. 2. **Bush.** The sign of a tavern; formerly an ivy-bush.— *Cotgrave.*

St. 3. **Solands.** A kind of goose of the pelican family.

St. 3. **Gammon.** "The buttock of a hog salted and dried;" a ham.

St. 3. **Buckler.** A shield for the arm.

St. 4. Notice the picture of a captain in the last eight lines.

St. 6. " For his best palfrey, would not I
Endure that sullen scowl."

Doubtless the poet intends an allusion to the wide-spread superstition of the evil eye.

St. 7. How well, incidentally, is the moral supremacy of the leader shown!

St. 8. St. Valentine's Day is the 14th of February. "About this time of the year birds choose their mates."— *Bailey.*

For an interesting account of the special celebration of this day in England, see Chambers's Encyclopædia.

St. 13. The omission of a foot in verses 15 and 18 adds force to the question and answer. The caesura of line 15 is effective.

St. 14. In verses 9, 12, 15, and 18 the omission of one foot adds a pleasant variety to the meter. There is a true poetic harmony between this variation and the explanatory nature of the last ten verses. Stanza 14 has the suggestiveness of Greek tragic poetry: the first nine lines tell a story; the last nine lines fulfil the prophetic office of the chorus.

St. 15. " But, *tired to hear* the desperate maid."

Tired of hearing, etc.

St. 15. **Though not a victim.** i.e., he expected the church to confine Constance, not to immure her.

St. 15. **Mulct.** Penalty; fine.

Stanza 16.   " All lovely on his soul returned."
The old story of " distance lending enchautment to the view."
St. 17.   " Fierce and unfeminine are there."
Fierce [looks] and unfeminine [looks].
Notice how well the greater length of this stanza suits revery.
St. 18. **Loch Vennachar.** In the county of Perth, and three and a half miles long.
St. 18. " For marvels still the vulgar love." i.e., the common people are superstitious.
St. 19. **A clerk.** A scholar.
St. 19. **The Goblin-Hall.** " A vaunted hall under the ancient castle of Gifford, or Yester, the construction of which has from a very remote period been ascribed to magic."
When " Marmion " was written, the Goblin-Hall was inaccessible by the fall of a stair. Sir Hugo died in 1267.
St. 19. " Gave you that cavern to survey." Gave you time, etc.
St. 19. **Dunbar** is at the mouth of the Firth of Forth.
St. 20.   " There floated Haco's banner trim
                 Above Norweyan warriors grim."
" In 1263, Haco, King of Norway, came into the Frith of Clyde with a powerful armament, and made a descent at Largs, in Ayrshire. Here he was encountered and defeated, on the 2d October, by Alexander III. Haco retreated to Orkney, where he died soon after this disgrace to his arms. There are still existing, near the place of battle, many barrows, some of which, having been opened, were found, as usual, to contain bones and urns." — *Walter Scott.*
St. 20. **Bute and Arran.** Islands off the west coast of Scotland.
St. 20. **Cunninghame and Kyle.** On the west mainland, on opposite sides of the Firth of Clyde.
St. 20.   " Upon his breast a pentacle."
" A pentacle is a piece of fine linen, folded with five corners, according to the five senses, and suitably inscribed with characters. This the magician extends towards the spirits he invokes, when they are stubborn and rebellious, and refuse to be conformable unto the ceremonies and rites of magic." — See Reginald Scott's " *Discovery of Witchcraft.*"
St. 21. **Racking Cloud.** Moving cloud.
St. 21.   " As born upon that blessed night."
" It is a popular article of faith that those who are born on Christ-

mas or Good Friday have the power of seeing spirits, and even of commanding them. The Spaniards imputed the haggard and downcast looks of their Philip II. to the disagreeable visions to which this privilege subjected him." — *Walter Scott.*

STANZA 21. **Soothly.** Truly.

ST. 21. **Buffet.** Blow with the fist.

ST. 21. **Malcolm.** Name of four Scotch kings.

ST. 21. **Down.** Bare, hilly ground, used for pasturing sheep.

ST. 21. **Fell.** Deadly.

ST. 21. **Edward.** Edward I. of England.

ST. 24. **Largs.** A seaport of Scotland, surrounded by beautiful hills. Largs is twenty-two miles W.S.W. of Glasgow. A great victory was gained here in 1263 by Alexander III. over Haco, King of Norway.

ST. 24. "Triumphant, to the victor shore."

Allusion to battle of Copenhagen, fought 1801.

ST. 25. **Dunfermline's Nave.** Abbey of Dunfermline, founded by Malcolm and his queen between 1070–1086. The body of Bruce was also interred here. Dunfermline is sixteen miles N.W. of Edinburgh. "The Host's Tale" inserted in the midst of a narrative, recalls "The Canterbury Tales."

ST. 26. **Quaigh.** A wooden cup.

ST. 28. **Darkling.** In the dark.

ST. 29. **Wight.** Person, creature; now used chiefly in contempt.

ST. 29. **Blithe.** Cheerfully.

ST. 30. What variation of meter is there in this stanza?

ST. 31. **Yode.** Used by the old poets for went.

CANTO FOURTH.

The Camp.

STANZA 1. "THE lark sang shrill, the cock he crew."

Ballad form. See Percy's Reliques. Lines nineteen and twenty by means of an extra half foot, unaccented, give the impression of haste.

The alternating trochees and iambi in line twenty-one increase the effect, and enhance the meaning of the verse.

ST. 1. **Friar Rush.** Will o' the Wisp. There is a book of great rarity called "The History of Friar Rush."

S<small>TANZA</small> 4. **Dome.** "A building of any kind ; a house." — *Britton.*

S<small>T</small>. 4. **Caxton.** Earliest English printer. Wynken de Worde was his successor.

S<small>T</small>. 5. "When thinner trees, *receding*, showed."

Growing less and less.

What grammatical errors are there in this stanza for the sake of the rhyme and rhythm?

S<small>T</small>. 6. What rhetorical figure in first verse?

S<small>T</small>. 6. "Gules, Argent, Or, and Azure glowing."

Colors common to coats-of-arms.

S<small>T</small>. 6. **Truncheon.** A short staff.

S<small>T</small>. 6. **Armorial.** Heraldic.

S<small>T</small>. 6. **King-at-Arms.** "The office of heralds, in feudal times, being held of the utmost importance, the inauguration of the Kings-at-Arms, who presided over their Colleges, was proportionally solemn."

S<small>T</small>. 7. **Cap of Maintenance.** A cap of dignity, anciently belonging to the rank of a duke; the fur cap of the Lord Mayor of London, worn on days of State. — *C. Macaulay.*

S<small>T</small>. 7. **Heron.** A bird, native to the greater part of Europe. The heron is found on the banks of lakes or rivers or in marshy places.

S<small>T</small>. 7. "With Scotland's arms, device, and crest."

Are arms, device, and crest used synonomously?

S<small>T</small>. 7. **Tressure.** In heraldry, an ornamental border.

S<small>T</small>. 7. **Sir David Lindesay** "was well known for his early efforts in favor of the reformed doctrines; and indeed, his play, coarse as it now seems, must have had a powerful effect upon the the people of his age."

S<small>T</small>. 8. "My *liege* hath deem'd it shame."

One to whom allegiance is due; a sovereign. Liege is a feudal term.

S<small>T</small>. 10. **Crichtoun Castle.** A large, ruinous castle on the banks of the Tyne, about ten miles from Edinburgh.

S<small>T</small>. 11. **Keep.** Tower.

S<small>T</small>. 11. **Whilom.** Formerly.

S<small>T</small>. 11. "Quarter'd in old armorial sort."

"Quartering in Heraldry is the bearing of two or more coats on a shield divided by horizontal and perpendicular lines, a practice not to be found in the earlier heraldry, and little in use till the fifteenth century. The most usual reason for quartering is to indicate descent from an heiress who has intermarried into the family. The expression 'quarterings' is often loosely used for descents in cases where there is no right to quarter from representation. The eight or sixteen quarterings which are sometimes ranged round the Scottish funeral escutcheon, and which are still important for many purposes in Germany, have no reference to representation, but imply purity of blood for four or five generations; i.e., that the father and mother, the two grandmothers, and four great-grandmothers, as also in the case of sixteen quarterings, the eight great-great-grandmothers, have all been entitled to coat-armour. The earliest instance of quartering in England is found in the paternal arms of Eleanor, daughter of Frederick III., King of Castile and Leon, and first wife of Edward I., as represented on her tomb in Westminster Abbey, the castle of Castile occupying the first and fourth quarters, and the lion of Leon the second and third."— *Chambers's Encyclopædia.*

STANZA 11. **Massy More.** A dungeon. "The Castle of Crichton has a dungeon vault, called the Massey Mole. The epithet, which is not uncommonly applied to the prisons of other old castles in Scotland, is of Saracenic origin. The same word applies to the dungeons of the ancient Moorish castles in Spain."

ST. 12. **Earl Adam Hepburn.** Second Earl of Bothwell, and grandfather to James, Earl of Bothwell, whose name is connected with that of Mary, Queen of Scots.

ST. 13. "Upon the Borough moor that lay."
The rhyming word of this line is awkward and redundant.

ST. 14. **Herald-Bard.** Sir David Lindesay.
Lines eight, nine, and ten are elaborated in Stanzas 15 and 17 inclusive. The original for this legend is found in the writings of Pitscottie.

ST. 15. **Linlithgow.** Linlithgow is one of the oldest towns in Scotland. It is sixteen miles from Edinburgh, and is on a lake. The palace stands on an eminence jutting into the lake, and was frequently the abode of the Scottish monarchs and the birthplace of Mary, Queen of Scots. The earliest record of its existence is in the time of David I., 1124–1153.— *Chambers's Encyclopædia.*

ST. 15. "The wild buck bells from ferny brake."
"Bell seems to be an abbreviation of bellow."—*Scott.*

ST. 15. "June saw his father's overthrow."
"The rebellion against James III. was signalized by the cruel cir-

cumstance of his son's presence in the hostile army. When the king saw his own banner displayed against him, and his son in the faction of his enemies, he lost the little courage he had ever possessed, fled out of the field, fell from his horse as it started at a woman and water-pitcher, and was slain: it is not well understood by whom. James IV., after the battle, passed to Stirling, and, hearing the monks of the chapel-royal deploring the death of his father, their founder, he was seized with deep remorse, which manifested itself in severe penances. The battle of Sauchie-burn, in which James III. fell, was fought 18th June, 1488."

STANZA 16. "The Thistle's Knight-Companions sate."

Thistle is the royal flower, and is here used instead of king.

ST. 16. **Limner.** An archaic term for artist; used chiefly for a portrait or miniature painter.

ST. 17.   "The Marshal and myself had cast."

Cast here means to contrive, to plan.

ST. 19. **Wold.** An open, unwooded, hilly tract; a down.

ST. 21.   "I well believe the last."

i.e., that the face he beheld was a dead face.

ST. 21. **For ne'er,** etc. i.e., became, etc.

ST. 21.   "The first time e'er I asked his aid."

i.e., the aid of St. George. His patron saint helped him before his prayerful thought was framed in words. The confusion of pronouns in lines 21-24 inclusive renders the meaning obscure.

ST. 22.   "Such chance had happ'd of old."

Such misfortune.

ST. 22. "And trained him nigh to *disallow*." [to reject.]

ST. 22. **Targe.** A large, round shield.

ST. 22. **Bowne.** Get ready.

ST. 23. **Dun-Edin.** An old name of Edinburgh.

ST. 24. **Whin.** Furze; gorse.

STS. 23 and 24. These stanzas are a pardonable digression from the narrative on the part of the poet, and have a certain pathos. They serve also as a contrast to Stanza 25.

ST. 25.   "But different far the change has been."

i.e., the change has been very great.

ST. 25. **Bent.** Declivity.

ST. 25. **Borough-moor.** "The Borough, or Common Moor, of Edinburgh was of very great extent, reaching from the southern walls of the city to the bottom of Braid Hills. It was anciently a forest, and in that state was so great a nuisance that the inhabitants of Edinburgh had permission granted to them of building wooden galleries projecting over the street, in order to encourage them to consume the timber, which they seem to have done very effectually. When James IV. mustered the army of the kingdom there, in 1513, the Boroughmoor was, according to Hawthornden, ' a field spacious and delightful by the shade of many stately and aged oaks.' Upon that and similar occasions the royal standard is said to have been displayed from the Hare-Stone, — a high stone now built into the wall, on the left-hand of the highway leading towards Braid, not far from the head of Burntsfield Links. The Hare-stone probably derives its name from the British word *har*, signifying an army." — *Walter Scott.*

STANZA 26. **Hebudes.** The Hebrides.

The fifth line is but a repetition of the first four, and recalls the style of Beowulf, Judith, and other early compositions.

ST. 27. **Wain.** Anglo-Saxon, waen. A four-wheeled wagon.

ST. 27.   " And there were Borthwick's sisters seven."

" Seven Culverins, so called from him who cast them." Culverin it a kind of cannon.

ST. 28. Line 5 seems to be explanatory of line 6.

ST. 28.   " The ruddy lion ramp'd in gold."

" The well-known arms of Scotland. If you will believe Boethius and Buchanan, the double tressure round the shield mentioned, counter fleur-de-lysed or lingued and armed azure, was first assumed by Echaius, king of Scotland, contemporary of Charlemagne, and founder of the celebrated league with France." — *Walter Scott.*

ST. 30. A beautiful and spirited description of Edinburgh and its environs.

ST. 30. **Demi-volte.** An artificial movement of a horse, in which he raises his fore-legs in a peculiar manner. — *Buchanan.*

ST. 31. **Clarion.** A kind of trumpet.

ST. 31. **Sackbut.** A brass wind instrument of the trumpet species.

ST. 31. **Psaltery.** A stringed instrument.

ST. 31. **Prime.** Dawn; morning.

ST. 31.   " To the downfall of the deer."

The first foot of this line is an anapest, and gives a rapid movement.

ST. 32. **Presaging.** Foreboding; foretelling.

ST. 32. **Stowre.** Contention; conflict.

CANTO FIFTH.

The Court.

STANZA 1.   **Palisade.**   A defence or barrier made of stakes driven closely together into the earth and having pointed tops.

ST. 1.   " And carried pikes as they rode through."

i.e., the warders must have carried the pikes.   If Scott were a grammarian the above would be the only possible meaning; but the poet's great carelessness of construction makes it necessary, in doubtful passages, for the student to depend solely on his common-sense.

ST. 1.   **Pike.**   A weapon with a wooden shaft ten to fourteen feet long, with a flat, pointed steel head called the spear. — *Stocqueler.*

ST. 1.   " The cloth-yard arrows flew like hail."

"This is no poetical exaggeration.   In some of the counties of England distinguished for archery, shafts of this extraordinary length were actually used.   Thus, at the Battle of Blcakheath, between the troops of Henry VII. and the Cornish insurgents in 1496, the bridge of Dartford was defended by a picked band of archers from the rebel army, 'whose arrows,' says Holinshed, 'were in length a full cloth yard.'   The Scottish, according to Ascham, had a proverb that every English archer carried under his belt twenty-four Scots, in allusion to his bundle of unerring shafts." — *Walter Scott.*

ST. 2.   " With faces bare."

The Scottish burgesses wore " bright steel caps without crest or visor."

ST. 2.   **Brigantines or Brigandines.**   A coat of mail or scale-armor quilted.

ST. 2.   **Gorget.**   A piece of armor defending the neck.

ST. 2.   **Mace.**   Club.

ST. 3.   **Crossbow.**   A weapon for shooting arrows formed by placing a bow athwart a stock. — *Carew.*

ST. 3.   **Hagbut.**   Hackbut.   A mediæval and very heavy gun.

ST. 3.   **"** To till the fallow land."

Ploughed but not sowed, or land left to rest after tillage.

ST. 4.   **Slogan.**   The war-cry of a Scotch clan.

ST. 4.   **Pricker.**   A light horseman.

ST. 4.   "O! could we but on Border side." i.e., the Scotch side.

Stanza 4. **Brown Maudlin.** Probably some woman of the camp.

St. 4. **Pied.** Variegated.

St. 4. **Kirtle.** A loose jacket.

Stanza 4 reminds one of some of Scott's humorous descriptions of his own ancestors.

St. 5. **Garish.** Gaudy.

St. 5. **Trews.** Trousers.

St. 5. **Buskins.** Half-boots.

St. 5. **Fen.** Marsh.

St. 6. "The bar that arms the charger's heel." A spur.

St. 6. **Falchion.** A broad sword with a slightly curved point.

St. 6. "A banquet rich and costly wines."

"In mediæval times in all transactions of great or petty importance, and among whomsoever taking place, it would seem that a present of wine was a uniform and indispensable preliminary."

St. 6. **Weeds.** The word here means outer garments. •

Sts. 7, 8, and 9. A spirited and finished description.

St. 8. "Toledo right."

i.e., genuine Toledo. Toledo, like Milan, was famed for its weapons.

St. 9. "The pressure of his iron belt."

"Few readers need to be reminded of this belt, to the weight of which James added certain ounces every year that he lived. Pitscottie founds his belief that James was not slain in the Battle of Flodden, because the English never had this token of the iron belt to show to any Scottish man. The person and character of James are delineated according to our best historians. His romantic disposition, which led him highly to relish gayety approaching to license, was, at the same time, tinged with enthusiastic devotion. These propensities sometimes formed a strange contrast. He was wont, during his fits of devotion, to assume the dress and conform to the rules of the order of Franciscans; and when he had thus done penance for some time in Stirling, to plunge again into the tide of pleasure. Probably, too, with no unusual inconsistency, he sometimes laughed at the superstitious observances to which he at other times subjected himself." — *Walter Scott.*

St. 10. "Sir Hugo the Heron's wife held sway."

"Historians impute to the king's infatuated passion the delays· which led to the fatal defeat of Flodden." — *Walter Scott.*

Notice the languorous effect of the last two verses of this stanza, produced by varying the regular four feet with the iambic pentameter measure, — the so-called heroic verse.''

STANZA 11. **Wimple.** A covering of silk or linen for the neck, chin, and sides of the face, also a neck-handkerchief.

ST. 12. **Lochinvar.** — **Lady Heron's Song.**

ST. 12. **Eske.** River of Scotland emptying into Solway Frith.

ST. 12. **Brake.** A thicket.

ST. 12. **Galliard.** A sprightly dance.

ST. 12. **Croupe.** Behind, on horseback.

ST. 12. **Lochinvar.** A lake in Scotland in Kirkcudbright, three miles in circumference. Here are the remains of the Castle of the Gordons, knights of Lochinvar.

Walter Scott busied himself for years in collecting both the written and unwritten ballads cherished among the Border people.

ST. 13. This stanza is truly dramatic. Marmion's fortune, like that of the king, consistently hinges on his connection with various women.

ST. 14. Contrast this picture of Douglas with that of the king in stanza 9.

ST. 14. **Angus.** Now Forfarshire, a maritime county bounded east by the North Sea and south by the Firth of Tay.

ST. 14. **Lauder.** A river giving name to the western district of Berwickshire, i.e., to Lauderdale.

ST. 14. **Archibald Bell-the-Cat.** '' Archibald Douglas, Earl of Angus, a man remarkable for strength of body and mind, acquired the popular name of Bell-the-Cat upon the following remarkable occasion: James the Third, of whom Pitscottie complains that he delighted more in music and ' policies of building ' than in hunting, hawking, and other noble exercises, was so ill advised as to make favorites of his architects and musicians, whom the same historian irreverently terms masons and fiddlers. His nobility, who did not sympathize in the king's respect for the fine arts, were extremely incensed at the honors conferred on those persons, particularly on Cochrane, a mason, who had been created Earl of Mar; and, seizing the opportunity, when, in 1482, the king had convoked the whole array of the country to march against the English, they held a midnight council in the church of Lauder for the purpose of forcibly removing these minions from the king's person. When all had agreed on the propriety of this measure, Lord Gray told the assembly the apologue of the mice, who had formed a resolution that it would be highly advantageous to their community to tie a bell round the cat's neck that they might hear her approach at a distance; but which public measure unfortunately miscarried from no mouse being willing to undertake the task of fastening the bell. 'I understand the moral,' said Angus, 'and, that what we propose may not lack execution, I will *bell-the-cat.*'"— *Walter Scott.*

STANZA 14. **Liddesdale.** A valley of Scotland, County of Dumfries, named after the river Liddel which is on the border.

ST. 14. "To fix his princely bowers" [where Bothwell's turrets, etc.].

"Angus was an old man when the war against England was resolved upon. He earnestly spoke against the measure from its commencement; and, on the eve of the Battle of Flodden, remonstrated so freely upon the impolicy of fighting, that the king said to him, with scorn and indignation, 'if he was afraid, he might go home. The earl burst into tears at this insupportable insult, and retired accordingly, leaving his sons George, Master of Angus, and Sir William of Glenbervie, to command his followers. They were both slain in the battle with two hundred gentlemen of the name of Douglas. The aged earl, broken-hearted at the calamities of his house and his country, retired into a religious house, where he died about a year after the field of Flodden."— *Walter Scott.*

ST. 15. **Tantallon Hold.** "The ruins of Tantallon Castle occupy a high rock, projecting into the German Ocean, about two miles east of North Berwick. The building formed a principal castle of the Douglas family."

ST. 15. **Dunbar.** A seaport town on the eastern coast of Scotland.

ST. 15. **Cochran.** In the summer of 1482, the nobles of Scotland, headed by Douglas, seized Cochran and several of the king's other favorites, and having hanged them before his eyes, returned with their royal captive to Edinburgh castle. — *Cyclopædia Britannica.*

James III. was at that time thirty years old.

ST. 15.   " A cloud of ire, remorse, and shame."

i.e., for his father and his race.

ST. 16. **Bruce.** Robert Bruce, most heroic of Scotland's kings, born 1274.

ST. 17. **Tamworth.** In Central England, a few miles south of

Lichfield. There is a castle here reputed to have been founded by a daughter of King Alfred. Tamworth is on the ancient Watling Street.

STANZA 17. **Nottingham, Yorkshire, Derby.** In the north-east of England.

ST. 17. **Ouse and Tyne.** Two rivers in the north-east of England.

ST. 17. **A hall! a hall!** "Ancient cry to make room for a dance or pageant."

ST. 20. "And all the city hum was *by*." Past.

ST. 20. "To *bowne* him for the war." Prepare.

ST. 21. **Dispiteously.** Maliciously.

ST. 21. **Martin Swart.** "A german general, who commanded the auxiliaries sent by the Duchess of Burgundy with Lambert Simnel. He was defeated and killed at Stokefield. The name of this German general is preserved by that of the field of battle, which is called, after him, Swartmoor. There were songs about him long current in England."

ST. 21. **Gueldres.** A town of Rhenish Prussia.

ST. 22. "A stranger maiden, passing fair." Constance de Beverly.

ST. 22. "The *falconer* and huntsman knows."
A hunter who hunts by means of a falcon.

ST. 22. **Tame.** A small river rising in Yorkshire; course, eighteen miles.

ST. 23. "Should scheme." [For, in favor of.]

ST. 24. **Wolsey.** Cardinal Wolsey.

ST. 25. "A pillar'd stone." Shaped like a pillar.

ST. 25. **Malison.** A curse.

ST. 25. "As fancy forms of midnight cloud."
As the imagination forms out of the clouds at midnight.

ST. 25. "This awful summons came."
"This supernatural citation is mentioned by all our Scottish historians. It was, probably, like the apparition at Linlithgow, an attempt, by those averse to the war, to impose upon the superstitious temper of James IV." — *Walter Scott.*

ST. 26. "Ross, Bothwell, *Forbes*, Lennox, Lyle."
The rhythm requires Forbes to be divided into two syllables.

ST. 26. "What time, or how, the Palmer *pass'd*." Went away.

ST. 28. "Although the pang of humbled pride
The place of jealousy supplied."

That is, the fact that Marmion had been able to humble De Wilton's pride, made him forget to be jealous.

STANZA 28. Lines 13, 14, 15. Is this picture consistent with a previous description of Marmion's love for Constance de Beverly? Do these lines contradict line 25?

ST. 29. "Before a venerable pile."

"A convent of Cistercian nuns, founded by the Earl of Fife in 1216."

ST. 29. **Bass.** A large, insulated greenstone rock of Scotland at the mouth of the Firth of Forth. It is a mile in circumference, and four hundred and twenty feet high.

ST. 30. "Will bring us to the English side" [where female attendance can be provided, etc.].

ST. 30. "To curse with candle, bell, and book."

"In the Romish Church, the ceremony of excommunication was formerly attended with great solemnity. Lamps or candles were extinguished by being thrown on the ground, with an imprecation that those against whom the excommunication was pronounced might be extinguished by the judgment of God. The summons to attend this ceremony was given by the ringing of a bell, and the curses accompanying it were pronounced out of a book by the priest. Hence the phrase of 'cursing by bell, book, and candle.'" — *Strong and McClintock.*

ST. 31. "Drove the monks forth of Coventry."

"This relates to the catastrophe of a real Robert de Marmion."

ST. 31. "St. Anton' fire thee!"

See St. Anthony's fire in Strong and McClintock's Biblical Cyclopædia.

ST. 32. "In that inviolable dome."

i.e., in a church, where, according to the then English law, homicides and other criminals were safe. See also Leviticus.

ST. 34. **Wark.** In Northumberland.

ST. 34. **Wooler.** North of Warkworth.

ST. 34. **Flodden Field.** After Henry VIII. had been two years on the English throne, a rupture occurred between him and James IV. of Scotland.

"James had demanded reparation for an alleged outrage on the Scottish flag; Henry had returned a contemptuous answer. He had further irritated the Scotch king by countenancing certain English border chieftains, who had been accessory to the murder of Sir Robert Ker ; he had also declined to deliver a legacy of jewels bequeathed to Queen Margaret by her father [Henry VII. of England]. Long and angry negotiations followed, which ended in James's rash and fatal invasion of England in the summer of 1513. The disastrous battle of Flodden [in Northumberland] was fought on the 9th September of that year. The body of James was found on the field after the battle. He died in the forty-first year of his age, and twenty-sixth of his reign." — *Chambers's Cyclopædia.*

CANTO SIXTH.

The Battle.

STANZA 2. "The bloody heart was in the *Field.*"
"The surface of a shield, so called because it contains those achievements anciently acquired on the field of battle." — *Dryden.*

ST. 2. **Mullets.** "The rowel of a spur [in heraldry], used to distinguish the third son."

ST. 2. **Bartizan.** A small projecting turret on the top of a house or castle.

ST. 2. **Bastion.** "A large projecting mass of masonry at the angles of a fortified work, and so constructed that every part of it may be defended by fire from some other part of the works."

ST. 2. **Vantage-Coign.** Corner or point of advantage.

ST. 3. **Fretted.** Variegated.

ST. 3. **Breviary.** Book containing the daily service of the church of Rome.

ST. 5. **Targe.** Shield.

ST. 5. **Corslet.** "Light armor for the fore part of the body."

ST. 6. **Beadsman.** "Man employed to pray for another; a monk."

ST. 7. **Slough.** Skin; the cast skin of a serpent.

ST. 8. **Postern.** Small door. "Passage under a rampart affording communication from the fort into the ditch, etc."

ST. 9. "This eve anew shall dub me knight."
In early mediæval times, one already a noble could dub another knight.

STANZA 9. "When the dead Douglas won the field."
See the ballad of Otterbourne in the Border Minstrelsy.

ST. 9. **Twisel Glen.** Where James encamped before the battle of Flodden Field.

ST. 9. **Surrey.** Commander-in-chief of the English.

ST. 11. **Embrasure.** Loop-hole.

ST. 11.   "A bishop by the altar stood."

"The well-known Gawain Douglas, Bishop of Dunkeld, son of Archibald Bell-the-Cat, Earl of Angus. He was author of a Scottish metrical version of the Æneid and of many other poetical pieces of great merit. He had not at this period attained the mitre." — *Walter Scott.*

ST. 11. **Mitre.** A kind of Episcopal crown; often used to designate the office of bishop, — as, "attained the mitre."

ST. 12. A spirited picture of chivalric feeling and usage.

ST. 13. The last three lines of this stanza are often quoted.

ST. 14. This stanza is justly famous.

ST. 14. **Bothwell** is a few miles from Glasgow.

ST. 14. **St. Bride** or **St. Bridget.** Patroness of Ireland, and born about middle of fifth century.

ST. 15.   "A letter forged !"

"Lest the reader should partake of the earl's astonishment, and consider the crime as inconsistent with the manners of the period, I have to remind him of the numerous forgeries (partly executed by a female assistant), devised by Robert of Artois to forward his suit against the Countess Matilda; which, being detected, occasioned his flight into England, and proved the remote cause of Edward the Third's memorable wars in France. John Harding, also, was expressly hired by Edward I. to forge such documents as might appear to establish the claim of featly asserted over Scotland by the English monarchs." — *Walter Scott.*

ST. 15.   "Saint Jude to speed."
Does this oath allude to Marmion's treachery ?

ST. 15. **Clerkly skill.** Scholarly.

ST. 16.   "Against the Saracen and Turk."
During the Crusades.

ST. 16.   "The Earl did much the Master pray."
That is, his eldest son.

ST. 16.   "Thou sworn horse-courser."
One who keeps or studies race-horses.

STANZA 17. Lines 27 and 28 are often quoted.

ST. 18. **Saint Bernard.** Of Clairvaux.

"One of the most eminent names in the mediæval church. Saint Bernard was born of noble parents, near Dijon, in 1091. Luther says of him, 'If there has ever been a pious monk that feared God, it was St. Bernard.' Bernardine monks were the same as the Cistercian, and were named after St. Bernard, who greatly extended the order."

Compare lines 26, 27, 28, for movement with "The Falls of Lodore."

ST. 20. **Bannockbourne.** The battle of Bannockburn was fought June 24, 1314, between the English under Edward II. and the Scotch under Robert Bruce, accepted by the Scotch as their king, for supremacy in Scotland. The most important of the Scotch fortresses, Stirling, still held out for Edward. "The army which Bruce had gathered to oppose the inroad [of the English] was formed almost wholly of footmen, and was stationed to the south of Stirling on a rising ground, flanked by a little brook, the Bannock burn, which gave its name to the engagement." The English army finally "broke in headlong rout." The flower of the English chivalry fell into the hands of the Scotch.

ST. 21. **Basnet.** Also "bascinet" and "basinet." A light, basin-shaped helmet worn in England in the fourteenth century.

ST. 22.   "The pheasant in the falcon's claw
             He scarce will yield to please a daw."

A fine figure. The royal pheasant is Clare, the falcon Marmion, the peaceful daw the Abbot.

ST. 23.   "Hence might they see the full array."

"The reader cannot here expect a full account of the battle of Flodden; but, so far as is necessary to understand the romance, I beg to remind him that, when the English army, by their skilful counter-march, were fairly placed between James and his own country, the Scottish monarch resolved to fight, and, setting fire to his tents, descended from the ridge of Flodden to secure the neighboring eminence of Brankstone, on which that village is built. Thus the two armies met, almost without seeing each other, when, according to the old poem of 'Flodden Field,'

              'The English line stretched east and west,
              And southward were their faces set;
              The Scottish northward proudly prest,
              And manfully their foes they met.'" — *Walter Scott.*

STANZA 24. " My sons command the *vaward* post." Van, the fore.
ST. 24.   " With Brian Tunstall, stainless knight."

" Sir Brian Tunstall, called in the romantic language of the time
Tunstall the undefiled, was one of the few Englishmen of rank slain
at Flodden. He figures in the ancient English poem, to which I may
safely refer my readers." — *Walter Scott.*

ST. 24.   " Edmund, the Admiral."

" The English army advanced in four divisions. On the right,
which first engaged, were the sons of Earl Surrey; namely, Thomas
Howard, the admiral of England, and Sir Edmund, the knight marshal of the army. Their divisions were separated from each other;
but, at the request of Sir Edmund, his brother's battalion was drawn
very near to his own. The centre was commanded by Surrey in person ; the left wing by Sir Edward Stanley, with the men of Lancashire, and of the palatinate of Chester. Lord Dacres, with a large
body of horse, formed a reserve. When the smoke, which the wind
had driven between the armies, was somewhat dispersed, they per-
ceived the Scots, who had moved down the hill in a similar order of
battle, and in deep silence. The earls of Huntley and of Home commanded their left-wing, and charged Sir Edmund Howard with such
success as entirely to defeat his part of the right wing. Sir Edmund's
banner was beaten down, and he himself escaped with difficulty to
his brother's division. The admiral, however, stood firm; and
Dacre, advancing to his support with the reserve of cavalry, probably
between the interval of the divisions commanded by the brothers
Howard, appears to have kept the victors in effectual check. Home's
men, chiefly Borderers, began to pillage the baggage of both armies;
and their leader is branded by the Scottish historians with negligence
or treachery. On the other hand, Huntley, on whom they bestow many
encomiums, is said by the English historians to have left the field
after the first charge. Meanwhile the admiral, whose flanks these
chiefs ought to have attacked, availed himself of their inactivity, and
pushed forward against another large division of the Scottish army in
his front, headed by the earls of Crawford and Montrose, both of
whom were slain, and their forces routed. On the left, the success of
the English was yet more decisive ; for the Scottish right wing, con-
sisting of undisciplined Highlanders, commanded by Lennox and
Argyle, was unable to sustain the charge of Sir Edward Stanley, and
especially the severe execution of the Lancashire archers. The King

and Surrey, who commanded the respective centres of their armies, were meanwhile engaged in close and dubious conflict. James, surrounded by the flower of his kingdom, and impatient of the galling discharge of arrows, supported also by his reserve under Bothwell, charged with such fury that the standard of Surrey was in danger. At that critical moment, Stanley, who had routed the left wing of the Scottish, pursued his career of victory, and arrived on the right flank, and in the rear of James's division, which, throwing itself into a circle, disputed the battle till night came on. Surrey then drew back his forces; for the Scottish centre not having been broken, and their left wing being victorious, he yet doubted the event of the field. The Scottish army, however, felt their loss, and abandoned the field of battle in disorder before dawn. They lost, perhaps, from eight to ten thousand men; but that included the very prime of their nobility, gentry, and even clergy. Scarce a family of eminence but has an ancestor killed at Flodden; and there is no province in Scotland, even at this day, where the battle is mentioned without a sensation of terror and sorrow. The English lost also a great number of men, perhaps within one-third of the vanquished, but they were of inferior note." — *Walter Scott.*

STANZA 25. "The cloud enveloped Scotland's war."
Scotland was the aggressive party.

ST. 26. The Gordons were one of the most renowned clans.

ST. 27. "The Howard's lion fell."
Howard was Admiral of England.

ST. 27. "The pennon sunk and rose."
"The pennon, in the Middle Ages, was the banner of a knight, *baronet,* or esquire." — *Brande.*

ST. 27. "May bid your beads." To count prayers by beads.
The action expressed in this stanza is spirited. Scott's practical knowledge of military tactics served him well in the composition of "Marmion."

ST. 30. Lines 1–6 inclusive are often quoted.

ST. 30. **Runnel.** A small stream, or run.

ST. 30. "To dubious verge of battle fought."
That is, a battle whose issue is still dubious.

ST. 30. "To shrieve the dying."
To receive the confession of the dying.

ST. 31. "Then the dark presage must be true," and "A simple

heart makes feeble hand," are examples of the many passages in Scott's prose and poetical works showing the vein of superstition which he possessed in common with most Scotchmen. George Mac-Donald uses this same native propensity most freely and skilfully in his writings. Superstition is a Celtic trait ingrained into the very blood of both high and low, the literate and the illiterate. Buckle's " History of Civilization" gives many curious examples of its expression.

STANZA 32.   " Shake not the dying sinner's sand! "

An allusion to the hour-glass, and here, of course, used figuratively.

The poet's art is shown in Stanza 32.   Marmion, with all his faults, dies like a warrior, and in full possession of the reader's sympathy. As the hero of the poem, it is right that he should throughout claim more interest than De Wilton.

ST. 33. **Fontarabia.** " A fortified town of Spain in Biscay, on the boundary between France and Spain, and chiefly interesting because of its historical associations."

ST. 33. **Roncesvalles.** " A valley in Navarre. where Charlemagne's army, in the eighth century, was defeated by a combined force of Arabs, Navarrese, and French Gascons.   In this action Roland, the famous paladin, fell.   Many generals and chief nobles were also killed; and the whole baggage of the army fell into the hands of the victors." — *Chambers's Cyclopædia.*

ST. 34.   " Though *bill*-men ply the ghastly blow."

A **bill** is a battle-axe; also, a hatchet with a hooked point.

ST. 34.   " Linked in the serried phalanx tight."

The **phalanx** was of Macedonian origin, and was used effectively by Philip, father of Alexander the Great, in the fourth century before Christ.   The phalanx was invincible only on level ground.   The first five rows of the phalanx presented an impenetrable wall, as the spears used by the last row were twenty feet long, and of the preceding four sufficiently long to reach to the front.   The spears of each row rested on the shoulders of the men in front, and were couched in such a manner that the front row of men presented a wall of spears.   The phalanx in ancient warfare was replaced by the Roman legion.

ST. 34. " They melted from the field as snow,
            When streams are swoll'n and south winds blow,
            Dissolves in silent dew."

Notice the melody of these lines, due to the skilful admixture of vowels, liquids, and consonants. The figure is classical in its style and beauty.

STANZA 34. " To [gain] town and tower, to [gain] down and dale,
    [In order] To tell red Flodden's dismal tale."

Contrast the picture of defeat in this stanza with the picture of Roncesvalles in the preceding one.

ST. 35.   " Reckless of life he desperate fought."

" There can be no doubt that King James fell in the battle of Flodden. ' He was killed,' says the curious *French Gazette,* ' within a lance's length of the Earl of Surrey ; ' and the same account adds that none of his division were made prisoners, though many were killed, — a circumstance that testifies the desperation of their resistance." — *Walter Scott.*

ST. 35.   " But, O ! how changed since yon blithe night."

This line serves as a point of connection, and aids the unity of the poem.

ST. 36.   " The fair cathedral stormed and took."

" This storm of Lichfield Cathedral, which had been garrisoned on the part of the King, took place in the great Civil War. Lord Brook, who, with Sir John Gill, commanded the assailants, was shot with a musket-ball through the visor of his helmet. The Royalists remarked, that he was killed by a shot fired from St. Chad's Cathedral, and upon St. Chad's Day, and received his death-wound in the very eye with which, he had said, he hoped to see the ruin of all the cathedrals in England. The magnificent church in question suffered cruelly upon this and other occasions, the principal spire being ruined by the fire of the besiegers." — *Walter Scott.*

ST. 36. **St. Chad.** Bishop of York in the seventh century; afterwards bishop of the See of Lichfield. " His name is still preserved in the calendar of the Church of England (March 2); and the cathedral of Lichfield is named St. Chad's."

ST. 37. Lines 19–25 are rather prose than poetry.

ST. 37. **Commune** is an example of " wrenched accent."

ST. 38. **Holinshed, Hall.** Famous writers of chronicles.

ST. 38. " To whom it must in terms be said." In so many words.

ST. 38. **Wolsey.** Cardinal Wolsey.

ST. 38. **More.** Sir Thomas More, martyr, author, philosopher, statesman.

S<small>TANZA</small> 38. **Sands.** Edwin Sandys, D.D., Bishop of Worcester, next of London, then Archbishop of York.

S<small>T</small>. 38. **King Hal.** Henry VIII.

S<small>T</small>. 38. **Catherine.** Catherine of Arragon, first wife of Henry VIII.

L'ENVOY.

S<small>T</small>. 38. **Rede.** Story.

INTRODUCTION TO CANTO FIRST.

S<small>TANZA</small> 1. **Linn.** Waterfall.

S<small>T</small>. 2. " The sheep before the *pinching* heaven."

A bold and graphic metaphor.

S<small>T</small>. 6. '' Who victor died on Gadite wave."

Admiral Nelson, who died on the sea of Cadiz, or Gades, Oct. 21, 1805. Nelson gained a victory over the combined navies of Spain and France in the Bay of Trafalgar. In this brilliant engagement he lost his life. Gades is the Phœnician name of Cadiz, and it was a flourishing colony of that ancient seafaring people in the time of the first Punic War, in the third century, B.C. Modern name for Sea of Cadiz is Bay of Trafalgar.

S<small>T</small>. 6. **Levin.** Lightning.

S<small>T</small>. 7. **Hafnia.** Copenhagen. Admiral Nelson gained a brilliant victory over the Danes at the Battle of Copenhagen.

S<small>T</small>. 7. " Nor mourn ye less his perished worth."

William Pitt, the younger, died 1806.

S<small>T</small>. 8. Lines 5–12. Notice the similes and metaphors in the lines. Metaphors are often more effective when following similes.

S<small>T</small>. 9. Lines 11–14 inclusive ruin the clear flow of the thought, and give the effect of the dullest prose.

S<small>T</small>. 10. Fox was the Whig leader. Walter Scott was a Tory in his sympathies and political principles. In the contest with Napoleon, in which all Europe and finally England took part, Pitt and Fox dropped party rivalries, and worked hand in hand for the salvation of their country. They died in the same year.

S<small>T</small>. 11. One of the most famous oracles of Greece, that of Dodonian Zeus, was in Thessaly. Lines 21 and 22 are famous.

STANZA 12. This is a blot upon what precedes. It is as if Scott perfunctorily returned praise for praise.

ST. 13. This stanza is beautiful throughout if we except the line, "It *will* not be, it *may* not last." The meaning would be clearer thus: It *may* not be, it *will* not last.

ST. 14. A literal picture of the manner in which Scott most frequently sought recreation after literary labor.

ST. 14. **Cairn.** A heap of stones, a mound, a barrow, supposed to have been raised in prehistoric times for sepulchral purposes.

ST. 15.   "By warriors wrought in steely weeds."
In clothes or garments of steel.

ST. 15.   "As when the champion of the Lake," etc.
See poems on Morte d'Arthur.

ST. 16. For a picture of the corruption in Dryden's and other writings of Charles II.'s time, read Leigh Hunt's essay on The Drama of the Restoration.

The last two lines of this stanza recall the sonorousness of many in Dryden's famous Ode on St. Cæcilia's Day.

Stanzas 17 and 18 by themselves would have formed a most suitable prologue to Marmion.

ST. 19. **Ytene.** Ancient name of the New Forest, Hants.

ST. 19.   "Of Ascapart and Bevis bold."

"The 'History of Bevis of Hampton' is abridged by my friend, Mr. George Ellis, with that liveliness which extracts amusement even out of the most rude and unpromising of our old tales of chivalry. Ascapart, a most important personage in the romance, is thus described in an extract: —

> This geaunt was mighty and strong,
> And full thirty feet was long;
> He was bristled like a sow;
> A foot he had between each brow;
> His lips were great, and hung aside;
> His eyen were hollow, his mouth was wide,
> Lothly he was to look on than,
> And liker a devil than a man.
> His staff was a young oak,
> Hard and heavy was his stroke.

"I am happy to say that the memory of Sir Bevis is still fragrant in his town of Southampton, the gate of which is sentinelled by the effigies of that doughty knight-errant and his gigantic associate." — *Walter Scott.*

STANZA 19. **Red King.** William Rufus, born 1056.

ST. 19. **Boldrewood.** Now New Forest.

ST. 19. **Partenopex.** Poem by W. S. Rose.

The mingling of names and subjects of the poems of Mr. George Ellis and W. S. Rose in this last stanza, renders the interpretation very confusing. Poetry, according to Noah Porter, should be simple, sensuous, passionate — so simple as to be easily comprehended; sensuous, as dealing in pictures; passionate, as appealing to the heart.

INTRODUCTION TO CANTO SECOND.

STANZA 1. **Rowan.** Mountain-ash.

ST. 2. **Newark.** On the Newark River, a small tributary of the Trent. Northwest of the town are the stately ruins of an ancient castle where King John died in 1216.

ST. 2. **Gazehound.** "A hound that pursues by the eye rather than by the scent."

ST. 2. **Bratchet.** Slowhound.

ST. 2. **Quarry.** Prey, game.

ST. 2. **Harquebuss.** Arquebuse. A sort of hand-gun used by infantry before the invention of the musket.

ST. 3. **Ettrick.** "A mountainous region of Scotland, seventeen miles southwest of Selkirk. Ettrick forest is 'a beautiful pastoral tract of country, watered by the Ettrick and its tributaries. It formed originally a part of the great Caledonian Forest, and now is almost co-extensive with the county of Selkirk.'"

ST. 3. **Yarrow.** "A parish of Scotland, County of Selkirk, containing Ettrick Forest and several petty villages. Walter Scott resided in the Ettrick Forest for ten years; and Hogg, the Ettrick shepherd, lived and died in this parish."

ST. 3.   "Where erst the outlaw drew his arrow."

The outlaw Murray, the Robin Hood of Ettrick."

ST. 3. **Holt.** A forest or a hill.

ST. 3.   " In classic and in *Gothic* lore."

Walter Scott and several of his friends, when young men, studied German together, then little thought of by the Scotch and English literary world.

STANZA 3. **Bowhill.** A seat of the Duke of Buccleuch on the Yarrow.

ST. 3.   " Fair as the Elves," etc.

A local tradition in the Scott clan, whose representative in the poet's time was the Duke of Buccleuch.

ST. 3. **Forest Sheriff.** Allusion to Scott, who held the office of sheriff.

ST. 3.   " No youthful baron's left to grace."

Allusion to the son of Scott's warm friend, the Duke of Buccleuch.

ST. 3. **Oberon.** See Shakespeare's Midsummer Night's Dream.

ST. 3.   "And she is gone." Duchess of Buccleuch.

ST. 4.   " Her long-descended lord is gone."

The Duke of Buccleuch died several years before Scott.

ST. 4. Lines 9 and 10 are very quotable.

ST. 4. **Wallace.** Famous Scotch chieftain and patriot of the thirteenth century.

Stanzas 5, 6, 7, and 8 are properly one in the development and completion of one train of thought and sentiment.

ST. 5.   " By lone St. Mary's silent lake."

The sheet of water from which the Yarrow takes its course. " Near the lower extremity of the lake are the ruins of Dryhope Tower, the birthplace of Mary Scott, . . . and famous by the traditional name of the Flower of Yarrow."

The chapel of St. Mary of the Lowes was situated on the eastern side of the lake, to which it gives name. It continued to be a place of worship during the seventeenth century. The vestiges of the building can now scarcely be traced; but the burial-ground is still used as a cemetery." The clan Scott, in a feudal strife, injured the chapel.

" At one corner of the burial-ground of the demolished chapel, but without its precincts, is a small mound called Binram's Corse, where tradition deposits the remains of a necromantic priest, the former tenant of the chaplainry."

ST. 9. **Loch-skene.** " A mountain lake of considerable size, at the head of the Moffat-water. The character of the scenery is uncommonly savage, and the earn, or Scottish eagle, has, for many ages, built its nest yearly upon an islet in the lake. Loch-skene discharges itself into a brook, which, after a short and precipitous course, falls from a cataract of immense height and gloomy grandeur, called, from its appearance, the 'Grey Mare's Tail.' The Giant's Grave, afterwards mentioned, is a sort of trench which bears that name a little way from the foot of the cataract. It has the appearance of a battery designed to command the pass." — *Walter Scott.*

STANZA 9. **Moffatdale.** In the county of Dumfries.

ST. 10. **Isis.** A river which joins the Thames at Dorchester.

INTRODUCTION TO CANTO THIRD.

STANZA. 1. Notice the Virgilian succession of similes in this Stanza. The stanza is also a good description, not of the introductory epistles, but of the poem proper of "Marmion."

ST. 3. Is the third verse good poetry ? What foot is used ? Where is the cæsura of the foot in the verse?

ST. 3. " For Brunswick's venerable hearse? "

When Napoleon threatened Austria, the combined armies of Austria and Prussia were placed under the Duke of Brunswick, who assumed the aggressive, and marched against the enemy.

ST. 3. [Though] "The star of Brandenburgh arose!"

ST. 3. **Brandenburg** is one of the more important political divisions of Germany. Brandenburg through its electors was prominent in the sixteenth century.

ST. 3. " For ever quench'd in Jena's stream."

"The great battle of Jena was fought in the neighborhood of the town on 14th October, 1806. The Prussian army, numbering about seventy thousand men, was under the command of the Prince of Hohenlohe; while the French, commanded by Napoleon, amounted to ninety thousand. The former was completely defeated. On the same day, Davout defeated the aged Duke of Brunswick at Auerstädt, with thirty thousand French against sixty thousand Prussians, and these two battles decided for a number of years the fate of the Prussian Kingdom and of the North of Germany."— *Chambers's Cyclopædia.*

ST. 3. "**Jena** was the Trafalgar of the Prussians, and from that time they ceased for some years to be a military power." — *White's History of France.*

ST. 3. " And crush that dragon in its birth." Napoleon.

ST. 3. " And snatched the spear, but left the shield."

i.e., lost the victory.

What figure of rhetoric in the last eight lines of this stanza ?

STANZA 3. **Arminius.** Leader of the North German tribes against the Romans in first century, A.D. " By the testimony of his Roman foes, he was undeniably the liberator of Germany; and he was, perhaps, the first man who ever conceived the hope of German unity." — *History of Germany, Lewis.*

ST. 4. **Red-Cross hero.** " Sir Sidney Smith foiled Bonaparte's projects in Syria by his defence of Acre." — *Green.*

ST. 4. " The invincible." Napoleon.

ST. 4. " When stubborn Russ, and metal'd Swede." France had taken the island of Malta from the Knights of St. John. The czar considered himself the patron of the knights. He therefore instigated Sweden and Denmark to join Russia " in a league of armed neutrality."

ST. 4. " On the *warp'd* wave, etc." Curving wave.

ST. 4. " The conqueror's wreath with dying hand." Sir Ralph Abercromby.

ST. 5. " When she, the bold Enchantress, came," Joanna Baillie and a very intimate friend and correspondent of Sir Walter Scott, who was prone to overestimate his friends.

ST. 6. Line 7, *warps;* twists.

ST. 7. " And still I thought that shatter'd tower." Smailholm tower in Berwickshire.

ST. 7. " Far in the distant Cheviots blue." Cheviot Hills.

ST. 7. **Wassel-rout.** A carousal; a merry festival enjoyed by a select company.

ST. 7. " From the thatched mansion's gray-hair'd sire ! " Robert Scott, grandfather of the poet.

ST. 7. " Whose doom, etc." Judgment, opinion.

ST. 8. " And in the minstrel spare the friend." Retain your friend as a minstrel.

INTRODUCTION TO CANTO FOURTH.

STANZA 1. " That motley clown," etc. Allusion to Shakespeare's " As You Like It."

ST. 2. **Ettrick Pen.** Mountain of Scotland, twenty-two hundred feet high.

ST. 3. " Through heavy vapors dark and *dun*." Obscure.

STANZA 3.   " To shelter in the brake and rocks."
A thicket of brambles.
ST. 4.   " His rustic kirn's loud revelry."
Scottish harvest-home.
ST. 5.   " As he, the ancient Chief of Troy."
" See the Iliad. Sir William Forbes of Pitsligo, Baronet, unequalled,
perhaps, in the degree of individual affection entertained for him by
his friends, as well as in the general respect and esteem of Scotland
at large. His "Life of Beattie," whom he befriended and patronized
in life, as well as celebrated after his decease, was not long published
before the benevolent and affectionate biographer was called to follow
the subject of his narrative. This melancholy event very shortly
succeeded the marriage of the friend, to whom this introduction is
addressed, with one of Sir William's daughters." — *Walter Scott.*
ST. 5.   " Pandour and Camp, with eyes of fire."
Two dogs. Camp was a favorite bull-terrier of the poet.
ST. 6. **The laverock.** The lark.
ST. 6.   " Not Ariel," etc. See Shakespeare's " Tempest."
ST. 7. " Then *he* whose absence we deplore." Colin Mackenzie of
Portmore.
ST. 7.   " And dear loved R——."   Sir William Rae.
ST. 7.   " For, like mad Tom," etc.
" Common name for an idiot; assumed by Edgar in ' King Lear.' "—
Walter Scott.

INTRODUCTION TO CANTO FIFTH.

To George Ellis, Esq., Editor of Specimens of Ancient English
Romances.

STANZA 2.   " Caledonia's Queen is changed."
The old town of Edinburgh was secured on the north side by a lake,
now drained, and on the south side by a wall, which there was some
attempt to make defensible even so late as 1745. The gates, and the
greater part of the wall, have been pulled down, in the course of the
late extensive and beautiful enlargement of the city. My ingenious
and valued friend, Mr. Thomas Campbell, proposed to celebrate
Edinburgh under the epithet here borrowed; but the " Queen of the
North " has not been so fortunate as to receive from so eminent a pen
the proposed distinction." — *Walter Scott.*

STANZA 2. "A wicket churlishly supplied." A small gate.

ST. 2. " For thy dark cloud, with *umber'd lower.*"

Umber is sometimes used to define peat. The line probably means a smoky atmosphere caused by the burning of peat.

ST. 2. A salient illustration of Scott's exceedingly careless construction. Notice the connectives and ellipses.

ST. 3. "Erst hidden by the aventayle."

The movable front of a helmet through which the air was breathed. See Spenser's "Fairy Queen," Book III. Canto 9.

ST. 4. "*For* fosse and turret proud to stand." In place of.

ST. 4. **Knosp.** An architectural ornament, representing an unopened bud.

ST. 4. "To Henry meek she gave repose."

Henry VI. of England, who sought refuge in England after the fatal battle of Towton." — *Scott.*

ST. 4. "Great Bourbon's relics sad she saw."

Many French officers were in Edinburgh in 1814. The battle of Edinburgh, which ended Napoleon's triumph, was fought in 1815.

ST. 5. This stanza is beautiful.

ST. 6. "The minstrel and his lay approved." Philip de Than.

ST. 6. **Marie translated.** " Marie of France, who translated the "Lais of Brittany " into French. She resided at the court of Henry III. of England, to whom she dedicated her book." — *Scott.*

ST. 6. "Who, when his scythe *her* hoary foe."

Her must relate to minstrelsy personified.

ST. 7. This stanza could well apply to Scott during the last six years of his life.

ST. 8. "Achievements on the storied pane."

Some of the mediæval stained glass has never been equalled in gorgeousness and depth of color.

INTRODUCTION TO CANTO SIXTH.

STANZA 1. **Iol.** "The Iol of the heathen Danes (a word still applied to Christmas in Scotland) was solemnized with great festivity. The humor of the Danes at table displayed itself in pelting each other with bones; and Torfæus tells a long and curious story, in the History of Hrolfe Kaka, of one Hottus, an inmate of the Court of Denmark, who was so generally assailed with these missiles that he constructed, out of the bones with which he was overwhelmed, a very respectable intrenchment against those who continued the raillery." *Walter Scott.*

STANZA 2. **Scalds.** Scandinavian poets of semi-barbaric times.

ST. 2.   "Saw the *stoled* priest the *chalice* rear."

Stole. A narrow embroidered or jewelled band worn across the shoulders. **Chalice.** Cup in which wine of the eucharist is administered.

ST. 2. **Kirtle sheen.** Silk petticoat or dress.

ST. 2. **Underogating.** Without sacrifice of dignity.

ST. 2. **Post and pair.** Old game at cards.

ST. 3. **Brawn.** Boar's flesh.

ST. 3. **Blithely trowls** [trolls]. Sings.

ST. 3.   "Traces of ancient mystery."

"It seems certain that the *Mummers* of England who (in Northumberland, at least) used to go about in disguise to the neighboring houses bearing the then useless ploughshare, and the *Guisards* of Scotland, not yet in total disuse, present, in some indistinct degree, a shadow of the old mysteries which were the origin of the English drama. In Scotland (me ipso teste) we were wont, during my boyhood, to take the characters of the apostles, at least of Peter, Paul, and Judas Iscariot; the first had the keys, the second carried a sword, and the last the bag, in which the dole of our neighbors' plum-cake was deposited. One played a champion, and recited some traditional rhymes; another was

> ' Alexander, King of Macedon,
> Who conquer'd all the world but Scotland alone.'

These, and many such verses, were repeated, but by rote and unconnectedly. There was also occasionally, I believe, a St. George. In all, there was a confused resemblance of the ancient mysteries, in which the characters of Scripture, the Nine Worthies, and other popular personages, were usually exhibited." — *Walter Scott.*

ST. 3. **Mumming.** Masking.

ST. 3. **Richly dight.** Clothed.

ST. 6.   "Though *Leyden* aids."

A personal friend of the poet.

ST. 6. **Ulysses, etc.** See Odyssey.

ST. 7.   "And shun the spirits' blasted tree."

" Alluding to the Welsh tradition of Howel Sell and Owen Glendwr. Howel fell in single combat against Glendwr, and his body was concealed in a hollow oak." — *Walter Scott.*

STANZA 7.   " If asked to tell a fairy tale."

"The *Daoine Shi'*, or Men of Peace, of the Scottish Highlanders, rather resemble the Scandinavian *Duergar* than the English Fairies. Notwithstanding their name, they are, if not absolutely malevolent, at least peevish, discontented, and apt to do mischief on slight provocation. The belief of their existence is deeply impressed on the Highlanders, who think they are particularly offended at mortals who talk of them, who wear their favorite color, green, or in any respect interfere with their affairs. This is especially to be avoided on Friday, when, whether as dedicated to Venus, with whom, in Germany, this subterraneous people are held nearly connected, or for a more solemn reason, they are more active and possessed of greater power. Some curious particulars concerning the popular superstitions of the Highlanders may be found in Dr. Graham's Picturesque Sketches of Perthshire." — *Walter Scott.*

ST. 7.   **Franch'mont.** This castle of Belgium was a noted stronghold as early as the twelfth century.

ST. 7.   " His *hanger* in his belt is slung."

A short broadsword and curved at the point.

ST. 9.   " While *gripple* owners still refuse."   Tenacious.

The Students' Series of English Classics.

T O furnish the educational public with well edited editions of those authors used in, or required for admission to many of the colleges, the publishers announce this new series. *The following books are now ready:*

LEACH, SHEWELL, & SANBORN, Publishers,
BOSTON, NEW YORK, and CHICAGO.

www.ingramcontent.com/pod-product-compliance
Lightning Source LLC
Chambersburg PA
CBHW030623030726
47497CB00006B/1615